OAK AND IVY

REBEKAH ISERT

To Kenneth—
Who taught me how to me how to make boundaries.

To Coach—
Who taught me how to maintain them.

And to Dad—
Thank you for being absolutely nothing like the fathers in this book. I love you.

OCTOBER 20

He wasn't what I expected a psych patient to look like. There's typically a haunted look about them, particularly at medication time. It's like the alien world that's constantly encroaching on their thoughts is a little closer — muted voices whispering insistently through the cracks in their sanity.

This man didn't look haunted. He looked annoyed.

I stood in the hallway outside the ward, gazing transfixed through the window in the door. The man, all dark eyes and broad shoulders, sat at the far side of the room on a worn blue sofa, staring back at me with a sort of dogged tenacity that made me wish I had some drapes to pull between the two of us.

I stepped back, unable to break my gaze, caught somewhere between voyeur and victim.

"Ah, Nurse Margot, I see you've noticed Thomas," a low female voice said from behind me.

I jumped, my concentration breaking as I twisted toward the source, trying not to appear as surprised—or as embarrassed—as I was.

Matron stood there behind me, staring past me to Thomas. *Matron* was her title, but there wasn't much that was matronly about her. Long auburn hair complimented creamy skin and a white coat, making her stand out against the dark inlaid wood paneling of the hallways like a nightlight in a dark room. She looked like she wasn't much older than forty, and yet there was something endless in her eyes that belied any assigned age.

She was also my brand-new boss, and even if she hadn't had an otherworldly quality about her, there was something about her job title that kept me from wanting to look at her too long. My first day nerves, which had been suspended by the man in the ward, slammed back into me.

I brushed a nonexistent piece of hair out of my face, smiling sheepishly and glancing back into the ward. "Um, yes. He's not . . . he doesn't look like the usual type that you see in this kind of place."

Matron's smile was controlled, but the ever-so-slight crinkles around her eyes showed fondness as she gazed at the patient.

"Yes, Thomas is quite distinct, even for a facility like Our Lady." She motioned me down the hall. "He'd go to the abyss and back before he admitted that he isn't in full possession of his faculties, and if you look at only the surface he is quite easy to believe. But his delusions can't be ignored. That's why he's a permanent resident, like the rest of his ward mates."

"What is his condition?" I asked.

Matron smiled again, and continued down the hall, her steps slow and metered, the perfect speed for walking and talking. "All in good time. As I previously explained, you'll be on the night shift for The Boughs. Nurse Gwen will brief you on each of the patients and their conditions." For a moment I wondered what she was talking about, until I remembered that she was continuing the conversation from where we'd left off before we'd walked up to the ward door to look through at the patients.

Too late, I realized there had been other patients there than Thomas. The urge to frown was stronger than before, and Matron caught the end of it as I wiped it from my face.

Thankfully, she misinterpreted it. "This won't be a difficult job, but for your first couple of weeks, we wanted to slowly ease you into the way of doing things here."

"I appreciate that," I lied, groaning a little inwardly. I'd known that this particular institution was of the highest caliber —which was partially why I'd chosen to move here in the first place—but I was an experienced nurse. I didn't need easy, nor did I want it. Easy meant time to think, and that was the last thing that I was looking for.

Not that I'd been in any better circumstances at home. Swamped with the health situations of Mom and Bill, and then Mom, and then Bill, I'd been teetering on the edge of buying a one-way ticket to Tibet. Then Beth—my coworker at Safe Harbor Regional Medical Center—had pulled me aside and handed me a notice about a job at Our Lady of the Wood Psychiatric Hospital, several hundred miles north of my hometown of Three Rivers, Michigan. Our Lady was an intensive care unit. Longer hours, interesting cases. A perfect place to get away and forget.

I'd left the next week, four days ago.

I'd arrived in Carterhall, Michigan, my new town, three days ago.

I followed Matron down the dimly lit halls, lined by wall fixtures that looked as though they could have once held candles instead of electric bulbs. Despite the dated—and frankly rather creepy—appearance, the hospital didn't seem to be that bad. It was modern hiding behind history and atmosphere, and while I wouldn't have chosen the aesthetic for myself, I could appreciate it.

Even with the bright lights and the smiling faces of the patients in the wards, and the calm, reassuring presence of the other nurses and doctors, the dark wood hallways in between made me feel as though I was wading in shadows. At one point, driven more by curiosity rather than conviction, I reached out and poked the wall, feeling the solid wood under my finger, barely retracting it in time as Matron turned back to see that I was still following.

The rest of the hospital was fairly standard as far as private institutions went—each ward was separate and contained, with five to ten patients to a ward, obviously clinical but pretending to be homey. In each ward there was a motif of some sort of plant. Blue flowers for the Delphinium Ward, yellow for the Daffodil Ward, and so on, each room as clean and sterile as the last.

After the tour was finished, Matron took me back to the main office, the scent of industrial strength cleaner and autumn leaves trailing behind us. A woman dressed in blue waited on the wooden chairs outside, hands clasped in her lap as she rubbed her thumbs together, ID clipped onto the neckline of her scrubs. Before I could read it, she saw us and stood. Letters flashed at me, and I read *Nurse Gwen* on the tag before it flipped out of view again.

"Matron," the nurse said, nodding deferentially.

Matron motioned to me, her expression warm but businesslike. "Nurse Gwen, please meet Margot Knight. Nurse Margot, as I stated earlier, Nurse Gwen will be responsible for training you in The Boughs for the next couple of weeks. We're a little shorthanded currently, so after your training you will be on your own until we come by a couple more people. I'm sure you'll do splendidly, though. Your professional history speaks for itself."

"Welcome, Nurse Margot," Nurse Gwen said, smiling. It was an odd smile. It registered as friendly but was too cool to be particularly inviting.

Between that and the decidedly weird rule that—at least in front of patients and Matron—I was to be called Nurse Margot, and in turn call all staff by their appropriate names, I had to fight the urge to put an equally cool smile on my face. *Give her a chance*, I reminded myself. *This is your first day. You're probably just imagining the coldness. Or she's just as nervous to meet you.*

Gwen continued. "Let's go introduce you to everyone. They're excited to meet you." Her expression shifted for a second. She didn't look particularly pleased, but I didn't know whether that was at the prospect of introducing me, training me, or simply going back to the ward.

That was . . . promising.

While we walked through the hospital, having bid Matron goodbye, Nurse Gwen gave me the side-eye. "You are not what I expected," she said matter-of-factly.

I looked over at her before I could stop myself, sending a critical eye over her appearance. She *was* what I expected. From the tip of her immaculate but utilitarian brunette ponytail to the points of her sensible shoes, she looked like Nurse Barbie, with a slender elfin face and clear blue eyes. Self-consciousness flooded over me a second later, and I glanced down at my own white, slightly-scuffed tennis shoes. They were clearly broken in, but apart from that I couldn't think of a single reason why anyone might take issue with my appearance. This was the uniform of a nurse, and I was a nurse.

"Oh?" I asked, steeling myself against the sudden insecurity, wishing there were a mirror somewhere in this place. I knew why there wasn't, of course—safety always came first—but it would have been nice to at least do a teeth check and put my unfounded worries to rest. I shook myself. First-day nerves were one thing, but this was ridiculous. It wasn't like I hadn't done a full check in the rearview mirror of my car—or eaten anything since.

"I was under the impression that you came from a similarly small hospital?" She said it like it was some sort of explanation.

"Yes," I said, not following. "I went to school in Detroit, but I came right back to my hometown to work."

"In Psych?"

"Yes," I said, feeling defensive and not knowing why. "Why?"

"You seem . . . happy," Gwen stated, frowning, walking the last couple of steps to the doorway that Matron and I had stopped in front of before. The panel beside the door shouted 'THE BOUGHS WARD' at me in straight, carved letters.

Given that my nerves felt like they'd been in a blender since I walked in, I couldn't think how she'd come to that conclusion. Nevertheless, I looked over at her, one eyebrow raised. "Is that a problem?"

She didn't answer. Something flickered in her eyes that I couldn't name, and she swiped her card to open up the heavy metal door. It swung out toward us, revealing the main room of the ward. All laminated wood and heavy woven covers, the left half of the room heavily resembled a cafeteria disguised as a living room, complete with a counter running along the left hand wall, but without any sharp edges, possible projectiles, or anything that could be possibly be classified as "unsafe."

There was a strip of worn blue carpet that ran from the back of the room where there was a couch and a door that was labeled "Restroom" to where I was standing in front of the ward entrance. To the right were three open doors. A glimpse into the first lent me a view of the edge of a bed and a group of wooden shelves. Bedrooms.

At the top of the walls a mismatched green border crawled around the edges, the odd leaf just large enough for me to identify it as some sort of ivy. It didn't match the carpet or the walls, the carpets and the walls didn't match the furniture, and as I looked around at the patients, the people didn't match either the furniture or the decor.

All in all, it just felt cold.

"All right, you three!" Gwen said, clapping her hands sharply. "We're going to introduce you to Nurse Margot, and then we're going to get ready for bed." She raised a finger to the older man in the ward who had just opened his mouth. "No exceptions, Randal."

The man was older than I had expected for this type of ward—between sixty or seventy, probably. His gray hair was sticking up in all directions, and there was a strange sort of insistence in his eyes as he spoke in an aged but pleasant baritone voice.

"Nurse Gwen, the night is young. How are we supposed to revel in the light of the stars if we cannot stay up to see them?"

"It's not time to revel," Gwen said firmly. She glanced at me with an odd look—something approaching embarrassment, but not quite, as if she were warning me against believing him. Or obeying him.

Thankfully, I knew better.

Gwen continued. "It's time to meet Nurse Margot, and then time to go to sleep."

Randal sighed and shook his head, his voice sad. "Your generation has no respect for the old ways."

Gwen ignored that, instead pointing to me. "Randal, this is Nurse Margot." Her voice brooked no argument. She turned that severe look to me and motioned toward Randal. "This is Randal. He's been here at Our Lady the longest of all our patients. His family couldn't take care of him any longer, and after a brief and apparently horrific stay in a retirement home, his family sent him here to be looked after and to . . . manage his condition."

Randal looked between Gwen and me, his bushy salt and pepper brows lowered in confusion, his voice childlike as he spoke. "But my family is here. It's not like I'm crazy—Matron says so, and I can always trust her, and I have, ever since she was a little girl." He laughed a little. "Oh, little Gwennie, you don't make any sense sometimes."

Gwen's expression didn't change, and she turned away, as if she hadn't heard Randal, directing her gaze to the only woman in the ward. The young woman was sitting at a round, plastic table, placing pieces in a large puzzle that was almost finished. She was small and fair-haired, with hunched shoulders, as though she was deeply uncomfortable, and was dressed neatly in what seemed to be her 'day clothes'—crisp purple scrubs with a white knitted cardigan over top. The cardigan was obviously a keepsake; there was a dotted reddish stain down the front, with a matching spotting on the sleeve. She didn't acknowledge us standing there, watching her. In fact, if I had known any better, I could have sworn that she hadn't noticed that we were there.

"Polly?"

Gwen's voice wasn't particularly loud, but the blonde woman jumped, looking up at Gwen with large, frightened eyes the color of a stormy sky. Polly didn't speak or look at me, she simply stared at Gwen, as if waiting for something. Something bad, going by her body language.

Gwen motioned to me. "Polly, this is Nurse Margot," she explained, her voice far too loud and deliberate. "She is going to be the new nurse, okay?"

Polly glanced at me, her eyes lingering on something just above my head, and nodded slowly, as though the idea was just beginning to settle in her brain.

"Polly is relatively new here in the ward—been here just under a year," Gwen said to me. "She'll function normally most of the time, but as you can see, she has slower days where she needs a bit more help. It's why she's here in The Boughs instead over in The Tulip Ward or somewhere more short term."

"I see," I said, nodding. I didn't, of course, but considering I'd been in the room barely twenty minutes, I was willing to give myself a little more time to get settled in.

"No, you don't," another voice cut in. At the far edge of the room, Thomas stood up from the worn blue couch. His voice was strong and rich and, to my surprise, British. He was also extremely tall, his shoulders practically the width of the door frame. I wasn't small, but even this far away from him I felt about half my size. I didn't like it. Straightening up a little, I lifted my chin to stare back at him. He noticed, and a wry smile flashed across his face.

"Don't worry, Nurse Margot, you have nothing to fear from me," he said easily. He narrowed his eyes at Gwen. "I can introduce myself."

"Be my guest," she replied.

It wasn't exactly animosity that I sensed between the two of them, but it wasn't respect. At least, not on Thomas's part. Crossing the room in three enormous strides, he held out his hand. I shook it firmly.

"Tam Lynn," he said.

"Tom?"

"No, Tam." His voice turned irritated. "It's Scottish."

That didn't make any sense, and I still wasn't sure whether I'd heard him correctly, but I answered as though I had. "Oh, okay. I'm Margot Knight. Nice to meet you."

"I didn't really have a choice," he said, his voice dropping deeper, "but thank you for being here. Please listen carefully, I am being held here against my will. I am not insane, and you're in very great danger." As he spoke, he leaned in a little to where his dark green eyes were even with mine, intense and almost pleading.

I blinked, and it took all my training to not yank my hand from his. What? "I'm sorry?"

Gwen sighed. "Thomas—"

"Tam."

Gwen looked at him darkly. "Thomas. Thank you for your input. Feel free to go back to your activities."

There was an icy silence, and I was sure that Thomas was going to ignore her and keep talking to me. Then, stiffly, he nodded to me, turned on his heel, and went back to the couch.

"Thomas believes that he's being held prisoner here," Gwen said quietly. "He's quite convinced that the staff are some sort of mythological creatures or something. He was committed by the police—they found him wandering around the forest, on a white horse of all things."

I glanced back over at him. He was glaring at the two of us over a book.

"Um, does he know that his book is upside down?"

She frowned. "He knows. He says he's trying to get around

the actual order that was given to prove that he can do what he wants. Because he's apparently under some sort of spell."

"How do you get around that?"

Gwen looked at me sharply. "You won't have to. The most you'll need to do is help them get to bed on time."

Wow.

"Sorry," I held my palms out, "I realize that. I mean, how do you keep the peace with him? Maybe make it so he doesn't feel so threatened?"

She laughed, and all three patients looked up, their expressions ranging from concerned to downright nervous. Judgment thundered on the heels of defensiveness in my brain, crowding out the nervousness, and I glanced at them, fighting the concerned frown that was threatening to emerge on my face.

Gwen laid a hand on my arm. "Nurse Margot, would you take a little friendly advice?"

"I will always listen to free advice."

"The way to get things done around here is not to cajole." She said it loud enough that all three patients could hear her. "Or make friends. Give orders, expect to be obeyed, report it when you are not. Those are the most efficient ways to get things done around here."

A dozen thoughts flashed through my brain, not all of them strictly complimentary. After a moment, though, I nodded and forced a smile. "Thank you for your advice. I will definitely keep that in mind."

She must have noticed the fact that I had definitely *not* committed to follow her advice. "You're here to treat these people," she reminded me, "not make friends. Keep that in mind."

"Yes, ma'am," I said, changing my tone immediately. I didn't need to get on Gwen's bad side my first day. More than that, I *did* need to do my job effectively in order to keep it. I didn't know the purpose of the rules, but usually they were there for a reason. Furthermore, I'd uprooted my entire life to be here, and unless I found myself willing to start over again, it would be wise to remember that I didn't have to know everything about a rule before I followed it.

"Good," she said. Then, narrowing her eyes, she looked around the room. "Now, while I've got your attention, it's time to get ready for bed. Everyone, pajamas. Polly, you're first on the schedule. Randal, you're next."

"That was yesterday," Randal said, bouncing a little impatiently, his voice twisting up into a surprisingly juvenile whine. Gwen shot him a look. He stopped bouncing immediately.

Across the room, Thomas cleared his throat. "Sorry, Nurse," he said in a low, but unexpectedly deferential voice, "but I believe he's right."

Gwen looked like she was going to disagree, but she took a deep breath instead, glancing at me for a second. "Fine," she said. "Randal first, Thomas second. Polly, you need to be ready, so go get your things now."

Polly nodded, and with the slightest whisper of movement, she stood up from the table. Blankly, almost as though she were floating through a dream, she walked toward one of the three doors on the wall next to me. She ignored me completely, entered the middle door, and closed it behind her. Randal traced the same route, entering the door on the right, closest to the ward's entrance, but he emerged a second later with his toothbrush, toothpaste, and a set of clothes.

Thomas similarly moved through his routine but, after he'd grabbed his pajamas and basket of toiletries and settled himself back on the couch, he glanced over at me every now and again, as if watching me to see if I'd react.

I looked around the room instead. I'd been working in psychiatric wards of varying degrees of severity for the last ten years. There wasn't much that was different. Except—

"You let them keep a lot of stuff in their rooms." I noted the desk and large heavy lamp in Randal's room. Keeping my face carefully neutral, I shifted in my stance to face her a little better.

"I would've thought that some of those things might be considered dangerous."

Gwen shrugged, a glimmer of respect on her face. For noticing? "Not so much. None of them are suicidal or homicidal, and there's always a nurse on duty. This is largely an advanced assisted living ward to keep them in a secure environment. They're fine in here, but they don't do so well out on their own."

I glanced over at Polly's door, nodding. I'd had more experience in that regard than I'd ever wanted.

Randal had to be sent back into the bathroom twice, once to actually change into his pajamas—apparently reveling in starlight was still on his mind—and once to pick up his toiletry tote and bring it back out with him. After that, wrapped in a faded, blue-striped robe with white tube socks on his feet, he shuffled out into the main room with a magazine under his arm and a sulky expression on his face.

"You, madam," he said, pointing the magazine at Gwen, "have no respect for the old ways. Or culture. Or your elders." With great aplomb, he flopped down on the sofa next to the spot Thomas had just vacated and flipped open his magazine. He stared down at it for a good thirty seconds, then glanced up at me and Gwen. He seemed a little surprised, as though disconcerted that we were still standing there, and his frown intensified before he refocused on his magazine.

Thirty seconds later, he glanced up again.

"Does he think we're going to leave?" I asked quietly, leaning toward the other nurse.

Gwen shrugged. "Probably. Randal Kingman, you're not going out tonight. My last word."

He huffed, neck and fists tight, and chucked his magazine to the side. "Very well. But I think you are doing all of us a disservice. How else can we prepare for All Hallows Eve unless we are able to look to the stars and align ourselves with their will?"

"The stars can take care of themselves." Gwen rolled her eyes almost imperceptibly. "And other people will prepare for the bonfire. It's not your responsibility."

"It used to be," Randal said sulkily. "Before you young ones usurped the old, and made it as though I were not fit to do my duty."

Gwen didn't try to hide her eye roll this time. "Randal, it's a bonfire."

"It's *special*," he insisted. "And you know that. It's the All Hallows Eve bonfire. Your disrespect disturbs me. Rest assured, I will be speaking to Matron about this." He looked petulant for a moment longer, and then he caught sight of me. He'd acknowledged me before, but as he looked at me with an oddly clear gaze, it seemed like this was the first time he actually saw me and understood exactly who I was.

"Nurse Margot," he said, his voice so suddenly childlike that it was jarring, "will you be coming to our Hallowe'en party?"

I looked between him and Gwen and shrugged. "Well, Randal, I'm not sure. I don't really know anything about it, or if I'll be allowed. What happens at the party?" There would apparently be a bonfire, but I didn't know whether he wanted to tell me about it himself, or just get it by inference.

"Well, there's the bonfire," he said. "Sometimes games. The Solemn Feast—"

"You're straying, Randal," Gwen interrupted. "Nurse Margot has no time to listen to your rambling." She turned to me, telling me by her posture not to encourage him.

At the same time, Thomas exited the bathroom, dressed in the same type of blue pajamas as Randal, topped by an almost laughably small robe. He looked between me, Gwen, and Randal curiously, having heard the last few lines of the conversation. "Nurse Margot uncovering all our secrets already?"

Gwen scoffed, her expression ultimately fed up. "At the Hallowe'en party we usually have some games, a nice dinner for the patients, and then a bonfire."

"It's only twelve days from now," Randal looking toward the door wistfully.

Gwen noticed, taking an extra sidestep in front of it.

Randal continued, evidently not noticing. "A holy number. One that would lend us special power if only we were out among the stars."

Thank goodness Gwen was going to be here. It wasn't as though I hadn't met others with similar manias, but even if Randal wasn't dangerous, I could see why a regular retirement home couldn't handle him.

"Well, Randal," I said, keeping my tone light and conversational, "if it's only twelve days from now, I'll probably be there. I guess it'll depend on what time I come in. It gets dark pretty early right now, you might have the bonfire before I get here."

There was a small gasp, and we all turned toward the bathroom door. Polly stood there, looking at us with large, horrified eyes.

"Fire?" she whispered at us.

Thomas's eyes widened a little, and he took a step toward her, but Gwen spoke up first.

"Yes, Polly. Hallowe'en is in twelve days. Are you ready?"

"Ready," she whispered.

I narrowed my eyes slightly. Was that an answer or was she simply repeating the last word that she had heard?

Thomas noticed my expression, and when I glanced at him, he raised an eyebrow with an air of satisfaction, as if something had been proved to me. Ah, right. He was convinced he was being threatened by something. Mythological creatures? Did Polly think the same?

Gwen looked at the pajamaed crew in front of her. "All right. Meds, then bed."

Randal kept on chattering away about Hallowe'en night as we all followed Gwen over to the medicine cabinet. He was talking about past bonfires. It was clearly the only part that he remembered, and it was kind of endearing in a way. I couldn't help but smile as I listened, even while I watched Gwen carefully to see which medications went to each patient.

"The bonfire's your favorite part, isn't it, Randal?" I asked, holding out his cup of pills.

He looked up at me, a brilliant smile on his face. "It's like magic," he said. "The best part of the whole year."

Thomas huffed, but not in a sarcastic or mocking way. "Magic is a good word for it. It will definitely be a night that none of us will forget." His low voice rumbled, his eyes far away, drifting in Polly's direction. She sat at the round table again, staring off into the distance while she waited for her medication.

"What do you mean?" I asked, handing Thomas his medication.

Gwen gave me a faintly disapproving look for engaging in the conversation but she let it slide. Did she never talk to these people? Thomas stared down at me, expression inscrutable.

"What do you mean, 'what do you mean?'" he challenged.

I shrugged a little. "People usually mean one of two things when they describe something as 'magic,' It's either because something is more wonderful than they ever expected, or it's unexplainable. Usually in a positive way."

A smile quirked up one of his cheeks. "Always in a positive way," Thomas countered.

"You didn't use it that way," I pointed out.

He looked a little ruffled, as though I wasn't supposed to have picked up on that detail.

I smiled. "Sorry. Do you need water with your meds?"

Looking me dead in the eye, Thomas dumped the pills into his mouth and swallowed them dry. We stood looking at each other for a minute, my smile growing. There had been about ten tablets in the tiny cup, most of them the size of horse pills.

"How was that?" I asked, after a moment of silence.

He sighed. "Water would be good, thanks." His voice was a little weak.

Chuckling slightly, I turned and filled a paper cup from the dispenser and pushed it into his hand. He nodded in thanks, and then nodded to Gwen.

"Nurse, I'm headed in."

Gwen nodded in return. "Very good. Polly, you going in?"

Polly rose, as if in a trance. "Yes," she said softly. "In." Then, crumpling the empty paper cup in her hand without looking at it, she floated into her bedroom. The door slid shut, and a moment later the light in the door's window went dark.

"Poor girl," Gwen whispered in the sudden silence. "Today's even worse than I thought. Hopefully she'll be better tomorrow. The meds will help her sleep."

I nodded my head in agreement. I'd seen the prescriptions, and I knew what they did.

Thomas disappeared into his own room soon after Polly. Randal sat up on the couch for as long as he could, which ended up being about ten minutes before he started to nod off despite his excitement, his head bobbing down to his chest. A few minutes later, when he started to snore, Gwen and I towed the older man to bed.

"He was excited tonight. He's not always like that." Gwen walked over to an old beat-up file cabinet that was an odd shade of mossy green and opened the top drawer. It protested with a screech that sent a shiver up my spine.

Pulling out three files and pushing the drawer back in, resulting in a similarly dinosaur-like screech, Gwen turned back to me and motioned toward the table. "The patients are allowed to sit up as long as they can or want to after they take their meds, but if you're in here by yourself, it's more convenient to have them go to bed. Here, you can sit there. I'll show how you to do the charts, but I want a bit of tea first. Want a cup?"

Her tone had changed somewhat now that we weren't in front of the patients. That made sense, in a way. She certainly wasn't the first nurse that I'd met with the perspective of being tough on the patients and chummy with the nurses. I had friends in both camps, but I definitely favored connection over command.

"Yes, please. Strong tea, if you could." I sat down at the table. I'd only been at work for a couple hours, but it was now eleven at night, and my brain was starting to tell me that it was time to simmer down myself. I shifted a little in my seat, trying to wiggle into wakefulness. For crying out loud, it was like my body was convinced I'd never done this before.

Mom was right, your body did catch up with you in your thirties. *Mom* . . . I pushed the thought away and tuned in hard to what Gwen was saying.

"I just have individual tea bags, so you can let it steep for longer if you'd like," Gwen said, handing me a steaming teacup and saucer. The set had a pretty design, with an ivy pattern around the rim and some kind of berry on the side. Holly? I smiled.

"Thanks," I said, taking the warm set. A scented puff of steam floated across my face. The tea smelled wonderful—some sort of peppermint, mixed with another scent that seemed to push wakefulness into every corner of my brain.

"Drink it before it gets cold," she advised, and then placed her folders down on the table. We went over the charts, which were similar to the progress charts that I'd been dealing with since I'd started to work in psychiatric hospitals. She let me read through some of the previous entries.

Thomas was straightforward. He believed that the entire staff was faeries, he was being held against his will, and that they —the staff—were planning on doing him harm. Looking at Polly's file, it was odd for me to imagine the fair-haired young woman having the conversations and intense dreams detailed in her file. At the same time, they revealed a quiet soul that was very sweet and sensitive to the needs of those around her. Randal was off on his own path, but mostly benign. He rambled more, and he often got worked up, but he wasn't dangerous. Not any more than any other seventy-three-year-old with hallucinations and a manic fascination with . . .

"Faeries? Again?" I whispered.

Gwen looked up. "What was that?"

I shook my head. "It's just interesting to me that both Ta—Thomas and Randal have obsessions with faeries."

"It isn't coincidental." She pointed back to the filing cabinet, "If you look at the earlier files, they were both put here because they don't drive each other crazy—they just play off of each other harmlessly. They've both been through a lot of therapy, though, and it's gotten to the point that we've been keeping them well-maintained. At least, the data says that we have. No manic episodes for a while now for either of them."

"I see." I looked back at the pages.

"You disagree?" she asked with interest.

I shook my head. "Not necessarily. It's just interesting that you would put two people with the exact same mania and paranoia in one ward."

She shrugged. "I just treat them."

"Oh, I know. I guess it's just one of those things," I said, smiling.

She shrugged again. "I guess. You have . . . experience with faeries?"

My mouth dropped open a little, and I laughed a little, slightly embarrassed. "No. Well, yes, I guess. My parents were convinced they were real. They escaped some cult when they were younger that was focused around fae."

"So . . . they taught you about them?" Her fingers curled around her teacup, and her eyes, a sharp blue even in the dim night lighting, seemed to cut into me.

She probably thought I bought into it too. "Yeah," I admitted. "I even believed it for a while, but let's put it this way: college has a way of stamping out most fairy tales, especially the ones that aren't real. It's been a long time since I've believed anything like that."

Gwen's expression was still a little concerned.

I leaned forward. "Gwen, I promise, there's no chance of me turning into one of the patients."

There was a flicker of something behind her eyes, and a rather teasing smirk crossed her face. "Careful, careful, Margot. The only difference between us and them is how well we control our reality."

I took another sip of the tea, and smiled. For all her gruffness, maybe Gwen wasn't all that bad. I sighed, rubbing my eyes and resisting the urge to look at the clock. "So. Hallowe'en party —dinner, games, bonfire? Do we arbitrate as staff? Am I about to be drafted into being a pumpkin?"

"Some of us help." Gwen leaned back, a genuine smile crossing her face at last. She tapped her pencil thoughtfully on the table. "But most of those assignments have already been made. It's the biggest celebration we hold at the hospital—the bonfire is enormous, and often times we have a dance around the fire too, for some of the more stable patients."

She spoke a little bit wistfully, like Thomas and Randal had, and I smiled. "It sounds like it's your favorite as well," I said teasingly.

She threw a half smile over at me. "What can I say? I enjoy a good party, even if sometimes I have to dress up like a pumpkin." Now she grinned. "The dinner's catered, though, so that's something. Anyway, you're right. Since you're on nightshift, you'll probably be asked to work it."

I yawned a large, long yawn. "I think my goal should be to get on day shifts. Not sure if night shift really agrees with me."

"Who knows? Maybe you'll find you enjoy it more as you get used to it."

I smiled ruefully and picked up Randal's file again. "Here's hoping."

OCTOBER 21

The next morning, I dumped my half-drunk tea down the sink and headed on home. I'd burned my brains out learning all the paperwork protocols—which apparently hadn't caught up to the twenty-first century yet, as there wasn't a single computer anywhere in Our Lady. Then I'd paced until around two in the morning, forgetting the shot of caffeine that sat invitingly on the table.

Gwen had been merciful then and had let me take a much-needed hour-long nap on the couch. I'd woken up when the bathroom door opened and closed, and as I'd rubbed the sleep out of my eyes, I saw a bleary-eyed Thomas shuffling across the dimly lit room. He looked at me questioningly, but as soon as he was there, he was gone. Feeling a little bit ashamed of being caught sleeping, I got up off the couch and started to search for ways to stay awake. I'd remembered the tea and warmed it up in the microwave, but I could only manage a sip or two more before the flavor—or lack thereof—was too much for me. Like most herbal teas, it smelled better than it tasted, especially after steeping for so long.

And that was all that had happened the entire night. As the shift drew to a close, and under Gwen's supervision, I made the notes in the files. Just before six in the morning, before the morning nurse—apparently named Kristen—showed up, Gwen shooed me out of the room, hushing my protests by insisting that it was my first day on night shift and it wouldn't do any harm. So, before the autumn dawn began to lighten the sky, I rolled toward the tall, wrought-iron security fence. There was a guard waiting for me.

"ID card?" he asked, holding out his hand.

I looked at him oddly for a moment. Was he turned around? I was heading *out* of the hospital. Or maybe they were worried about people escaping?

"Oh, sorry," I said, pulling my ID card lanyard over the top of my head and holding it out to the guard.

He took it and examined it thoroughly, as though not convinced I was the person on the card. It wasn't really fair of him—that was by far the best ID picture ever taken of me.

I pulled my hand back inside the car and rubbed it against the early morning chill, adjusting the thermostat accordingly. The Range Rover's heater worked, it just took three to five business days to get up to a reasonable temperature.

The guard also took his time, and I sighed, looking toward the closed fence in front of me. Oak leaves were part of the design, the curves creating an unnatural depth to the fence, like it was several feet deep instead of only a couple of inches. I found myself quite entranced by it, staring at it dreamily until the guard nudged the ID card against my arm. I jumped.

"Here," he grunted.

Trying to pretend I hadn't nearly achieved orbit by jumping so high, I took my card, nodded in thanks and drove my car through the gates before turning onto the highway toward Carterhall.

Home.

It was a fifty-minute drive and, despite the slow brightening of the sky from black to deep blue, I had to turn my music up to keep myself awake. I didn't need to die driving home after surviving my first day—or night—at work. Thankfully, on normal days I wouldn't have to stay much longer than this. Most days—nights?— my shift started at eight thirty and ended at six. Tonight, though, Gwen had told me I didn't have to report until nine.

Just as I was about able to separate the silhouettes of trees from the night sky, I saw the lights of the town ahead of me. Carterhall was a one-stoplight town that at every angle and from every perspective seemed to plaintively cry, "Take me out of the eighties!" I surveyed the houses that lined both sides of the street as I passed, taking in the grocery store and the gas station, and the one bar that I could say with some certainty that I was *never* going to set foot in.

When I finally got to my overly-cheerful white house, I trudged up the three concrete steps, and locked the door behind me. I stumbled to my bedroom, pulled the blackout curtains over the window and collapsed, fully clothed, into bed.

❦

I was none too pleased when I woke up at two in the afternoon to the annoying, cheerful tune of my phone ringing. Rolling over on my bed, I picked up the phone, and tried to focus on the caller ID.

Edward Campion.

My stomach suddenly began roiling, and I hit 'Decline.' After turning the phone to vibrate, I flopped back onto my stomach, closed my eyes, and pulled my pillow over my head.

The phone began to vibrate again. It buzzed and buzzed and buzzed, and, whispering nice-girl epithets to myself, I firmly ignored the buzzing phone.

"Freaking lawyer. I hope his coffee creamer curdles. I hope he has traffic on all the ways to work! I hope his beard grows in patchy." In the dissipating fog of sleep, I remembered he didn't have a beard. "I hope it grows in patchy when he wants one!"

The vibrating lasted for a few more minutes, and by the time it stopped rattling against the bedside table, I lay utterly awake in my bed, any ability to sleep firmly behind me. After laying in the pretend darkness for a couple more moments fuming to myself, I gave up, and stumbled toward the bathroom to shower.

It was all for the best, really, as my house's interior was still in an anxiety-inducing state of disarray. I spent a couple of hours unpacking and cleaning and making a "lunch" to hopefully help keep me awake during the night. Then, I left the house after the last little bit of light had dimmed from the sky. Grumbling in displeasure, I flipped my headlights on as I left my driveway. Steeling myself against humanity, I tried not to rev my engine at the driver that cut me off at the stoplight, staring out at the darkness.

I'm never going to drive in the daylight ever again, am I? I thought morosely.

Stop it, Margot. I physically shook my head. *You're just tired. Fix your attitude, or this day is only going to get worse.* After plugging in my MP3 player, I turned on my favorite song, blasting it on repeat until I got within hearing distance of the iron gates. By that time, I actually felt like a decent human again.

That is, until I made it up to The Boughs at five minutes to nine.

I hadn't met the day nurse yet, due to my late introduction to the ward the night before. So, I was a little confused when a beautiful redhead in scrubs looked up from the table where Polly and Randal were playing cards. Standing up swiftly, she met me at the door, a glower on her face.

"*There* you are! I thought you were never going to get here."

I frowned and checked my watch. "Nurse Gwen told me to get here at nine. Why, has something happened?" I asked, alarmed. I hadn't missed any calls from the hospital—or any unknown callers. "Has something gone wrong with the patients?"

The young woman shook her head and sighed, a look of realization dawning on her face. "Classic Gwen. She was supposed to call and tell you to get here at eight-thirty to relieve me. There was an emergency with one of the nurses in another ward, and since Nurse Jeffrey and Nurse Velma were already out, she had to take over Delphinium Ward for the night."

I blinked. "Wait, I'm on my own?"

Randal shifted, a weird expression his face, clearly listening to the conversation. I ignored him, vehemently praying that wasn't an omen of the near future. The woman, whose name badge said Eileen, put her hand on my shoulder. "Are you actually complaining?" I couldn't decide whether it was comforting or condescending, until she said, "This is the easiest ward in the hospital. Get Thomas to help you if you have trouble with Randal. Polly's having a good day, so she won't be any trouble either."

"But—"

"Nurse Margot, I'm already late," the redhead snapped, shutting her bag decisively. "You can call Gwen over the office phone if you need help."

I sighed, putting my hands up, trying to keep from snapping back. "Fine. No problem. Have a good evening."

She smiled then, her mood turning on a dime, as if to thank me for staying—even though I was contractually obligated to stay. "Sweet girl. Have a good evening! Oh, Gwen left a note on the file cabinet with the schedule in case you need it."

I nodded in forced gratitude, but Eileen was already gone, the door clicking shut and beeping behind her. I stood there, looking around the white and blue room and suddenly feeling ridiculously out of my element.

Nonsense, I thought. *You've been a nurse for ten years. You've seen it done, now it's time to do it yourself. It's not the end of the world.* I'd seen Gwen do it yesterday, and she had left a schedule that I could refer to if I needed. I could do it. And I could do it well. No one would die, no one would get maimed, and I could finish the shift on a high note.

Easy.

"You all right there, Nurse Margot?" Thomas drawled from the other side of the room. He drew my name out, overpronouncing the *oh* at the end. Polly glanced up at us.

I sighed. "Yes, thank you." I ran a quick hand over my hair, sighing again. At least after a day like today I wasn't working a high-risk unit. *Thank you, night shift.*

"You're quite formal," he noted.

I looked over at Thomas. He sat on the arm of the rough blue sofa with a book in his hand, glancing through the pages unconvincingly, perched as though he could move at any time.

"You're not," I noted in return.

"Life's a bit too short to get overworked about details like formality," he said matter-of-factly, his crisp accent enunciating each syllable like he was a long-suffering nineteenth-century nobleman.

I raised an eyebrow. "Is that so?" I thought of his greeting the night before. His statement about life certainly wasn't the sort of thing that I usually heard from someone with paranoid delusions.

"Of course," he responded coolly. "So if I do get overworked about something, you can rest assured that it's really worth it."

There it is.

"Good to know." Somehow, I managed to push the sarcasm down to where it wasn't obviously audible, and he didn't seem to notice. Small mercies. Heaven knows I didn't need to get in a shouting match tonight with a patient who was twice my size. So, instead, I left Thomas to his reading and the others to their card game, and went to put my stuff down and check out the schedule on the door of the office.

As expected, the schedule was pretty much the exact same as it had been yesterday: get ready for bed at 10:00, lights out between 10:30 and 11:00. It also listed the medications that everyone was to take as well—something I was grateful for. I'd been administering medications for years, but it didn't mean I'd memorized on first sight what everyone was taking.

"Nurse Margot?" A soft female voice spoke directly behind me, and I whipped around to see Polly. Her pale blonde hair fell in waves around her face. She looked a little guilty when she saw my expression and began to fiddle with the hem of her white sweater. "Oh, I'm sorry, I didn't mean to frighten you."

My heart rate had picked up, but I shook my head soothingly. "You didn't. What can I do for you, Polly?"

Her pink lips curved upward. "Randal and I wanted to know if you would like to play cards with us?" she asked, clasping her hands tentatively.

I looked at her for a moment, and then down at the schedule. "You know, I need to read through the notes that Nurse Eileen left about today, but I will when I'm done, okay?"

She seemed to think about it for a moment, but a dissatisfied expression crossed her face. "But then it'll be time for bed."

I looked at the clock. It was just past nine. "No, it won't," I said. "It shouldn't take me more than a half hour to get through everything, unless one of you had an emergency today. Anyone?"

Randal shook his head solemnly. Thomas grunted.

Polly shook her head. "No, today has been a good day."

"Well then, it shouldn't take me too long to catch up."

A cautious smile crossed Polly's face. "Thirty minutes, yeah?"

"Yes," I said. "If I forget, remind me. I'm serious."

She grinned suddenly, and somehow it lifted the weight of my earlier mood. "I will," she promised, then she crossed the room back over to where Randal was shuffling the deck of cards.

Just as I'd thought, not much had happened during the day. There'd been a horseback riding excursion earlier with all three patients, and nothing had gone wrong. Someone had left a note saying that Polly might be sore, and it was all right to add an anti-inflammatory to her medications, but that was the extent of it.

So I played cards.

And I got trashed.

"Where in the world did you learn how to play cards like this?" I demanded after losing the third straight hand.

Randal chuckled, shuffling the deck again. "Polly here is the daughter of a card shark. Comes from Vegas. Me? I've just got hundreds of years of experience."

"I call baloney," I said. "You're only seventy-three. I've seen your file."

"Ah, that was the age that I was *assigned*," he said, lifting a finger. "Do you think the average seventy-year-old would look as young as I do?"

I grinned. "You look young?"

Someone snorted from the other side of the room, but when I looked up, Thomas's face was impassive behind his book. I noted that it was right-side up this time.

Randal harrumphed good-naturedly. "So this is why nurses don't get close to their patients—they're rude!"

"Every single one of us." I held out my hand. "It's also my turn to deal."

"But I like dealing," he said, pulling the cards close to his chest.

"Yes, well, I'm pretty sure you're cheating." I wiggled my fingers. "Now hand them over."

Sighing dramatically, Randal handed the cards over. "It's my moral obligation," he said sniffily. "If you didn't notice, then you deserve what's coming to you."

"Rubbish," I said good-naturedly. "Why test out whether or not I can spot you cheating? What if I'm just bad at cards in the first place? Or are you just trying to take advantage of me because I'm the new nurse?"

One of Randal's eyebrows rose. He leaned across the table, and said softly, his voice remarkably deep and serious, "And if I'm simply testing your aptitude? Perhaps I'm seeing how well you can spot trickery."

I stared at him, hair raising on the back of my neck in the sudden silence, utterly at a loss for how to respond.

Suddenly his face split into a smile. "I got you!" he said, cackling in a good-natured way that didn't entirely soothe the uncomfortable weightless feeling from a moment ago.

Forcing a smile on my face, I shook my head and my finger at him. "Don't you go playing nasty tricks, Randal."

He grinned in response. "I'll make you a deal," he said, tipping his head playfully to the side. "I will never play the same trick on you twice, if you catch me."

"I—"

"Randal, don't be ridiculous. You know better than to make deals with the staff," Thomas broke in, cutting me off.

I jumped, looking up at him towering over me. I wasn't sure how I could have missed someone as large as him approaching, and yet here he was, enormous and looming over the back of my chair. Instinctively, I pushed the chair back and stood to face him.

Up close, he wasn't quite so massive as he'd seemed, but he was still a good five inches taller than me, and a lot broader. I fought down the discomfort that crawled under my skin, but I still shifted slightly.

"I thought I told you that you have nothing to fear from me," Thomas said, his deep voice rumbling. His green eyes looked almost curious. "Don't you trust me?"

"Can't, Thomas," I said a little regretfully, tapping my work badge. "Sorry."

He took a half step back, nodding as if he realized something for the first time. I felt a pull of shame, like I had disappointed him in some way. I fought down the urge to take it back, to tell him *of course* I trusted him, and that everything was okay. It reminded me of—

"Can we play another hand, Nurse Margot?" Polly asked.

Thomas backed up deferentially, and I nodded, relieved.

"Of course," I said, glancing up at the clock. "We have time for another hand or two. Do you want to join us?" I directed the question at Thomas.

"No, thank you," he said, that same small smile still on his face, returning to the couch. "I would prefer to read."

"No problem," I said, unbothered. He seemed content in what he was doing, no need to take him away from that.

We played another round quietly but quickly. I got smashed again. As I glared down at my hand, Randal smiled and leaned back in his chair.

"You are a good sport," he said. "That's nice. Most of the nurses that we have in here are overbearing or fidgety. I can't remember the last time Nurse Gwen played cards with us. She was probably too worried that she wouldn't be able to control us."

"And I'm not worried about that?" I asked.

Randal shrugged. "You're nice, so I'm nice. Call it an exchange."

I raised an eyebrow. "So, you're difficult with Nurse Gwen because she's stern with you?"

His eyes flicked up to mine and shrugged carelessly. "I will neither confirm nor deny anything," he said gleefully. Which meant yes.

I smiled and shook my head. "Aren't you worried they're not going to let you go to the Hallowe'en Party if you make trouble?" I asked. "At all the hospitals that I've worked at before, usually there was a privilege system. If you caused trouble on purpose, there were usually consequences."

Randal seemed to think about that, but then he shrugged. "It's never had that effect before. I'm too special, I think," he said, a grin returning to his face. "And what wonderful Hallowe'en nights we've had, Nurse Margot." A sparkle ignited in his eyes, and the grin turned blissful. "The most beautiful night of the year. The stories I could tell . . . The bonfire roaring as big as a house. People dancing and singing. The drinks and the food. Truly a night you'll never forget as long as you live."

I frowned. "They'd let the bonfire get that big? It seems a little . . . dangerous, considering the needs of some of the patients here."

"Not everyone goes," Randal said. "There are some people who are . . . well," he looked around the room, "unstable. It wouldn't be safe for them."

"I see." And I did.

"Well, well, Nurse Margot," Thomas said from across the room. "You managed to say that without a hint of irony. I'm impressed."

"I'm not allowed to understand?" I threw back.

"He is the unstable one," he said harshly, meeting my eyes over the top of his book. I raised an eyebrow.

"Is he?" I asked. "He seems able to understand how to be safe and to follow orders. Why shouldn't he have regular privileges?"

He narrowed his eyes. "You're defending Randal."

"And you're acting defensive," I pointed out. "All I'm saying is what he says makes sense. Different people with different capacities are given different activities—including Randal. That's not foreign to me or, I think, to you."

Thomas's dark eyes studied me carefully.

"Fine," he said, and his gaze dropped back down to his book. I had the feeling that he didn't disagree, but it was almost was as if he'd stopped himself, as if he felt he'd engaged too much.

Randal had kept on talking during my conversation with Thomas, not realizing that I wasn't paying attention. He was speaking about the Hallowe'ens of years past—in great detail.

"And this year will be magnificent," he was saying. "It's the seventh year of the cycle, and so everything will be enormous, and grand, and—and—and *special*. The bonfire will be bigger than ever, the food will be sweeter, the lights and the magic will be something you will never forget, even if you never remember anything else."

I smiled at the absolutely blissful expression on his face. It was enchanting, the way he spoke about the party, and I could almost see it in my mind's eye.

"What makes the seventh year so special?" I asked, shuffling the cards quickly and then dealing out.

"It's the year that Matron kills someone," Polly said matter-of-factly, reaching out to grab her cards.

I froze. Randal did as well, looking up at Polly with such vicious anger that my heart began to race and my breath caught in my lungs. The lights flickered, just for a moment, and then Randal surged to his feet, bolting around the table. He grabbed Polly by the shoulders, shaking her hard enough that her head whipped back. Polly screamed, reaching up toward Randal's face to push him away. I leaped out of my seat after Randal, grabbed one of his arms, and pulled it away from Polly with far more difficulty than I thought it should take, his strength completely at odds with his frail appearance.

Randal shook me off and continued jerking Polly back and forth. "Silence! Silence, do you hear? You know nothing! Nothing!" His shouts, half roar and half sob echoed through the ward. The lights flickered again, flashing painfully bright before the electricity died completely.

Suddenly, there in the dark, my brain started again, compelling me to move, and move quickly.

"Randal!" I reached out to where I remembered him being, seizing one of his wrists by sheer luck, and yanked it behind his back with one arm. I tried to drag him backward, but when that didn't work, I reached for Polly's silhouette in the light of the emergency exit sign and shoved her out of harm's way. She stumbled back, gasping and blinking hard, as if breaking out of a daze as the emergency lights came on.

A large pair of hands joined mine, bringing Randal's other arm behind his back, pinning them in place and bringing Randal up to his tiptoes.

There was a moment of silence. Polly looked at all three of us with an expression that was frightened, but not quite aware. A second later, the regular overhead lights came back on, the power restored. I blinked in the harsh light, breathing hard.

"You can see to Polly," Thomas's voice said from beside me. "I'll hold onto Randal until he calms down. It won't be long now."

Breathing hard, I nodded and hesitantly let go of Randal, checking to make sure Thomas's grip was secure before moving to Polly, glancing over her to ensure no immediate medical assistance was needed.

"I will not calm down!" Randal seethed. "Polly must apologize. She must apologize, or she will be smitten for her ignorance!"

"You have no authority to smite anyone!" I snapped.

"I have every authority!" he shrieked.

I straightened, one arm protectively around Polly's shoulders. He'd fooled me once. Randal had fooled me once. He had completely gotten the better of me, but if he came at me now that I knew what to expect, it would end very differently.

"Randal." The tone had a razor edge, and I took in a deep breath, calming myself. Deescalate. Deescalate until you have no other choice. "Randal. You told me that because I treated you kindly, you were treating me kindly. It was an exchange to you, yes?"

Randal narrowed his eyes at Polly and didn't answer me.

"Randal!"

He huffed and nodded. "I did say that it was an exchange."

"Don't exchanges go both ways?" I asked.

His eyes rose to mine in a glower that seemed to be dimming. "Yes," he said, his tone softening.

"I'm responsible for Polly. Do you think it's kind to me to threaten someone that I am responsible for?"

Randal's shoulders were relaxing, and I could see Thomas's grip on Randal's arms loosen a bit. Randal looked down, and I heard him sigh. "No."

"No," I agreed, feeling Polly tremble under my arm.

I saw Randal's bottom lip extend. A moment later he let out a doleful sniff.

"I think you should apologize to Polly." It took effort to force my voice to be calmer, lowering the pitch so it was almost a whisper.

"But she—"

"I know she *said* something hurtful," I said, although I wasn't exactly sure what it was, "but you hurt her physically. She will apologize to you, too. But you did more harm."

Randal looked away, tears glimmering in his eyes. "She doesn't understand."

"I know." I sighed. I didn't either. "But I need you to apologize."

"Sorry, Polly," he said, shuffling his feet and not meeting anyone's eyes.

Polly shifted, pulling the ends of her cardigan together. Her knuckles were white. "Sorry, Randal," she whispered.

Randal gave a stiff nod.

"Good," I said. I nodded at Thomas. He slowly released Randal's arms.

Randal hugged himself, looking piteously over at me. "Polly doesn't know what she's talking about. Nurse Margot, *please* believe me."

"I believe you, Randal," I said gently. "How about we call it a night, eh? I bet everyone's tired."

"It's not ten yet," Randal whined. The clock read nine fifty-five.

I folded my arms. "Only tired people do mean things, Randal," I said, trying to keep my voice patient, but not conde-scending. He was acting like a child, but a moment ago he'd been shaking Polly so hard he could have given her whiplash.

"I'm first," Thomas said, quietly, still standing behind Randal. Randal turned back to look at him. "It'll be past ten when you start getting ready for bed. No going early required."

"Can I read my magazine?" Randal asked Thomas meekly.

Thomas pointed to me. "Nurse Margot's in charge, not me."

Randal looked at me, eyes pleading. It felt like I was rewarding him for bad behavior, but there was just something about those eyes. Big and soulful, and genuinely sorry.

"Sure," I said, keeping the sigh from my voice. "As long as you're quiet, you may read your magazine until it's your turn in the bathroom. And then it's straight to bed."

"No looking at the stars tonight," he said, nodding, as if agreeing to something that I had never actually spoken.

Remembering his obsession the night before, I suddenly felt very cold and very out of my depth. "No. No looking at the stars," I agreed, fighting down the sudden knot in my chest.

"I promise."

Thomas was quick getting ready for bed, then he settled down on the couch with his book. After Polly finished and came out, Randal went in. I glanced at him, wondering if it were appropriate to ask Thomas to watch the door while I made sure Polly was all right.

"See to Polly, Nurse," he murmured, flipping a page. "I'll make sure that Randal stays where he ought to."

I pressed my lips together. It wasn't strictly appropriate, but he'd been helpful earlier, and I was on my own. I'd just have to make do. And if that wasn't a running theme of my life, I didn't know what was.

"Thank you," I said finally. I went to the cabinet first, putting together the medication cups. After locking up Thomas's and Randal's, I grabbed Polly's and a paper cup of water.

She looked at me through the window as I tapped gently on her door. Recognition lit in her eyes, and she opened the door. "Nurse Margot."

"I brought you your pills. And I wanted to make sure you were all right from where Randal grabbed you earlier."

There was a little bit of confusion in her eyes, but she nodded and stepped aside, allowing me into her room. It was rather plain, with a cot-like bed and a bedside table with curved corners and a plastic lamp. She also had a small writing desk, a shelf with a couple of books that looked like journals, and a solitary picture of Polly standing with a dark-haired woman, both grinning widely.

I gave her the pills and the water first, then checked her eyes for any abnormal dilation from being shaken so hard, and then her neck and arms for bruises. Small pinpoints of blue were starting to show up on her arms and I winced on her behalf.

"Do your arms hurt?" I asked after I'd come back with some ice.

She shook her head.

"Do you have a headache?"

She shook her head again.

"If you get one, will you tell me?"

She nodded, swallowing her pills one by one with tiny sips of water.

"Good," I said. "Leave the cold pack on your bedside table when you're done with it. I'll leave a note for someone to put it away tomorrow morning." I stood and slipped the door open. A sudden question piqued in my mind, and I turned back to her.

"Polly?"

"Yes?"

"What did you mean when you said the Matron kills someone every seventh year?"

Polly looked up sharply. "Did I say that?" she asked with concern. "That's awful!"

I blinked a couple of moments, until the reality dawned on me. Of course. Her memory. Trying not to feel disappointed at the lack of an explanation, but also fighting back a wriggle of unease, I smiled and patted her gently on the shoulder.

"Don't worry about it," I said. "I must be mistaken. Have a good night, Polly."

She smiled tentatively and turned out the light as I left.

I grabbed the next medicine cup and paper cup of water

from the medicine cabinet. A moment later, Randal walked out of the bathroom, glancing over to me.

"Medicine, and then off to bed," My voice was firm. Maybe too firm. Visions of Gwen flicked through my brain, and I sighed. I was going to have to be sure that I wasn't reactionary. It wasn't fair or professional.

Randal shuffled his way over without protesting, day clothes and toiletries tote tucked under one arm. He threw back the pills and then went to bed.

As the door clicked shut and the light flicked off, I took in a deep breath and sunk down into the chair.

"You doing all right?" Thomas's voice rumbled from the couch.

I jumped, hand smacking against the tabletop. Groaning a little, I nodded. "Yeah, I'm all right."

And I was. Sort of. Coming down off the adrenaline high from Randal's outburst, my voice was ever so slightly jerky, my thoughts were jumbled, and I hoped beyond hope that Thomas wasn't going to have an episode as well. But I just needed a minute to recalibrate. It wasn't the worst day I'd had in a psych ward, not by a long shot. More than anything, I was just ready for my time alone.

"Would you tell me if you weren't?" Thomas's accent softened the consonants of his words, making them almost float across the room. I caught myself relaxing, and then I straightened.

"Probably not," I admitted. "My problems aren't usually something I try to share with my patients. But today, I'm fine. And you can believe that."

"Randal can be unsettling. Even Polly, in her own way."

I nodded because I wasn't exactly sure what else I was supposed to do.

There was a moment of silence before Thomas spoke again. "That was a mean wrist lock. You had really good control—I wasn't doing much. "

"Thanks." It hadn't felt that way.

"You have training?"

"A bit."

"That could mean anything," he said.

"It could." I smiled despite myself. It wasn't that I minded talking about myself, but I didn't have the brain for it quite yet. "A few years. Why are you Thomas to the staff?"

"They call me by my given name because that's how they control me. A name gives faeries power over a person. People aren't careful enough about who they give their names to, and unfortunately, I was no exception. Not," he added grimly, "that I was given a choice."

"So your full name is Thomas Lynn?"

"Yes."

And that's how you think the staff controls you. "But you want to go by Tam."

"If you please."

I could tell that he was smiling even in the dim light. "Okay, then."

"What, just like that?"

"Why would I call you something that you hate? Besides, I don't need or want to manipulate you. I'm hoping that we can work together to help get you better."

Tam's eyes widened at me just a bit. "Who are you?" he whispered.

How was I supposed to respond to that? "I'm your nurse, Thom—Tam."

Apparently, a reply didn't come to him after that because we sat in silence for a while.

Eventually I glanced up at the clock. "Do you want your meds now, or closer to eleven?"

Tam gave me a half smile, a slight dimple appearing in one cheek. "A little later, I think," he agreed, settling back onto the couch, but not bringing his book up to read again. We sat there looking at each other for a couple of moments, as if neither of us was entirely sure what to say.

"Thank you," I said. "For stepping in earlier."

"You needed the help," he said matter-of-factly. "I've done that before."

"Still. It shouldn't have happened. I mean, I shouldn't have been here alone. It's not . . . protocol."

Tam smiled. It wasn't gentle, more like subdued, and he looked away as soon as he noticed that I had seen it.

"What?" I asked.

"Nothing." This time his voice *was* gentle. He closed his book and stood. "Actually, I think I'd like to take my medicine now. I'm getting tired."

"All right." I walked over to the medicine cabinet, unlocked it, and pulled out Tam's cup with his ten pills and filled him a cup of water without asking if he wanted it.

I handed him the medication and the cup. "Tam?"

He raised an eyebrow. He didn't feel quite so big now, or at least not quite so threatening. I pushed away the thought. *Expect the unexpected.*

"Yes, Nurse Margot?"

"Do . . . well, this is probably going to sound crazy—"

"You're in a mental hospital, Nurse Margot. If you don't sound crazy, you don't fit in."

I didn't want to fit in, but I shrugged. "All right. Why did Randal react the way that he did? I mean . . . Polly couldn't be serious, could she?"

Tam looked down at me with an unreadable expression. Shaking his head, he tipped his head up, downing all the pills in one go. "She was serious," he said mildly after swallowing. Then he smiled at me. A sad, resigned smile. "And the one who'll die . . . is me."

❦

I t was possibly the worst night to be alone in a psychiatric ward. I sat at the table, filling out the night's incident report in each patient's individual file—none of which would be digitalized—and tried not to shiver at what Tam had said.

That's not the whole story, I told myself. *You know that. First Randal and Polly, then the lights—it wasn't just Tam. Besides, Tam's a paranoid, delusional man who thinks this world is inhabited by faeries that are out to get him, and he reminds you of . . . Bill.*

Even thinking his name made the dimly lit room seem to press in a little closer, and the knot that I'd felt in my chest earlier reappeared higher, in my throat. I scooted nearer to my lamp, frowning and swallowing hard. *Nothing you haven't dealt with before. Now put that thought away before you dwell on it any longer.*

I finished the reports and shoved the files back into the file cabinet, wishing the ancient relic wasn't quite so loud. Still, I was grateful to be done. Slumping onto the couch in Tam's spot, part of me wished that the paperwork would have taken me a little bit longer, just to fill up a little more of the night and leave me with less time to be alone with my thoughts, at least until I could sleep the next morning.

Maybe it was time to eat. Food always seemed to solve a lot of problems. Pushing myself up again, I pulled out my "lunch" and heated it up in the office microwave. Then I returned to the table and stared at the chair that Randal had been sitting at.

I didn't know why his reaction to Polly's words unsettled me so much, or why I'd frozen. I'd dealt with violent patients before. During a really bad confrontation when I was still a new nurse, I'd been pushed to the ground and cracked a bone in my arm. It was just part of the job, even if it wasn't pleasant. Recently, I'd even . . .

I shook my head, running a hand over my hair. I was tired, not insane. Bringing up past trauma—real trauma—was just asking for trouble.

I whispered my mother's favorite adage: "If you want light, don't seek out the darkness." I could picture my mother in my mind's eye, sitting on the old green couch with the white crocheted lace cover. She'd repeated that adage more times than I could remember, but *that* time she'd said it to me, she'd sat grasping my hand, her prematurely white hair a glorious halo around her head in the golden hour of the evening.

It was as if she'd known it would be the last time.

"It's hard when the darkness comes looking for you, Mom," I whispered in the present, pushing the food around its container.

The clock read twelve. Six more hours. I sighed, put down the spoon and rested my head in my hands.

There was a beep from outside the ward, and I stood to go check it out. It was after lights out and past visiting hours, so it was bound to be a nurse. I didn't know if I'd have to let them in. However, as I approached the door, it swung outward and Gwen stepped into the room. Relief relaxed the knots in my shoulders.

She looked around the room, impressed. "Well, everything is still standing. How did it go?" she asked.

I just shook my head.

"Polly or Randal?" she asked.

I lifted an eyebrow. "Randal."

She looked me up and down. "You hurt?"

"No."

"Anyone else?"

"Polly has a couple of bruises, but nothing more severe, at least as far as I could tell." I pointed to the cabinet. "I put it all in the report."

Gwen glanced toward the file cabinet. "Good. Exactly what I would have done."

A question was forming in my brain. It half coalesced before disappearing like smoke. It must be late. I asked a different question that I actually remembered. "I thought you were watching another ward tonight?"

She rolled her eyes, motioning for me to join her at the table.

She sat down and stretched her feet out in front of her. "Apparently, the Delphinium Ward nurse thought that she could come in any time she wanted. Matron wrote her up when she finally got here, but I'm here for the rest of the night."

Relief surged again. I wished that the other nurse had gotten here a little earlier, so Gwen could have helped me with the Randal situation. Then again, I'd come off all right.

"What was the fight about?" Gwen asked.

I looked up, blinking a little in fatigue. "Oh, Randal said that this year was a special year. I asked why and Polly said that Matron was going to kill someone. Randal got mad. He said it was hurtful. I assumed that she was lying."

"She wasn't."

I blinked. "What?"

Gwen shook her head, as if taking it back. "I didn't put that well," she said sheepishly, "But seven years ago, someone *did* die at the bonfire. It was a patient, I think his name was Rider, and he somehow fell into the fire. I was just new here, then. He died of his injuries later. I guess Polly translated that into murder?"

I shuddered. "That's awful."

Gwen shrugged. "Polly is in her own little world. She probably heard about it from Randal, and the combination of paranoia and schizophrenia . . . In a way it kind of makes of sense."

I fought the urge to swallow.

Just then there was a murmuring from one of the rooms. The middle one. Polly. Was she having a nightmare?

"Speak of the devil. Don't let it worry you, Margot." Gwen reached out and patted my arm as she stood. "It was an accident that happened a long time ago."

But it haunted my thoughts for the rest of the night, when I filled out my morning reports, and on the drive home. I stomped up the front steps of my white house, brain buzzing, fumbling a moment with the keys in the almost-grey of the coming morning. Once inside, I paused in the entryway. I looked toward my bedroom, and then toward my office where my computer sat, debating.

I wasn't going to sleep if I didn't check.

I sat down in front of my desk, pressed the power button, then pulled my knees up against my chest as I watched the screen light up. After waiting a couple more seconds for the booting to finish, I typed into the browser's search bar.

"Rider" death "Our Lady of the Wood Hospital"

The results popped up. The news report from the *Carterhall Oracle* was short, but the published police report was shorter. Thomas Rider, who had been a patient at Our Lady for almost seven years had fallen into the bonfire at their celebration and had died at the scene shortly after.

I looked at the accompanying picture of the victim—thankfully not of the crime scene—and frowned. "Tam?"

The brown hair and strong build—even the shape of the eyes was familiar. On closer inspection, though, Thomas Rider was not exactly the same as Tam. Rider's blue eyes had more lines at the edges, suggesting he was older, perhaps in his mid-forties. Tam had a more defined jaw and broader shoulders, but the two could have been brothers. It almost made me wonder . . .

I jerked back and shut off the computer, whispering furiously to myself. "Go to bed, Margot. This is why you hate the night shift."

OCTOBER 22

"I just wanted to let you know," Gwen said in a low voice as we watched Polly and Randal play cards, "Matron was very impressed with how you handled the situation last night. There's not much more I need to guide you on, so Matron has authorized you to handle the ward from here on out. This is my last day training you."

I blinked, noting out of the corner of my eye that Tam was looking up at us from his position on the couch. "What?"

"You're a consummate professional," Gwen said, taking my protestation as a lack of self-confidence. "You're resourceful and capable, and neither Matron nor I think you'll have any problems managing the ward."

"What about the patient-nurse ratio? I've read the hospital policy. Shouldn't there be someone else in here with me? What if something happens?"

"Nothing is going to happen."

I frowned and lowered my voice, leaning forward. "Gwen, there's already been a fight. Last night with Randal—"

"A fight that you managed to deescalate before it ever got started. Besides, Randal is so easy to handle most of the time.

Even if you worked another five years, I doubt you'd have another incident like that."

I looked at Gwen disbelievingly—clearly, she was either delusional or lying to me—but she reached out and patted my hand.

"It's probably just because of the changes in staff and the season, Margot. Everything will be fine. Besides, I can't change Matron's decision. We're short staffed, and these three seem to be doing just fine with you."

I sighed but nodded. I knew the hospital was short staffed—that was definitely obvious. But a ward all to myself . . . That didn't seem safe.

"Margot?" Gwen asked, her hand tightening on mine and I looked over at her. A questioning, even concerned, look was on her face.

I felt a pang of guilt. Matron and Gwen were depending on me. In any case, Gwen was probably right. I probably just had a small sample size of experience with Randal. And they'd hire new people soon, right? It wasn't like I hadn't been warned when I'd first been hired.

"Okay," I said reluctantly.

"Attagirl." Gwen beamed at me. Standing, she clapped her hands to get the patients' attention. "Time for bed everyone. Polly, you're first. Hop to it!"

Polly got up without any sort of pushback, though she gazed regretfully at the unfinished card game. She had seemed a little more put together today, even cracking a joke or two with Randal. She didn't seem to remember what had happened the night before, thank goodness. She was moving a little more freely, too. It was almost as if I got a glimpse of who she might have been.

Randal looked up at me, and guilt flashed across his face. He'd given me pretty much the same expression the whole evening, and because I knew that his guilt was directly related to what had happened to Polly, I felt a little bad for being quite as relieved as I was. But if he felt guilty, he wouldn't try anything like it again—or at least he'd think twice first—and I could do with any help that I could get.

A little later, we had handed out the medication and Gwen was in Polly's room, checking on her shoulders. I had just given Randal his pills and he had toddled off to his room, flicking his light out as he went. Tam was staring contemplatively at me from the table, his chin resting on his hand.

It took me too long to notice. Had he seen the relief, or rather the guilt about it, that I was feeling? Could he tell why? "What?" I asked.

There was a line between his eyebrows, and he shook his head slightly. "You look . . . uneasy."

"Oh. Not really," I tried to lie. He raised an eyebrow and I shook my head. "It's nothing."

"Is it?"

He didn't have to sound so patronizing. I frowned at him.

"I guess . . . I'm still a little worried about Randal," I admitted, eyes straying toward Randal's door.

Tam followed my eyes and then turned back to me. He seemed to consider my words, and then he shrugged a little, his voice quiet. "I doubt that it'll happen again."

"How can you be sure?" I asked. Then I scolded myself inwardly immediately. I was the nurse. I was trained to deal with stuff like this. If I was going to discuss these kinds of situations at all, it should be with my fellow ward nurses, or Matron. Not with a patient.

"I think it's because Hallowe'en is his favorite holiday. He just doesn't want anything to spoil it."

I thought about that, and sighed, nodding. "How long has he been here, anyway?"

Tam smiled a little bit. "Longer than anyone else here, that's for sure. Rumor has it he used to own the place until Matron made him step down. There are full-grown trees around here that are younger than Randal." He glanced toward the darkened window by the counter. He paused, as if picturing the view that was out there—the red, orange, and golden trees of the Michigan forests that were slowly fading into a dull brown.

"Tam, he's seventy-three. It's not actually that hard." My voice was a little drier than I had intended, but Tam smiled anyway. It gave me the impression that there was something I was missing, or at least something that he wasn't telling me. It rankled me a bit, but far less than when we were talking about my feelings, so I let it go.

"How long have you been here?" I asked. I'd only meant it as a follow-up question, but I immediately regretted it when Tam's expression fell.

He shook his head a little ruefully and gave a forced grin. "Almost seven years."

I blinked at him.

"This is the part where you think to yourself, 'Wow, he doesn't seem that crazy,'" Tam said good-naturedly.

That pulled me out of my thoughts, and I shook my head. "Tam, I've worked in psychiatric hospitals for over ten years. I've been trained out of thinking people are crazy."

He snorted. "Sorry if I have a hard time believing that."

I raised an eyebrow. "You can believe it or not believe it as much as you want. I don't control how you think."

He suddenly let out a laugh, swiping his pills off the table. "I like you, Nurse Margot. You've got spunk. I wouldn't be too sure, though. Remember the three rules of faeries—Don't eat or drink anything they give you, don't give them your name—"

"And don't make deals with them," I finished.

Tam looked as though I'd caught him off-guard.

"This isn't my first rodeo, Tam," I said, standing up.

At that moment, Gwen came out of Polly's room, flicking off the lights.

Looking from me to Gwen, Tam shook his head microscopically. "Be careful." With that, he tossed the pills back into his mouth and swallowed them down with the water before turning around and heading to bed.

❧

I had brought a book today. In a normal hospital, I wouldn't have dared—or even needed to—but here the hours seemed to drag, and there were only so many times I could go over the patient files. I'd checked with Gwen first, though. The novel was one of my old favorites, and it pulled me in immediately just as it always did.

A hand tipped the book toward me. I looked up to see Gwen peering at the cover.

"Fantasy?" she said, smiling. "I pegged you as a non-fiction type of girl." She walked over to the table, pouring herself a cup of water.

I smiled and closed the book. "Everyone needs a little escapism," I said, running my hand over the cover. "Sometimes I just need a little reminder that every so often things work out in spite of everything."

"Oof. That sounds like there's a backstory to it."

I shook my head. "Just family . . . stuff."

"Oh?"

I looked up at her and gave her a half smile. "I don't really want to talk about it. It's still pretty fresh, and it's not fully my story to tell."

"I see," Gwen said, her smile faltering a little, but as much as she looked like she wanted to press me, she didn't. It was comforting to know she could maintain boundaries when they were presented to her.

That realization jolted me. I'd been treating her like someone I'd simultaneously never met, but also someone that I'd known for a long time and just kept at arm's distance. It was an old problem, and the reason I didn't have tons of bosom buddies—I often distanced myself from people I'd just met, and that led to not a lot of people getting close.

I opened my mouth to say something to her—exactly what, I had no idea—when a scream ripped through the air.

Middle door.

Polly's room.

Gwen and I bolted toward her door and I threw it open hard enough that it recoiled back into me. Catching my balance, I flipped the light on. Polly was thrashing around, jerking the blankets here and there in manic movements.

"Where is the oak?" she screamed, pounding her fists against the walls. She turned toward the wall again and again, as if she didn't realize that the open side of her bed was behind her.

"Polly." I lifted my voice, but kept it calm. I reached out and grabbed one shoulder.

She recoiled, turning toward me with another scream, then pressing herself back against the wall. Her eyes were open, but she obviously wasn't awake. "I tried to find the oak!" she kept screaming. "I tried! I tried! I can't find it! Please don't!"

"Polly, it's me!" I said again, reaching out again.

She pushed away from me, holding her hands out to hold me off, desperation blazing in her eyes. "Do you know where the oak is? It's somewhere in here. They won't let me out if I don't find it. I'll be here until I find it." Her voice fell, becoming deep and throaty, her breaths rattling from the base of her lungs.

I blinked. "Polly? I don't—"

"I have to find it!" Her voice rose to a shriek again, and her hands clawed at me, fingernails tangling in the sleeves of my scrubs.

I shifted instinctively, catching her hands as they tried to grab my shoulders, pushing them gently down to the mattress. I knew that she wouldn't hurt me on purpose—I doubted that she could hurt me at all, but I preferred keeping that possibility off the table.

"Polly, you're dreaming," I said, clear and a little loud, trying to wake her up as gently as I could. My words didn't register.

"Where is it?!"

"I don't know, Polly. I don't know where the oak is," I said. I said it because I had no idea what else to say. Where was Gwen? Shouldn't she be here, helping Polly? I didn't know what Polly was talking about, or what she thought she needed to look for.

I didn't anticipate a hollow sob to emit from Polly's throat. "But you told me!" she pleaded, voice still high in volume and pitch. "'Leave by the oak leaf, never a bough. Leave by the oak leaf, never a bough, leave by the oak—'"

"Polly!" I grasped her hands tighter. I didn't want to risk her striking the walls again if she yanked away from me, but what I was doing wasn't working.

She looked into my eyes then, cloudy grey eyes boring into mine desperately. Was she still asleep?

"I'm so sorry! I couldn't find it!" Her tone changed, fear filling every syllable. "Please don't! Please don't!" She ripped her hands from mine and pushed herself away. Curling up in her bed, she sobbed lustily.

I didn't know what to do. If I tried to touch her now, she might hurt herself.

"Polly, I'm not going to do anything to you," I said quietly, consciously lowering my voice to calm both Polly and my pounding heart. If I talked softly for long enough, she would follow. There was no energy to feed off if I didn't give it to her. "It's me, Margot. Your nurse. Everything is going to be all right."

She swallowed hard, pressing her forehead into the wall, blinking furiously. Tears were streaming down her cheeks. Her breaths gradually began to slow, though, and after a couple of moments, steadied. Turning back, she stared at me, clearer than I had ever seen her look at anyone, though confusion was apparent on her face, as if I were the last person in the world she expected to see as she came out of her nightmare. And then, oddly, relief crossed her face.

"You're Nurse Margot," she said quietly, although her tone was surprisingly strong.

"Yes." I rested my hand on the side of her bed but didn't try to touch her again. "You were having a nightmare."

She blinked a few more times, a very concerned look on her face, and then nodded. She closed her eyes tightly, and when she opened them, the old Polly was back—sweetness mixed with all the clarity of mud. "Yes . . . a nightmare . . ." Her voice had softened into a floating breathiness. She frowned, looking down at her hands. "They hurt."

"Yes, you hit the wall," I explained.

Polly looked up at me in surprise.

"Do you want me to get you some ice?"

She thought about it for longer than she probably needed to. Then she nodded. "Yes, that would probably be good. Reduces bruising, you know. It won't look so bad later. Matron won't ask."

I hesitated. "I guess. It'll also help numb the pain."

She sighed and shook her head. "I don't mind the pain. It's sharp. It is—" she searched for the word "—real."

I frowned. "I'd mind the pain, Polly."

Half of a smile curled up her lip. "Not like that, Nurse Margot," she said faintly, staring over my shoulder. "I am quite mad, but not . . . that kind of mad."

I turned to see what she was looking at, and to my surprise, Tam was standing there with a wrapped ice pack in his hands. He held it out without entering the tiny room. I took it and put it over Polly's hands.

"Nurse Gwen is pulling out a sedative for Polly," he said by way of an explanation.

I frowned. Had Gwen been there the whole time? How long had I been here with Polly?

"I don't need one," Polly whispered under her breath.

I barely heard her, but Tam must have had the hearing of a bat because he shook his head. "Take the medicine, Polly."

"I don't want to. I just got to the point—"

"Take. It." Tam's voice brooked no argument. He and Polly glared at each other in a battle of wills. I would have expected Tam to win outright, but as I watched them, I was surprised by Polly's decisiveness.

"I'm just trying to help, Polly." Tam's voice dropped to barely a whisper as footsteps sounded on the linoleum outside. "It's the least I can do—"

Polly cut him off. "You don't—" she started to whisper.

"Here, Polly." Gwen's strident voice shattered the quiet intensity of the room, and both Tam and Polly looked away from each other at the same time as Gwen walked in. Oddly, I felt like I had seen something significant.

"I don't need them," Polly muttered, turning away from the small cup of pills.

"Polly." Gwen's loud voice quieted from jet engine to church mouse, but the intensity remained.

Polly glanced up, and I could see a clear dislike in her face as she sighed and held out her hands to take the pills.

"Good girl," Gwen's tone was suddenly velvet. Polly's hand closed over the pills, and she brought them to her mouth as though resigned. "No need to trouble everyone again tonight."

I frowned, half turning my head to see Gwen out of the corner of my eye.

Polly lay back down on her bed, swallowing hard against the memory of the pills. On impulse, I took her hand, squeezing it gently as she settled back against her pillow.

She didn't look at me, but I felt the gentlest squeeze back as she closed her eyes, waiting for the medication to take hold.

"Are you going to be all right, Polly?" I asked.

Polly took in a deep breath and let it out slowly. "Watch over me?" she asked quietly, eyes still closed, a slow tear trickling down the side of her face.

"That's why I'm here," I whispered to her, putting my other hand on her shoulder. I was conscious of Tam and Gwen behind me, watching me over my shoulder as I knelt on the floor. I held

Polly's hand as she slipped into drug-induced sleep. When her hand relaxed a couple of minutes later, I stood up, laid her hand across her chest, and then ushered the other two out of the room.

"Tam, go to bed," I said, though I was looking at Gwen.

Tam glanced between the two of us, his mouth pursed in concern, and then turned around and slipped into his room without a word.

"You should really call him Thomas," Gwen said, stiffening under my gaze, "Calling him Tam will simply make you two overly casual, which will only cause problems."

"Really?" I said flatly. "Because I have seen exactly zero indication that that is the case. Actually, since I've been here, they've all seemed to relax, which has to be better for their recovery. You're holding them at arm's length, emphasizing their roles as patients here—how is that supposed to help them get better? What about finding common ground? Working with them as much as possible instead of ordering them around? Pointing out the places where they're coping well, where they're normal? I haven't seen you do any of those things. What are you trying to do here, Gwen? What you said earlier— 'No need to trouble everyone.' We're here to help them! They can't do it without us. What if we miss something important because they're too afraid of *troubling* us?" I didn't let my voice rise above an almost-whisper, but the tone was clear.

Gwen glowered at me. "You forget, Margot—these people are here because they are *delusional.* Thomas thinks everyone surrounding him are faeries, Randal thinks he *is* some sort of faerie, Polly—who knows what Polly thinks? Frankly, I don't think she does think. I'm supposed to—" she broke off and looked down, as if rethinking what she was about to say. "Perhaps it's best that you're taking over this ward," she said finally.

I couldn't tell whether she was serious or not. "Maybe it is," I said. "If you come back to help in the ward, please keep in mind that we are here to help these people get better, not stick them somewhere where time can forget about them."

She might have rolled her eyes, but it was dim enough in the big room that I wasn't sure. Then she sighed. "Fine."

"Thank you."

She didn't reply to that.

I was secretly quite impressed with myself. I wasn't used to asserting myself like that, at least not with a person that I'd known for less than a week. Not my superior, anyway.

Suddenly, a little guilt trickled through me. "Look, I'm sorry."

She looked up, surprised. "Excuse me?"

"Not for what I said," I clarified. "But I could have probably said it a little nicer. I don't want to make it seem like you're not helping these people get better. I know long-term care is hard, especially when progress seems non-existent."

Gwen looked at me like I was crazy. "Yes," she agreed cautiously, almost as if she was expecting me to start scolding her again. "I guess I just forgot. You have my . . . commitment that while I am in here, I will keep what you have said in mind."

"Thank you," I said.

Still looking a little uncomfortable, she nodded.

"I'll write up the report." I nodded toward the table.

"I'll help," Gwen said. "They'll want a second witness report, since we had to medicate Polly."

"Does she usually not want to take the medication?" I asked, something niggling at the back of my brain.

"She says it makes it hard to think. I honestly haven't seen much of a difference. But maybe you'll be able to see something I haven't."

"Maybe," I said, pulling out the files. Her comment wasn't exactly challenging, but it definitely had an underlying meaning that I wasn't sure of. I didn't blame her for being offended. I probably would have been a little bit more resentful if she'd scolded me like I'd done to her.

Thank goodness there were better people than me.

We sat in silence for a while after that, filling out the forms in Tam and Polly's files. Randal had not appeared, surprisingly, even through all of the noise. To my knowledge, he didn't take a sleep aid. Maybe he was just a heavy sleeper.

After we were done, I flipped through Tam's file. There wasn't much in there, particularly from the last year or so. In fact, the further I flipped, the more it seemed that the most trouble Tam had gotten into over the last two years was when he skipped his sleeping pill and had been found reading late in his room. No psychotic episodes. Plenty of instances of him stepping out to help the nurses whenever Randal or Polly had had their own breakdowns. Even the times he mentioned his obsessive beliefs were few and far between.

"Gwen," I said. "Why was Tam—Thomas admitted?" I couldn't find it mentioned anywhere in the file.

She looked up. "What?"

"Why was Thomas admitted to long-term care? I know I've only been here, like, three days, but it seems like he could get by with a good therapist. He's extremely high functioning."

Gwen gave me a strange look. "He's delusional."

"So I've been told," I said, conceding. "But aside from a little bit of paranoia, I don't see anything that screams 'take this man out of society.'"

"I suppose you're right." Gwen put her pencil down. "From what I've heard, a lot of it has to do with how he was found."

"On the horse?" I vaguely remembered something about that from my first day.

Gwen nodded, shrugging. "Just wandering around the woods nearby. I wasn't there then, but they said he was rambling about faeries or something. Both he and the horse looked like they'd been out in the forest for a while. The official police report, as well as his attending doctor, Dr. Ingen, estimated that he was out there for a couple of days."

"Why a horse?" I asked, frowning.

Gwen shook her head, getting up to pull her snack from

her bag. "No clue. It wasn't stolen or anything. There weren't any reports of a stolen horse from here, *or* any of the surrounding states. The horse is still here, actually, down in the stables. I think its name is Acorn or something. Big old white thing."

"Huh," I rested my chin in my hand, staring at Tam's door.

"Matron and Dr. Ingen oversee most of his therapy, so it's possibly that any outbursts he's had are in his therapy file—which aren't part of ours." Gwen saw the interest on my face and quickly held up her hand. "Don't bother asking for a copy, though."

I fought the urge to roll my eyes. "Thank you, I'm familiar with HIPAA laws. Anything pertinent to our care would be in our file."

Gwen nodded. "If you're concerned, you could possibly ask Matron if she remembers any major incidents, but like you said, it would be in the file if it were really important."

I nodded, mentally making a note in case I needed to ask later.

Gwen slid back into her seat, prying the lid off her container. "Anyway, Thomas is still completely obsessed with faeries. He thinks all of the staff are faeries, and Randal too. Well, you know. Heaven knows what he'd do if we actually let him wander around." She grabbed a piece of fruit. "Grape?"

"No, thank you," I said, looking down at my paperwork, feeling more than a little uncomfortable after what she said about Tam.

"What is it?" she asked, resting her hand on her chin as she chewed.

I shook my head. "Nothing. He just . . . reminds me of someone."

"Hmm, hopefully not too much. Thomas is also convinced someone's going to try and kill him soon. Like, before the end of the year. Paranoid." She shook her head and ate another grape.

I pressed my lips together.

"Margot, you can't give me that look and tell me there's nothing," Gwen protested. "What was it—"

"A patient," I said firmly, avoiding looking at her in the eye. "His name was Bill. He had some of the same characteristics that Tam does."

"Like . . . looks?"

I looked up at her and shook my head. "No. Bill thought there were faeries everywhere. And that I was one. And that I was going to try and kill him."

Her face went blank.

I smiled a little. "I'm not a faerie, by the way."

"What did he do?" Gwen asked in a whisper.

I frowned and looked away. "He tried to kill me," I said matter-of-factly, ignoring the keen sting that accompanied the words. "It's part of the reason why I moved up here."

Certainly not the whole reason. If I had been able to speak it out loud, Gwen wouldn't have been the first person I told.

"That would be really difficult. You should never have had to deal with that."

"It is what it is," I said. "At least Tam seems more peaceful. Besides, forewarned is forearmed. I'm not particularly easy to take advantage of."

Gwen leaned forward and touched my arm. A troubled expression was still on her beautiful face. In the dim light of the room she seemed even more otherworldly than usual.

"You won't have to worry about Tam for much longer, Margot," she said, rubbing my arm. "He's probably going to be transferred soon to another facility."

"What? Since when?" I asked, lifting my chin.

Gwen shrugged. "Nothing's official yet, but Matron let me know a couple of nights ago, right before you came. Maybe you're right. Maybe he doesn't need such thorough care. I never thought of that."

"Huh." Matron hadn't mentioned anything like that to me—

shouldn't she have warned me if one of my three patients was supposed to be leaving soon? "Did Matron say why?"

"Not specifically. She did say he was going to be sent to a place better equipped to deal with him."

I frowned but nodded. "I understand."

"I guess don't get attached?" It was more of a suggestion than actual advice, but I nodded regardless.

"Wasn't planning on it," I said, smiling. I think she knew the smile was fake, but I was grateful that she didn't say anything about it.

OCTOBER 23

I had four missed calls when I woke up that afternoon, all from the same number. Edward Campion. Sighing, I cleared the notifications from my phone, grateful for the Do Not Disturb function.

It was dark when I left the house, most of the ambient light emanating from the Hallowe'en decorations on the house across the street. The orange jack o'lantern grinned at me from beside the front door, and the plastic witches and skeletons dangling from the porch roof waved in the wind that whispered through the trees.

I held my jacket closer but shivered anyway. It was getting colder. I wasn't surprised, of course. It was almost November and I was so far north that if I tripped, I would land in Canada. That didn't stop me from grimacing against the pinch in my cheeks or shuddering against the cold fabric of my car's seat. I'd have to dig my winter coat out of my stuff sooner rather than later. And possibly my hand warmers.

I frowned, hands resting on the steering wheel of my Range Rover. Where had I even put my hand warmers? I remembered packing them, but I hadn't used them in a couple years. Not since the last time I'd worked the night shift, which was before Mom got sick, and way before Bill—

"You are going to be late," I said to myself, pushing the keys into the ignition. The old grey car groaned to life, probably wondering why I wasn't staying in for the night like I used to.

"I don't know, buddy," I said, shaking my head. "I don't know."

The TV was on in The Boughs when I got in there. I didn't know why I was so shocked. Actually, I did know why.

"We have a TV?" I asked the small group of people huddled around the old box television. I vaguely remembered seeing it sitting up against one of the walls on a trolley, but it had been covered with enough dust that I had assumed it was never used.

"Just pulled it out," Eileen explained from the table as she scribbled on the files in front of her. "I needed a bit of time to do paperwork. That and Randal wouldn't stop bugging Polly about her nightmare last night, so I decided to pull out the TV to keep them from wearing at each other."

"That's fair," I said, putting my purse on the table and my food in the office fridge. "What are we watching?"

"The most interesting thing they could find," Eileen said, rolling her eyes. "The news."

I walked over to where the other three were sitting on the blue couch. Going by her posture, Polly felt practically crushed between the two men without actually touching either. I smiled a little—I'd never considered Randal particularly large but, squished into the end of the couch to try and keep from touching Polly, he looked about twice the small woman's size.

He didn't seem to notice. He was staring at the screen, forehead creased in concern.

"Margot, I'm leaving." Eileen waved exaggeratedly to get my attention.

I caught her eye and waved back absently. "Thanks, Eileen," I said.

"Whatever," she said, suddenly looking annoyed about something, and trudged out the door.

I pulled in my chin, frowning after her before turning back toward my three patients. I caught Tam looking at me, before he looked back at the TV with a frown on his own face.

"So, what's new?" I asked.

Randal shushed me, leaning forward to listen to the television, his worried expression creasing deeper into his face. It was the weather portion of the news. The weatherman was in front of his green screen, gesturing toward a thick puff of blue that was heading down from the north. I stood back against the wall behind Tam and leaned forward to register the reporter's words.

"Looking forward to next week, snow heading down in an early storm should hit sometime Hallowe'en night, so make sure your Trick or Treating tykes are dressed in their warmest. The polar system that—"

"No, no, no!" Randal murmured, shaking his head. "Not that night. Not Hallowe'en! It will ruin it." He suddenly shifted, jostling Polly, then stood up and began pacing. Tam moved to stand up as well, but I put a hand on his shoulder and walked over to Randal.

"Randal? What's going on?" I asked, putting a hand on his forearm.

He was breathing a little fast. "It—it's supposed to snow," he exclaimed, gesturing at the TV. His tone was appalled, as if his combination of words and gestures should explain everything perfectly.

I nodded. "On Hallowe'en, I heard."

"It will ruin everything!" He tried to storm off, but I guided him to one of the chairs at the table.

"Are you worried about the bonfire?" I asked, pressing him gently into his seat, and taking my own.

He nodded, his bottom lip puckering out a little bit like a child's. "If it snows, the fire will go out. Or-or-or they'll cancel the bonfire entirely and it will ruin everything! Everything!"

I doubted a flood could have put out the type of bonfire he was envisioning, but I nodded sympathetically. "I know it's important to you, Randal. I'm sure Matron knows as well. I bet if it snows on Hallowe'en, they'll be able to move it to a different day. It doesn't have to be cancelled altogether."

"It's not the same," he said, and tears were gathering in his eyes now.

"No, but it'll still be a wonderful time, no matter the day," I said softly.

"You don't understand!" He shook his head slowly, a sob bursting from him.

"You can't control the weather, Randal," I said, placing my hand on his arm.

"I used to be able to!" he shouted.

I drew back, and my back stiffened.

He didn't stop there. "There was a time when flowers sprouted where I walked, and nature itself would bow at my coming. Even the clouds in the sky would not dare to release their moisture without my leave! Now, look at me! Unable to turn the gentlest breeze, or change the weakest mind." He grit his teeth and put his head into his hands, pulling his hair so hard that I was afraid it was going to come out in chunks.

"Randal—" What was he trying to say?

"I was a god," he said with a growl, "And now I am *nothing*. *NOTHING*."

"Randal," I said, a little firmer, and he seemed to inflate in response, indignation building in his eyes as he glared at me.

"How dare—" he started to bluster.

I stilled, my heart skidding to a stop. Then, shifting my

weight slowly, I brought up my hands in a hopefully disarming gesture. I opened my mouth to speak.

"Randal?"

I started at the slight, feminine voice. Polly stood a few feet away, leaning into view, and looking down at Randal fondly. He met her gaze. The look he gave her wasn't his usual one—slightly disinterested mixed with a sharp sort of mischievousness. No, now he looked at her closely, as if she weren't exactly who he expected.

"Polly?" he responded, his voice shockingly calm, given his outburst a moment earlier. There was a shift behind me, and I glanced back to Tam's sober expression, book resting on the couch cushions beside him as he balanced on the edge of his seat.

Polly pulled up a chair closer to the both of us and gave him an easy smile, which he couldn't help but return.

"You seem a little bit stressed," she said, her voice gentle.

He nodded sadly and inhaled. I could tell he was about to go into the same reactive cycle that he had just been in. Before he could speak, though, Polly tilted her head to the side. "I wonder, Randal, could you tell me a story?"

He blinked. I did too. The two of us stared at her, not knowing how to respond.

"What?" Randal finally said, and Polly's smile brightened.

"You tell such wonderful stories. I thought it might help you feel better."

Randal looked conflicted for a moment, but then he nodded, as though he couldn't quite help himself. "Yes, I suppose it would," he admitted.

Polly smiled in response. "Will you tell the one about Queen Mab?"

Randal smiled and patted her briefly on the knee in an almost fatherly way. It normally wouldn't have seemed odd, but this was the same man who only three nights before had attempted to throttle her.

"No, I have another tale for you," he said. "You'll like this one, I think."

"I trust you, Randal," Polly said. "You're such a good storyteller."

He seemed to swell then, and in an instant, I could see the strategy behind Polly's request. I hid a grateful smile.

He looked at me. "Will you listen?" he asked.

Now I smiled openly. "I would love to. I've never heard you tell a story before."

"Well, if I do say so myself, this will be something you never forget." His face had relaxed, distress morphing into a deeper satisfaction. He said to Polly, "You need to move by Nurse Margot. If I have to look between the two of you, it'll ruin the effect."

She moved accommodatingly to sit beside me. "You're in for a treat," she said quietly to me.

I knew she was right the moment Randal leaned in, his eyes alive and sparkling.

"It was in the time of Old England. Henry the Eighth was on the throne when our tale begins." Randal's voice was low and mysterious. "A young girl, no older than six years old, was caught up by a holy well, and brought down to be taken captive by the faeries."

Beside me Polly shivered, but she was still smiling. "What happened to her?"

"Hush, my child," Randal said to Polly, "The girl, a future great lady of the manor, was playing on the grounds of her estate, chasing the butterflies as high summer floated through the hills. The child, held protected inside the thick iron doors of the gate, was warned never to leave the safety of her home, as the Fair Folk would take her and keep her in their halls, deep beneath the forest of the Great Wood."

"Underground?" I said. "Shouldn't they live in the trees among nature?"

Randal looked at me disparagingly. "The Fae are not *elves,*

Nurse Margot. While others may dance within the light of sunbeams, those who wish to practice the deep magic must live where it resides—deep within the Earth, among the roots, and the dark, and the foundations of mountains."

I blinked a little, and for the barest of moments, I could see the scene as if I were there. The stone walls, smooth under my fingertips, stretched for miles and miles underground. If I ventured too deep, there was no way I would ever find my way out.

Randal's voice pulled me back, though not completely. "One day, the gate was left open. The precious child, playing near the gates against the wishes of her father, looked up through those gates to see a beautiful woman just outside the wall, dancing to a song that the little girl could not hear. The woman's movements were smooth and joyful, and the longer the small maid watched, the more she could hear the music—the flute of the wind, the drums of the rustling leaves in the trees. She was not able to resist the call of the Great Wood, and she passed through the cold iron gates that kept her safe within.

"She intended only to dance on the path with the young woman, to join in the smooth movements of the Great Wood. But as the girl moved through the gate, the young woman seemed to move further and further away, following a path toward the heart of the Wood that the girl had never seen before.

"You see, the girl did not realize that this was not a young woman from the village, nor an wandering maid, nor any manner of mortal being. The young woman was in fact a member of the Fair Folk—a faerie, a wood nymph dancing to the tune of the wind—sent from the Lady's Deep Hall to capture a child. *This child.*"

I shuddered a little bit, and Polly took my hand but didn't look at me, still wrapped up in Randal's story.

"The girl followed the young woman, dancing in her own childish way, clear into the darkest reaches of the forest. By the time the child realized what had happened, she was lost, the nymph having disappeared in the way that they do, leaving their followers stranded to be eaten by wolves or to be retrieved by their masters.

"And so it was with the young girl. At the moment of highest despair, as night came on, and as the howling of wolves seemed to surround her, drawing ever closer, she saw a light. It came not from a lantern but rather floated on the breeze, followed by the most beautiful of all the creatures the girl had ever seen. A woman with flowing red hair and eyes the color of jade stepped from the woods, and bade the child follow her to help and safety.

"The child obeyed, following the regal woman through the Wood a short way to a large well. The woman touched the rim of the well and the stones sank back, revealing a door and a stair reaching down deep into the ground. The child was frightened, realizing now that she was far from home in the darkness; but the howls of the wolves and the haunted blackness of the forest were more frightening than the beautiful lady and her magic light, and so she followed the lady into the well."

"The child's disappearance did not go unnoticed," Randal continued. "The girl's older brother was a kind and attentive young man, who had been called away on business, but he had been eager to return home. Arriving early by several days, before the return of his father and their men, he discovered his sister was missing, and he demanded of the servants where the child had gone.

"They told him that they did not know, that she had been playing by the gate, and then had vanished in the very moment their backs were turned. The man remembered the fine day and the faint song that had drifted on the breeze as he had been traveling through the Wood, and he knew at once that it was the work of the Fae. He knew the legends of the Holy Well and the entrance to the Hall under the Hill. At once he tried to set out to find her, but the threat of darkness and the wolves forced him back within the walls of his castle. The next morning, not having slept a wink, he ventured into the forest, intent on retrieving his sister.

"Now, The Fair Folk have servants in the Wood—crows, creatures, and miscreants—who whispered to their masters about the coming of the young man. When the brother came to the Holy Well, there stood the fair, red-haired lady, dressed in her green robes. At once he knew her and cried out—'Lo! The Queen of the Forest! Where hast thou taken my sister, that I might find her and bear her away?'

"The Queen laughed, for she knew who this young man was —a knight of the realm, fearless and full of honor toward his God and fellowmen. But he was exactly who she sought, for the Fair Folk are people of cunning. Just as the nymph had ensnared the child, so the Queen of the Forest sought to entrap the young man, for she had searched for a willing captive, one who would generate the magic for another era. What better than a pure, loving man who would give up his own life for his sister?

"But, as I mentioned, the man was not unknowing of the ways of the Faeries, and he proposed an exchange—himself for his sister."

"But—" I exclaimed before I could help myself. Randal jumped and looked at me accusingly. Swallowing a little, I looked between Polly and Randal. "Sorry. You just said that he knew of the ways of the faeries, and he just . . . proposes the exchange?"

"Am I done with the tale?" Randal asked impatiently.

I pressed my lips together sheepishly. "No," I said quietly.

"Then hush until I'm done," he said. Shaking his head and making a 'tsk' noise, he turned back to his story.

"The Queen laughed at him—asking him what he could give to her. He responded that he would be a willing prisoner until his father's father's grave be removed, at which time he must be released unmolested, he and his family safe forevermore. The Queen smiled at him, thinking that she should have him while the castle itself stood—surely as long as the man's natural life. But then the Queen knew only what happened in her realm of the forest. She did not know the doings of men, for even as she brought the man deep into the Hill and ordered her court to return the sleeping child to her bed, the Lord of the Castle was on the road, returning with unlikely salvation.

"The young man felt the weight of honor upon his breast. His word was his bond until the moment, many days and nights past—though night or day he knew not, being cosseted in the deepest recesses of the Halls under the Hill—when he felt the binding of his words lift, and he knew his honor was satisfied. Triumphant, he emerged from his cell, with not a one able to stop him.

"The Queen appeared, demanding why he would break his word of honor. He turned to her, full of valiant light. 'Lady,' said he, 'I would rather raise my own knife to my breast than break my bonded word. But even now the bones of my father's father be removed from their resting place, to preserve them from the fen encroaching on the edge of my father's lands. 'Twas for such purpose that I went into the city, to find the man with such knowledge to accomplish the task.'

"The Queen was greatly angered, but she knew in her heart that the bond had been satisfied, and herself outwitted. Nodding and bowing to his foresight and a game well played, she escorted him to the gates of the Castle herself. There she left him, never to molest him or his family forever more."

Randal sat back then, a faint smile on his face. His eyes reminded me of the moon, luminous and mysterious. The spell that had been weaved about us slowly faded away like mist in sunlight.

I blinked. "Wait, that's it?"

Randal raised an eyebrow. "You need more?"

"She just let him *go?*" I demanded.

"Of course."

"That's completely unrealistic! If she was morally bankrupt enough to abduct someone—two people, actually—why would she honor—"

"Ah, but you are thinking of humans," Randal said, folding his arms and holding up a knobby finger. "The codes that the Fair Folk and humans live by are very different. To humans, compassion can supersede honor. So can greed, malice, or simple belligerence. To the fae, the contract is the highest and holiest of all interactions. If you make a deal with a faerie, you may expect it be honored to the very letter. And the greatest calamities be heaped upon you should you not live up to your own end of the agreement."

I stared at Randal, who stared at back at me with steely blue eyes.

"And . . . that's it?" I asked. "Honor or calamity?"

"Yes," he replied, a calm smile spreading across his face. He looked somewhere off into the distance over my shoulder.

I thought about it. It fit with what I'd been taught, but it had to be fiction, or at least exaggeration. It wasn't like I was a pessimist, but if I'd been able to trust people by their word, my father and I wouldn't have had nearly the issues—

I leaned back in my chair, clearing my throat. "That was amazing. You definitely have a gift. Where did you learn the story?"

Randal's smile was genuine, and his voice quiet and far away. "I learned the story from my father, who learned it from his mother. As for the telling of tales . . . all it takes is the right story and a little magic." He sighed then and closed his eyes, a deep smile on his face, as though the story had left him satisfied but exhausted. "I think I will prepare for bed."

He walked to his room, grabbed his little tote, and headed into the bathroom. I stayed in my chair, looking at the seat that Randal had just vacated, contemplating what I had just heard.

A small hand touched my arm. "Are you okay?" Polly asked gently.

I blinked and smiled a little sheepishly. "Yes," I said, standing up. I stretched my back, then glanced at the clock, wondering why I was so stiff. "It's almost ten?" I exclaimed in surprise. "It was barely nine when we started!"

"Randal is captivating," Polly said, glancing toward the bathroom where the older man had disappeared.

A thought struck me then, and I tilted my head as I contemplated Polly. "Randal was almost inconsolable before. How did you know asking him to tell a story would work?"

Polly shrugged and started to fold the blanket that she had spread over her lap earlier. Once neatly folded, she draped it over the back of the chair. "That's what I used to do when I was the one who took care of him," she said. In that moment, her voice was strong and clear and matter-of-fact, though I could hear a subtle vein of humor winding its way through her voice.

My heart turned ice cold as I registered her words. I stared at her, unable to move or breathe. She froze too, her body stock still as she stared, shocked, into the distance.

"What did you say?" I managed to ask, my voice dropping into a whisper. Her words were improbable. Unbelievable, even. And yet, as I searched her face, I wondered why they rang so true to me.

Polly didn't answer, still stiff and unmoving. Instinctively, thinking that perhaps she had not heard me, I reached out to her, touching her arm. Polly shied away, pulling her arm back.

"I'm—I'm sorry," she said, her voice suddenly quiet and raspy. She swallowed hard and lifted her chin like she was trying to force herself to look up into my eyes, but she gave up and looked down and away, as if trying to find somewhere else—anywhere else—to look.

"What—why—"

"I mess up sometimes. I'm sorry." Her voice broke, and she shook her head profusely.

"Polly—"

"I won't do it again, I promise," she whispered, her chin practically lowering to her chest. She looked absolutely terrified, like she had done something unforgivable. Her gaze flicked around the room, landing on Tam as he was coming out of the bathroom. Randal must have already finished.

"Polly, all I wanted to know is what you said," I said quietly.

Still shaking her head, she fled to her bedroom.

I stared after her, wondering what in the world I had said, or what she had thought she'd said, that could have produced such a reaction. Shaking my head, I prepared the nightly medications and handed the appropriate cups to Randal and Polly. After their doors were closed and their lights were off, I sat down to read the reports as I really should have done before Randal had started telling his story.

My mind wandered, first to Polly's reaction, and then back to Randal's story. Thanks to my bewilderment, it was almost eleven by the time I finished the paperwork and closed the last folder. I noticed Tam was still reading peacefully on the couch.

"Tam," I said quietly.

He twisted around to look at the clock, then nodded and stood. I gave him his pills and water, and he grimaced as the avalanche of pills worked themselves down his throat.

"I don't know why you don't take them one at a time," I said, grimacing a bit myself.

Tam smiled and sat back on the edge of the table. "I'd rather get it all over with at once."

"Yeah, but that 'all at once' seems awful."

He looked at me a little meaningfully. "Better than having things drag out forever."

I thought about that. "You're right. But you don't have to apply the same philosophy to everything."

"Don't I?" he asked.

"Of course not." I made my tone flippant. "I believe in building good relationships with people. My philosophy with friends is spending time with them and building a good rapport. My philosophy for other select individuals is to spend as little time with them as possible."

"Was he that bad?"

I started and shot a glare at Tam. "What?"

At least he had the decency to look a little abashed. "I'm sorry, I just assumed. I shouldn't have . . . it wasn't . . ." He shoved his hands into his pockets and pressed his lips together. "Sorry."

"No, it's—" It wasn't okay. And it wasn't particularly appropriate for me to answer, but . . . "It was a patient who got too attached. And then he turned violent, so I had to get him transferred to a new . . . more secure facility. And he blamed me for it." I swallowed, my throat suddenly closing, unwelcome tears prickling at the back of my eyes, and I turned away to throw the little paper cup away.

"That sounds hard."

"It is," I cleared my throat, "but I've been managing." Barely, it seemed like these days.

"I'm sorry. That must be . . . well, really difficult." One corner of his mouth pinched, and a dimple appeared in his cheek.

I never would have admitted it, but I was a little bit glad that I wasn't the only one feeling uncomfortable about this. I took a deep breath. "It is what it is. It's not a particularly new or original story."

"Doesn't make it any more pleasant."

"Thanks," I said quietly.

He raised his hand as though to put it on my shoulder but dropped it at the last moment. I thought about that for a moment. Tam's normalcy was at odds with the frank eccentricities of his wardmates. If we had been anywhere else, under any other circumstances, I wouldn't even have noticed that he had a mania. Here, compared with cases like Polly and Randal, Tam was so normal it was almost unnerving.

We stood there for a moment, as if not entirely sure what to do with each other before I looked up and asked the thing that was really on my mind.

"How did Polly come to be at Our Lady?"

He met my eyes, a curiosity and suspicion clear on his face.

He opened and closed his mouth for a bit. Tam wasn't particularly talkative on a regular basis—at least to me—but this seemed deeper than that.

"I . . . I wish you'd asked me before I took my medicine," he said quietly and more than a little regretful.

I blinked a little. "What?"

"I . . ." He held up his hands. They'd started to shake, just a slight amount. Fatigue? "I took a sedative tonight." Tam explained quietly. I looked at his hands. Of course he did. I knew his medications by now.

"I understand," I said quietly. Why was I feeling so uneasy?

"Ask me tomorrow?" Tam's deep green eyes bored into mine. "I might not remember you asking me. Once Randal and Polly are in bed tomorrow, ask me again."

"I'm gone tomorrow—it's my day off," I said, barely remembering in time.

"The next day, then."

"I will," I said quietly, pulled into stillness by those eyes.

Tam turned to go, but seemed to stumble a little—his medications were starting to kick in.

I moved to his side. "Here, hold onto me," I said, bringing one of his arms over my shoulder to let him lean on me. "I kept you out here too long."

"No worries," he said, a small honest smile crossing his face. He shifted his weight onto me, and we moved sideways a little as I juggled my balance with his weight. "I'm sorry, the one they have me on makes me very dizzy."

"Do you want me to ask if they can find an alternative? One that doesn't affect you so bad?"

"We've been through about six already. They all eventually stop working."

I frowned.

"Is tha' not supposed to happen?" His voice slurred ever so slightly.

"Actually, it's pretty normal. Have you had that much trouble sleeping?" I asked.

Tam stopped and pulled away from me, looking down at me seriously, holding onto my shoulders to keep himself from swaying.

"That's the only way I *can* sleep," he whispered. His voice low and eerie, sent a shudder down my spine. "This place, Nurse Margot. You have no idea . . . you have no idea."

With that, his eyes stopped focusing and he pitched forward into my arms. Huffing with the effort, I maneuvered him with great difficulty until he lay over my shoulders in a fireman carry. I grimaced. He was heavier than I thought he would be—or maybe I just wasn't used to carrying people over my shoulders anymore. I'd have to find a martial arts gym here or something. If Carterhall was big enough to have a gym.

Grunting a little, I sidled my way into Tam's room, then laid him gently down on his bed. I groaned a little when I realized that I'd placed him down on top of the covers. Back when I'd had to rely on sleep aids, I'd constantly been cold. I didn't know whether he had the same type of reaction, but I'd rather cover my bases all the same, so I retrieved two blankets from the cupboard in the main room and spread them over him.

I stood there for a while longer than was probably appropriate. Not that I was thinking about anything inappropriate. He was just . . . interesting. He was definitely good looking, but there was something else about him. His kindness—not that it was out of place, but it was at odds with the inherent vulnerability of his situation. He knew how vulnerable he was, too. I could see it in his stance, his way of speaking, and in his interactions with everyone. Even the fact that he kept so fit seemed to confirm the fact that he knew he was vulnerable, and he hated it.

I could relate.

A memory rose, and after fighting it for a moment I allowed it in. That last day with Bill—sitting with the older man, laughing with him, talking with him. Waiting for the other shoe to drop. I don't know how I knew it would be that day. Maybe it had been the thin glaze over his eyes when I walked in. Maybe it was the way he'd laughed too loud. Made too much of an effort.

I'd had that same sense of vulnerability. So had Bill. The only question had been who was going to act first?

He had.

And I couldn't fight back. Couldn't do anything but cover my head with my arms and scream.

Forty-one stitches in my head. Twenty in my shoulder. Five in my lip.

Cracked skull. Broken nose. Broken humerus.

Broken heart.

I hugged myself tightly and bit my lip, my tongue tracing the scar along the inside, swallowing hard. Part of me wondered that if I had done something earlier, or maybe something during, it would have shaken him out of it. Helped him realize what he was doing, and who he was doing it to.

The other part of me stressed firmly what I already knew: Bill had made his choices long before I ever came into the picture. His decisions hurt me—physically and emotionally—but there was no changing them now. As a matter of fact, I had known, even before the attack, that there was no changing his mind, ever.

I forced my arms down by my sides and turned to leave Tam's room, resisting the urge to wave a hand by my head like shooing a fly. Bill was gone now, and I'd left that memory behind on purpose. I knew better than to dredge things up again.

I pulled the folders out of the file cabinet and filled them out diligently. I opened Polly's last. After adding my short entry, hoping my handwriting was legible—seriously, what was wrong with a computer?—I flipped back through her file. There wasn't much. Hers was a fairly new folder, slim, only going back a year.

I knew from Gwen that once the files got too thick, they'd store them in the archives of the hospital. Tam's had three years of history and was only about halfway to archive-limit. Randal's was approaching its limit but only covered about two years. *Not dramatic, my foot.* I frowned, thinking of Polly's placid nature, and flipped to the front of her folder. It was dated from the year before in Gwen's handwriting.

October 19, 2025—Patient Polly Blanchman admitted to Our Lady of the Wood Hospital, transferring from St. Epipodius's Hospital in Lansing.

October nineteenth? She'd just passed her year mark. Strange, though. It wasn't as though Polly acted like she'd been here longer than that. No, it was Tam and Randal. *They* acted like she'd been here for years.

What was going on?

I sat back in my chair, tapping my lips with my pen. Then, Polly's smiling face entered my mind, her strong, clear voice echoing through my skull: *"when I was the one who took care of him."*

OCTOBER 24

I stomped my way down the stairs toward the staff lounge a little after six the next morning, determined to leave the weirdness of Randal's story and Polly's words behind me. Nurse Kristen, the morning shift nurse, had gotten there a little late, murmuring an excuse that was a little too vague and quiet for me to understand what had happened, but she was there, and I could leave, so I left.

Our Lady of the Wood Psychiatric Hospital was shaped like an 'L.' There was only one authorized entrance for guests, a separate one for staff, and both were through the administrative wing, inconveniently located on the opposite side of the hospital from the Boughs. Making my way through the long, dimly lit corridor—thanks to the nighttime lighting—I hitched my bag a little higher onto my shoulder and tried to remember that no one was watching me.

There wasn't much movement in the hospital at this hour, just the odd staff member leaving the night shift, or moving in between wards. I caught the eye of one male nurse in passing as I neared the grand staircase, whose finely-boned face would have looked more in place on a runway than in a psychiatric hospital. He smiled at me, brilliant brown eyes dancing as if he knew a secret, and inclined his head toward me ever so slightly as he passed.

It didn't help the creepy-crawly feeling that I was being watched, and I tried to surreptitiously hurry toward the enormous staircase, grateful that I was headed down the three flights instead of up. There was an elevator, of course, but that was reserved for those who couldn't walk, and much as I rued the fact right now, my legs were fine.

I started down the stairs. One of the most distinct features of the old building was the four-story staircase. If you stood at the top of the stairs on the fourth floor, they were built in such a way that you could see all the way to the first. Today, lit by the cut-glass chandeliers, a woman that I didn't recognize was standing at the bottom of the staircase dressed in a flowing, brilliant blue dress, with long hair as white as snow. As I watched, she rounded the corner to the staircase and started up toward me.

Blinking, wondering who would be up and around at this time of day—and sincerely hoping that they weren't an AWOL patient—I paused, trying to get rid of the graininess.

"Nurse Margot?"

I opened my eyes.

Matron stood a couple of stairs below the second-floor landing, the white-haired woman nowhere to be seen. I looked around, wondering if I'd fallen asleep on the step when I'd closed my eyes, craning my neck to see if a flash of blue fabric or white hair would be visible if I moved quickly enough.

Nothing.

I needed to get home and fast.

"Good morning, Matron." I said it far too late, moving swiftly down the stairs. "You're up early."

"You're leaving a little late," she said, meeting me on the second-floor landing. I checked my watch. It was already almost half past six. She wasn't wrong.

"Nurse Kristen got in a little later than I think she was

hoping." I shrugged. "Not a big deal. Today's my day off anyway."

"I see." A small smile played around Matron's rosebud lips. There was a moment of awkward silence as we stood on the landing, dark red carpet under our feet. After a moment, she tilted her head to the side. "If she's late again please inform me. I don't want her forming bad habits."

I thought about that a moment, wondering if Nurse Kristen had a habit. Uncertainly, I nodded. "If I notice, and it's excessive, I'll definitely let you know."

"Good." The word was definitive. Then, taking a step toward the next flight of stairs, she paused. "You looked distracted just now. May I ask what you were thinking about?"

I motioned to the left where the dark wood railing wrapped around the opening to the stairs, and the doors to the wards lining the hall every few yards. It was a copy of the fourth floor, where I worked, but oddly unfamiliar at the same time. I hadn't ever paused here before—either I was focused on the hike up to the Boughs, or blundering my way down in the morning much as I had been in the process of doing today. Maybe it was the railings that made the difference?

"Nurse Margot?"

I needed to go home.

"Sorry, Matron. I think I'm just tired. By the way, is there a patient that has long white hair here? I saw her a couple of minutes ago coming up the stairs, wearing a blue dress. You might have seen her: I saw her only a minute before I saw you. I'm worried she might be wandering around out of her ward." Not that if she was she'd automatically get hurt or anything, but it would have been irresponsible to let her just wander around.

Matron seemed thoughtful, eyebrows crinkling together delicately above deep blue eyes that seemed oddly familiar all of a sudden. "No, I can't say that I saw her. I can check with the staff to see if anyone matching that description was out of bounds."

"Do you know who it might be?"

"Many of our patients have white hair, Nurse Margot."

Matron reached out and touched my arm. I felt a small jolt of static electricity as her hand touched me, and I couldn't help but jump. "Oops!" Her voice held an undercurrent of apologetic humor. "Now run along. We want you to stay awake on your ride home."

Flashing her a smile that felt about as real as I was at ease, I made my way to the bottom of the stairs. At the end of the long hall, I passed through the staff rooms and a few of the offices, all bedecked with autumn and Hallowe'en decorations that ranged from chic to campy. I wondered how it would look come Christmas.

Finally, pushing my way out the staff door, I stepped into the freezing pre-dawn. The cold jolted me further into awareness, and I headed down the cement steps toward the parking lot, only pausing long enough to look up at the enormous building behind me. Had there ever been more flights of stairs in one building?

Finally, hands snugged deep in my pockets, I trudged to my car. I barely remembered exiting the gates—only the vague imprint of the deep oak leaf fence remaining—and the next thing I knew I was at home, taking the key out of the ignition.

I sat there, blinking in the overhead light that automatically flicked on, disturbed. I knew I hadn't been asleep, but I'd never zoned out that badly before. I realized retroactively that I hadn't even pulled my phone out from where it was snugged into my center console to turn on my music.

I was going to have to figure out something else to do when the hot weather months came and I couldn't keep my phone in my car anymore. The rules were clear: No phones in the hospital, not even in the locker room.

Throwing the door open and kicking out my leg to stop it from rebounding back into me, I slowly and stiffly climbed out of my car, and then climbed the stairs to the house. *My house,* I reminded myself. *You signed a mortgage and everything.* The night was turning to a lighter blue, the sun apparently just thinking about rising. It would probably be another thirty or forty minutes until it peeked up over the horizon.

As I reached into my pocket for my keys, which I had inexplicably slid into my pocket, my eyes caught sight of a small package leaning up against the screen door.

I frowned. It hadn't been there when I'd left at seven-thirty the previous night. I also didn't think that mail men made midnight deliveries. Specialty mail, maybe?

Sighing a little, more from fatigue than annoyance, I leaned down and picked it up.

There was no postage. The handwriting on the box looked a little familiar, but I couldn't quite place it. I shook the package lightly. Nothing moved. Frowning but interested, I tucked the package under my arm, unlocked the door to my home, and entered. Throwing the deadbolt lock closed behind me, I dropped my keys into the dish on my just-barely-cleared-off hall bureau and went into the living room.

I shoved aside the pile of clothes that needed pressing and hanging, kicked off my shoes and sank onto the plush couch, letting it enfold me in its soft nest. Then I ripped open the package and pulled out a light, striated wooden box. I recognized it immediately, and my mouth dropped open.

I looked into the package looking for some sort of note and was rewarded at once. There were two letters actually. The one on top—not in an envelope—was handwritten like the address. As soon as I saw the name on the bottom of the letter, I realized why.

Margot,

I realize that this is a little irregular, but since you're undoubtedly ducking my phone calls at this point, I figured it would be better to get these to you as soon as possible, while respecting your need for privacy at this time. Your father asked me to send these to you during one of our last conversations. He hoped that it will bring you the luck and protection that it gave your mother.

His words.

If you have any questions at all, or if you want to send either item back, please return it to my business address. I've included a pre-paid package label. As ever, I am willing to act as intermediary until you get to a point where you can deal with the situation.

Best wishes,

Edward Campion, Esq.

Attorney at Law

I took a deep breath, a frown dragging at the edges of my mouth. It wasn't like he was wrong. I had been avoiding him, and for exactly the reasons he'd implied.

Putting Mr. Campion's letter and the one beneath it down beside me, I opened the rowan wood box, looking down at the ring nestled inside. Mom's wedding ring. The polished wood, with the strip of polished metal inlaid in the center, gleamed back at me in the fluorescent light. I let my thumb brush over the ring. It was hard to believe that I'd seen it on its previous owner on a day only two months ago. Well, almost three months now.

The day she died.

I wanted to push the pain away, but the combination of the stresses of work, the fatigue, and that little nagging voice that seemed to belong to my therapist—telling me to not hold it in— cracked my resolve. Breathing in deeply, I held the rowan wood box tight to my chest and leaned my head back onto the couch. The tears didn't take long to surface. They rolled down the sides of my cheeks into my ears as I stared up at the plain white ceiling.

Early Onset Alzheimers. It started with the little things like momentarily forgetting the names of things, like her purse, or the sofa. Momentarily forgetting she had visitors in the middle of a party. Walking into a room and forgetting why she was there. Normal things. And then she started leaving her front door open at night when she came in from her walk. Started getting lost in her own neighborhood. Started forgetting my name.

She'd lasted five years to the day from her diagnosis. I'd known that she was going to die for a while before it had actually happened. I'd worked with countless late-term cases to know the signs. But it never hurt like this before.

Of course it hadn't—she was my mom.

My real parent.

The one that was always going to be there for me. No matter what. All the other craziness in my life could be put aside. Every sting could be soothed. And then all that reassurance and comfort had slowly, agonizingly faded.

I raised my head and used the sleeve of my jacket to wipe away my tears, sniffing hard despite myself. I pulled the ring out of the box, touching the smooth surface again with the tips of my fingers. I could hear her words in the back of my mind from a day in my childhood. I'd been holding her hand on the green couch after a rough night, asking why she never took the ring off.

"It's . . . like a good luck charm," she'd said. "Your father had it custom made for me after we were married. The Douglas fir wood and the cold iron symbolize protection, clear sight, and discernment."

"Does it work?" I'd asked, looking up at her, leaning against her.

She'd smiled down at me, running a hand over my head gently. "Of course it does, my love," she said quietly, kissing the top of my head. "Look at the bank loan last week. The bank officer was going to put a much higher rate of interest on the loan, but I noticed at the last minute. Then, at the grocery store last year, when you nearly got hit by that car that was backing out? I saw and pulled you out of the way at just the right time. And . . . other things." She had trailed off then, a slightly worried look on her face. Wondering.

"Mom?"

She often got that same faraway look in her eyes, and it had scared me, even though I didn't know why. She smiled down at me and pulled me tighter against her.

"It doesn't really matter whether it's true or not, my love," she had said it quietly. "When we see the right things at the right times and are able to do something about it, that is what actually matters. You don't need a ring to do that."

"It feels like it should matter," I'd said a little sulkily. I didn't like not knowing things—it was a trait that I had definitely carried through to my adult years.

Mom had laughed at that. "Yes, it probably does," she'd said. "But I've found the older I get, if I want to be content, I need to try to just accept things how they are. I can't spend all my time wishing how I want things to be."

I had let my eyes stray to the stairs. A voice, Dad's—I didn't call him by his chosen name then—was loud and strident as he spoke on the phone up in his room, formed a rough staccato against Mom's calm melodic voice.

"Does it help?" *With him?* I didn't voice the second part, but I'd known by the look on Mom's face that she understood exactly what I was talking about.

"Yes," she'd whispered. "Yes, it does."

I fell asleep on the couch, sunk deep into the blue cushions, and nestled in between my slacks and the one party dress that I owned. I was still hugging the ring box when I woke up, the light, patterned wood cradled in the crook of my elbow. Shivering a little in the cool air of the house, I swallowed hard against my dry throat and rubbed my crusty eyes as I sat up.

Glancing at the clock that was propped up in the oddly dim room, I squinted a little at it, rubbing the crick in my neck that I really should have seen coming. Five o'clock. For a moment, I inwardly groaned. If I didn't get up and start making food, I was going to run late.

And then, in a moment of blissful recognition, I realized that no, no I wasn't.

It was my day off.

I flopped down sideways, ignoring the hanger poking into my side, and sighed in relief. No Randal today. No Polly. No Matron. No Tam.

I was going to . . .

I woke up thirty minutes later. Apparently, I was much more tired than I thought. Not that it was a big surprise—night shift was always the worst, and I never quite fully adapted. I had never actually wanted to. Humans were diurnal for a reason, and whenever I was up all night on night shift, it felt like I was trying to break a fundamental part of my human-ness.

Sitting up again, I pulled the empty package from where it was starting to sink in between my cushions. There'd been another letter in there that I had set down before I had been distracted by Mom's ring. Maybe she had left some sort of letter—

I looked at the handwriting on the page, my heart dropping into my stomach before splatting down somewhere between the floor and the center of the Earth. It wasn't from Mom, it was from Bill.

Sighing in disappointment and frustration, I stuffed Bill's letter and the letter from Mr. Campion back into the box, followed by Mom's ring. Blinking away sudden, different tears, I cleared my throat. I needed something else to do. Something not in here.

"Soup," I said out loud, needing something to break the silence. "It's fall. I need soup."

Pushing myself up off the couch, I headed toward the door, grabbing my keys. Reaching the door, I was about to turn the knob to let myself out, when I glanced down at myself. My scrubs were still decently clean, albeit a little wrinkled from my accidental sleep on the couch. I should be fine.

I started to turn the knob.

But I was also in a small town, and unless I wanted to drive two hours or so to the nearest superstore in Marquette, I'd probably want to look a bit more presentable before I left my house.

Thirty minutes later, showered and in a slightly more public-appropriate outfit of jeans and a T-shirt, I tugged my jacket a little tighter and headed out the door.

I probably could have walked to the grocery store. It wasn't like anything in Carterhall was over three blocks away. But considering I hadn't done much other than bought pre-prepped meals or bare necessities since I'd moved here, I would probably need my car to haul my motherlode back.

Besides, I was going to make my mom's Stone Soup, which consisted of almost every vegetable in existence with fresh-made bread and butter. There was something that was extra filling about homemade food, like it filled up my soul as much as it did my stomach. It was never going to be as good as my mom's, but I'd gotten it to a point where it would at least soothe me when I was feeling frazzled.

Like now.

The trip through the small, three aisle supermarket was confusing. It took me a full thirty minutes to realize that the foods were arranged alphabetically, at which point things started to move much faster. By the time I'd gathered all of my groceries and headed toward the check-out stand, I'd garnered the attention of one of the cashiers—a tall gangly teenager with an unfortunate combination of acne and headgear—and an oddly familiar older plump woman with silver hair and a name tag that said 'Sharon' who was doing inventory by the checkout counters.

I'd gotten a cart, but my list was a little longer than the cart had room, so I pushed the handlebar with one hand and my hip, a five-pound bag of potatoes snugged under my other arm, grateful that smooth floors were an industry standard.

"Trey, you get over there and help her right now," Sharon said, making a swiping motion at the teenager. The teenager—Trey, I could only assume—nodded and moved toward me, his legs moving just faster than the rest of him, making it look like he was partially deflated.

"Here," he said, reaching out to grab the cart.

"Thanks." I followed him to the checkout stand, smiling as he started to run the barcodes through the scanner. As I watched him, pulling my wallet out of my bag, I saw the woman sidle over, work momentarily forgotten.

"You must be the new move-in on 2nd Street." Her smile was big, and would have seemed friendly, except for the inordinately satisfied look on her face. I suddenly felt very much like a pheasant in the sights of a bird dog.

"Um, yes, that's me," I confirmed. I opened my mouth to ask her how on earth she knew that, when I realized that she was the owner of the house across the street. I'd only seen her twice, both times on my moving day a week ago, once leaning out from behind the swinging skeleton on her porch, and then once more as she left the house to walk her dog, pretending to not be sneaking glances at me or the house.

"And what brings you to Carterhall?" Her voice brought me back to the present and I looked up, blinking.

"Oh, I work at the hospital up the road," I said. "I'm a nurse there."

"Over by Newberry?"

"Um, no." I fought down the feeling that I was giving up valuable information. "The psychiatric hospital. Our Lady of the Wood."

There was a moment of uncomfortable silence, where Sharon's mouth hardened into a thin line and the teenager's mouth dropped open, metallic brackets clearly visible. Then they both started to speak at once.

"That's really rather unfortun—"

"That's so COOL." Trey's voice carried over the older woman's, his rail-thin body almost trembling as he gripped a can of tomatoes. "You're there with all the faeries!"

I stilled, staring at him.

Sharon smacked the counter in front of him. "Now that's enough of that. Rumors are just rumors, and you are the worst gossip on the whole U.P."

Trey cast her a doleful look and looked away sulkily. "It's not a rumor if it's *true*," he muttered. Looking up at me, he grinned. "Has anyone disappeared yet?"

"Sorry?" I must have pulled in my chin a little more than I thought, because he shrugged a little self-consciously.

"I mean . . ." he trailed off. "People have been going missing from there for years. I'm surprised you took the job."

"Really, Trey." Sharon turned to me. "There've only been one or two disappearances, and none of them recently. He's winding you up. I don't know why I keep him around."

I resisted pointing out that, going by the population of Carterhall, he was probably the only kid his age in the area. "I'm not worried," I reassured her. "Besides, most of the time when there're missing people, there's a perfectly logical explanation."

"Not when there's a coven of faeries nearby."

"They don't gather in covens." It popped out of my mouth before I could stop myself. When both Sharon and Trey looked up, I shrugged. "It's a court. I read it somewhere. Covens are witches."

"Well, whatever they are," Trey said, his voice low, "I wouldn't stay at the hospital long if I were you. Strange things happen there around Hallowe'en."

"Are you done?" Sharon's voice was loud and rather abrasive, and I barely caught myself in time to keep from jumping.

"Yes, ma'am," Trey said, running the last item across the scanner with a meek sort of beep. He told me my total and I handed him cash, and a moment later he gave me the change.

Sharon walked with me toward the door. "You'll have to forgive Trey," she said gravely. "He's just out of high school, and very excitable."

"So, a couple people have gone missing?" I couldn't help but ask the question as I walked out into the parking lot, even though the logical part of my brain was begging me to let it go.

"A couple, I guess," she admitted, following me out. "Not for a while, though. And not always attached to the Hospital."

Polly's face flashed through my brain, and I paused as I set my grocery bags into the trunk. I straightened, folding my arms against the chill of the last light of evening, and turned toward her. "Do you remember any of their names?"

Sharon looked at me strangely.

I smiled sheepishly. "I'm a bit curious, sorry."

The old woman shrugged a little. "I don't exactly remember. The last one was a while ago—a year, maybe two? It was something like . . . Mark—no John? Johnny. I think. The one beforehand would have been three or four years ago. It was a woman, I think. Or maybe that one was the one a year ago." She sighed, shaking her head. "I'm sorry. I don't have the most reliable memory."

I briefly wondered if I should go inside to ask Trey, but was a little resistant to the idea of getting sucked into what were undoubtedly conspiracy theories.

"No problem," I said easily. "Just idle curiosity. Every new place has its mysteries."

Sharon smiled, but it wasn't so easy. She shivered a little in the darkness.

I frowned in concern. "Don't let me keep you, it's cold out here."

"No worries. You all set with your groceries?"

"Yep! Thanks so much, Sharon."

"You're very welcome, um—"

"Oh! Margot, Margot Knight," I said, reaching out to shake her hand. She took it, her hand gripping as lightly as she possibly could and still call it a handshake.

"Good to meet you. Um, good luck with everything."

I closed the door to my Rover and nodded to her. "Thanks."

OCTOBER 25

At the start of my shift, I shivered my way into The Boughs. My quick search this afternoon through my boxes marked 'Storage' had not produced my coat, and my light jacket simply didn't ward off the chill. I pulled the space heater a little closer to my chair as I reviewed what had happened during the day shift.

Nothing out of the ordinary.

I frowned and looked around the room suspiciously, but neither Polly, Randal, nor Tam paid me any attention. What was going to happen today? Was anything going to happen? Was I becoming paranoid?

I wouldn't have been surprised. As inconvenient as life could be if my paranoia got out of hand, I couldn't—wouldn't—try to squash it completely. Paranoia, or rather vigilance, kept me prepared and aware. Considering everything that I'd experienced, I was willing to put up with a little inconvenience if it kept me safe.

"You okay, Nurse Margot?" Polly asked from the other side of the table. She was shuffling her cards. Her pale hair shone under the fluorescent light, and her smile was sweet.

"Yeah." I quickly rearranged my face into a smile. If nothing was happening, I didn't believe in disturbing that balance. "I'm fine."

Her head tilted to the side, as if she wasn't entirely sure if she should believe me, but she dropped the matter almost immediately, turning her attention back to Randal to make sure he wasn't cheating. Tam was ignoring everyone, reading a different book than yesterday. The room was quiet. The only thing breaking the silence in the room were the soft sounds from the card game.

The quiet was . . . nice. I pulled my own book out, stretching my feet out under the table in front of me. For a couple of moments I was able to relax, losing myself among the pages, at least until Tam stood up to get ready for bed. While he was in the bathroom, I tried to rehearse how I was going to ask about Polly.

'Hey, Tam, do you remember when you were going to tell me how Polly came to the hospital?'

'Hey, Tam, do you remember the terrible gossip I am? Would you tell me some more?'

'Hey, Tam, what do you know about HIPAA violations?'

As it turned out, I didn't have to bring up the subject. After Tam had finished getting ready for bed, he sat down at the table in what was usually Polly's spot—directly across from me. His book obscured his face, but it seemed likely that he remembered our impending conversation.

Neither Polly nor Randal chose to stay up much after they were done in the bathroom, so after I gave them their medications, Tam and I were soon alone in the room. We remained silent, though, while Tam seemed to search for a place to stop reading.

I looked at the cover. "*The Secret Garden?*"

He looked up, an eyebrow raised. "Yes? What of it?"

"Isn't it a little . . ."

"What?"

"Light reading?" I asked.

A faint smile touched the edges of his lips. "Would you prefer seeing me read some Tolstoy or Hugo? *Anna Karenina* or *Les Miserables*? A little *Hunchback of Notre Dame* to brighten up my life and make my days a little better?"

I pursed my lips. "I get your point. I just didn't picture you reading middle-grade turn-of-the-century fiction."

"Oh? And what did you expect me to read?"

"I don't know. Asimov? Sanderson? Maybe Connie Willis?"

"I enjoy Willis for the most part," Tam said contemplatively. "Her lighter works appeal to me more at this point in my life."

"Her *Doomsday Book* is incredible," I pointed out.

He leaned back in his chair. "It's true. But considering I'm almost constantly contemplating my mortality nowadays, I prefer things that are not so . . . pointedly applicable to my current situation."

"And what situation is that?"

He looked at me, no trace of a smile on his face now. "You wanted to know about Polly? I need to be in bed by eleven."

I shifted a little. "Yes, sorry."

"You're not in a mood that makes me particularly want to tell you," Tam said a little tiredly, his accent crisp and even.

I looked up and my brow furrowed. "I'm sorry?"

"You're argumentative," he said. "Do you usually have such a smart response to everything?"

"Not on purpose," I said, a little abashed. I thought for a moment. "I was projecting what I would have expected you to read based on my interactions with you. I had no right, so I'm sorry."

"You apologize very easily." His eyes were a little surprised, though his voice remained deep in the quiet room.

"If I'm wrong, I'm wrong," I said. "I'm not going to hold onto a wrong view just because I'm the one who had it. Besides, it wasn't appropriate, and you were right to call me out on it."

Tam continued to stare at me. I couldn't tell whether it was because he was shocked at what I'd said or because there was something on my face. I doubted it, but I touched my cheeks surreptitiously and looked at my hands. Nothing.

"What?" I finally asked.

He blinked a couple of times, not answering.

"Tam?"

"People don't apologize here," Tam finally said. "It's conceding fault."

"But I *was* at fault," I said, confused. "And you've heard me apologize before."

"Not like that." He shook his head. "Stop it."

"Wha-why?"

"Because people aren't—" He blinked and broke off, then shook his head. "Never mind. You wanted to know about Polly."

I was still mystified, but I nodded. "Yes, please."

"Well," he said, "first and foremost, her name isn't Polly."

I frowned. "Tam—"

He stopped me with a glare, and I put my hands up, conceding. I could wait until the end.

"Her name is Janet. She used to work here." He stared at the space beyond my shoulder, a heavy frown weighing on his face. "She worked here for about seven years—since before the last 'special' Hallowe'en celebration."

At first, I wondered why his voice was heavily sarcastic. Then I remembered. "*I prefer things that are not so . . . pointedly applicable to my situation,*" he'd said.

That's right. He thinks he's going to die on Hallowe'en.

You, Margot Knight, are a jerk, I thought to myself. It was one thing to know that a patient had difficulty separating fantasy from reality, but it was quite another to forget it entirely while caring for them. I watched Tam, feeling my own expression drop into a frown. Not a disbelieving one—a confused one.

"But if she used to work here, how did she become a patient?" I asked. "And why would they change her name to Polly?" Even if that had been her preference, they would have kept her real name in the file.

Tam looked down, and heaved a huge, weary sigh. "That was my fault," he said, running a finger over the tabletop.

"How could that be your fault? It—"

"Nurse Margot," Tam said, though with a patient tone, "I appreciate your desire for answers, but if you ask more questions more frequently than I have the chance to speak, we'll be here all night."

I almost responded flippantly with, 'Great, then I'll have company,' but instead I forced myself to lower my eyes and say, "Sorry."

Tam didn't smile, but the lines in his face relaxed a little. "She knew things were off for a while, but . . . didn't know how to help. She—Janet—tried to break me out of here," he said quietly. Then he swallowed and continued. "When we finally figured out what to do... well, it was before last year's bonfire. Randal—he's right. Each seventh year is special. Last year was just a normal one, so she—we—thought security would be a little looser, that we'd be able to slip off into the dark. You see . . ." He looked at me pointedly for a moment, as though weighing his words very carefully. "I already told you that Polly—Janet—was right when she told you that the Matron kills someone every seventh year. It's a ceremony, where the soul of a young man—preferably sound in body and mind, unattached to the world—is sacrificed to fuel their magic for a time further. Matron has been very clear in telling me that I am an important part in helping her race continue."

"Her race?"

"She's fae."

"A faerie?"

Tam seemed to catch the borderline timbre of skepticism that colored my voice, even as I tried to wipe it out. For a moment, he narrowed his eyes, as though he was going to fire back something totally devastating, but at the last second, he sighed and continued with his story.

"Matron caught us. It was the nineteenth of October, and

Janet had taken me out for a midnight walk. We weren't even escaping that night, but somehow Matron knew we wanted to. She always knows." Tam closed his eyes briefly, his thumbs running along the edges of *The Secret Garden* as he seemed to think back to that night.

"She was furious and trapped Janet in her office. I don't know what happened to her then—Polly can't remember. Or just won't tell me. Matron brought me back up herself, all the while telling me why I was so important, and how I had promised to stay until someone claimed me. She then locked me in my room and told me to stay there until I was told I could come out.

"The next thing I really remember, a couple of days later, she brought Janet up to the ward. Then she broke Janet's mind where Randal and I could watch. I guess it was supposed to be a lesson to us both, and a warning to let no one know. I don't remember exactly how she did it, but . . . I remember it was terrifying. I think I'd rather not remember." Tam's eyes were far away. Such a deep frown was ingrained on his face that he looked almost furious.

Maybe he was.

"Afterward, Janet was made part of the ward, under the name of Polly. Matron couldn't afford to ship her out, you see, she had to keep her secret safe. You can still see Janet in Polly some-times. Like a couple of days ago with Randal. Sometimes when Gwen would be too highhanded or rude, Polly would stand up to her. That's when it's like she's Janet again. Maybe if she was away from all of this for long enough she'd come back completely. She still can't face Matron, though. After what happened, I can't blame her, but I can't tell you how much I wish—" He broke off, staring over my shoulder, probably at the darkened window, his scowl deepening until I wondered if he'd be able to change his expression.

Finally, he noticed my contemplative expression and swal-lowed. "You don't believe a word of it, do you?" he asked softly. He sounded almost heartbroken.

I couldn't answer right away, my heart in my shoes. What could I have said? That I had forgotten that he was a patient? That I wanted the real story? That even a hidden psychosis was still a psychosis?

I stood, pushing away from the table, going to the medicine cabinet, unlocking it and pulling out his medication. "I think," I finally said, my voice softer than I expected, "that it's time to go to bed."

"You don't, then." Tam stood quietly, the chair hardly making a noise as he pushed it back.

I didn't look at him. I couldn't. "I don't," I confirmed quietly. "Listen, Tam, it's not that I don't want to believe you, but what you're saying—"

"But it's the truth! Why would I lie?" Hurt filled his voice.

I turned back to him. "Tam," I said. I opened my mouth to spill out something about how sometimes our brain tricks us into believing things, and that there was some sort of reasonable explanation to everything, and that above all, things would just be *okay*. But then I saw Bill standing there, in Tam's place.

Bill, who believed in faeries. Bill, who would have done anything to protect me from them, including beating me with an iron-based lamp to expel a faerie that had supposedly taken over my body. Bill, who had cradled me in his arms in a pool of my blood, sobbing, realizing that he had been wrong.

Stone gripped my heart, and I swallowed. Tam was a patient. For my own safety, I had to remember that.

But I couldn't hurt him. Not when he had Bill's enthusiasm. And hope.

"Tam," I said again, holding out the pills to him, "thank you for the story. I think you should probably turn in."

He took the medication from me stiffly, looking down at the small plastic cup in his hands. Then he slowly put it down on the table.

"How can I convince you?" he asked.

"I'm not one who needs to be convinced."

"Why not? Is it something against me? Am I not trustworthy? Do I need to swear on some iron or something? Why wouldn't—"

"Because faeries are things from stories, Tam," I said quietly, though my jaw was clenched. *And from my nightmares.* After everything I'd heard, everything from Bill, from Mom, and now from what Tam had told me, even if I did believe him, why on earth would I want to step willingly into that?

"Rubbish," he spat, and took a step forward.

I instinctively moved my foot back, solidifying my foundation. *Steady, Margot,* I told myself. "Please don't move any closer, Tam," I whispered. "Just take your medication and go to bed."

"Something has you scared," he said, reading my face disturbingly well.

I nearly scowled at him but realized just in time that it would tell him far more than I wanted him to know. Taking a deep breath, I forced a smile onto my face. "Tam, you just told me that the last person in my position had her wits broken. Why wouldn—"

"Not that." He narrowed his eyes. "Not here. Someone else. Someone different. It's that patient from before. The one that won't let you go. Isn't it? Did he believe in the fae, too?" There was something burning in his eyes. It wasn't normal, or recognizable.

Something pricked in my chest, and I consciously relaxed my hands from the fists that were beginning to form. "Tam, take your medicine and go to bed."

"No."

"Tam," I said warningly, "I'm more than happy to agree to disagree."

"Do you know what I think?" Tam's voice was just above a whisper. He took a step forward, suddenly large and looming. "I think you do believe me, but you don't want to. You'd do anything to keep yourself from believing."

I brought my hands in front of me, between us. "Tam, I would like you to back away right now."

"Why? Because I'm right?"

"Because I want you to *back up*, and that should be a good enough excuse for anyone." A warning was building in my voice. "Now, are you done?"

He didn't answer for a second. He stared at me for a moment, and in a second his anger vanished away, replaced with . . . shock? Concern? What would he be concerned about? Was he shocked that I'd defended myself?

No, that wasn't it.

"Yes, I'm done," he said, stepping back, his voice raspy as he dropped into a chair.

I didn't move. I didn't need to. I hadn't touched him, nor had I done anything more forceful than put my hands up. "Before you say it, I know you weren't going to hurt me, but let me disabuse you of something: I am your nurse. I am here to help you get better. You can believe what you want. You can live in whatever reality that you choose, and that is your right. But do not think for a second that getting up in my face is going to change what *I* believe. Randal caught me by surprise the other day, but you can never do that. You're right—that patient, Bill, he messed me up pretty bad. That's *my* reality. But if you want to believe anything about me, believe that I have no qualms about medicating your backside until the Second Coming if you threaten me."

Tam tore his gaze from the floor and seemed to relax a little. Then he closed his eyes and breathed deeply before a small laugh burst out of his lips. "You would, too," he said quietly.

I frowned at that. "You okay?"

Tam shrugged and sighed.

I held out my hand. "I'm sorry."

"You're apologizing? Again? What if I *had* been trying to hurt you?"

"If you'd wanted to hurt me, you would have tried harder," I said. "Besides, you're not that kind of sick. I've worked with them before. I know what they look like."

Tam took my hand and shook it. "Said to a permanent resident of an isolated wing of a mental institution." He paused for a moment, as if searching for the right words. "I'm sorry. I should have respected your space, no matter how frustrated I was. Or how differently we see the issue."

I smiled sadly, taking a step back. "Seeing reality in a different way doesn't make anyone a bad person, Tam."

Sighing, Tam dropped into one of the chairs. Then he squinted up at me. "So did you learn self-defense before or after whatever happened?"

I looked down at him for a moment. Then, I sat down in the chair next to him, crossed my legs, and linked my fingers together in front of me. "What makes you think something happened?" I asked, curious. I hadn't touched him. I hadn't had to do anything more than put my hands up.

Tam's expression didn't change, really, although it might have fallen a little.

"You've been sizing me up since day one. That stance? I usually only see that from the security guys around here. My guess is jiu-jitsu, but that's just a shot in the dark from . . . dabbling once upon a time," he said, fingers teasing around the edge of his medication cup. "And you said Bill messed you up pretty bad. Plus, statistically speaking—or at least at the time I was admitted here—a large percentage of women learn a martial art when they feel threatened. So, again: was it before or after?"

I bit my lip a little and shook my head. I owed him absolutely nothing, but I couldn't quite keep myself from answering. "It was both."

He frowned. "Of all the unhelpful—"

"You wanted an answer, and you got one."

"How can it be both?" he demanded.

I looked up at him, and shrugged. "Sometimes you can see

something coming long before it ever shows up." I smiled, but it felt fake. "Take your medicine, Tam. It's time to go to bed."

"How can Bill still get in contact with you?" he asked, eyes still on me, but his fingers had closed around his medicine cup. "You said earlier you tried to avoid him as much as possible. If he's a patient who hurt you, how can he contact you?"

I pressed my lips together, feeling that scar on the inside of my lip. "He can't anymore. And that's the short version of a much longer story than we have time for. And definitely more than I should tell you as a patient."

Tam looked at me a little regretfully. "Very well. I'm not taking back what I told you—it's the truth—but I am very sorry for the way that I acted, Nurse Margot." He paused. "And I'm sorry . . . well, for everything that you've gone through. Whatever it is."

I couldn't look at him. It's not like I would have known what to say if I could. Instead, I stood and took the files out of the cabinet. Tam downed his pills in one go, then went to his room and didn't look back, even when I did.

The reports took forever. I'd never heard of paperwork that seemed to take longer the more you did it, and yet here I was, up to my eyeballs in forms that at my current rate would be done sometime in my nineties. I reported the incident with Tam, noting that it ended peaceably. I noted the story that he told me, in a little more detail than I might have otherwise done, and perhaps I was feeling a little insecure about that because I added a comment that I realized that the story was fiction and that the patient showed a bright, imaginative mind. Maybe more stimulating day activities would help keep his psychosis at bay?

I didn't recommend any sort of discipline. I was sure that the most Tam would have done was get up in my face. I'd been trained to deescalate, and he'd responded to my efforts. And apologized, even.

I still felt rather uncomfortable about the whole thing. I wished there was another person up here. Someone with whom I could share the patients, so that Tam didn't have the chance to become overly familiar . . . and so that I didn't either. Then again, maybe it was a good thing that it only ever seemed to be me, the morning nurse Kristen, and Eileen up here day in and day out now that Gwen was in a different part of the facility. At least for now. Maybe no one would ever know about what had happened, and how I'd willingly listened to a madman.

When I got into the ward the next day, there was a note on the office door with my name on it telling me to report to Matron's office as soon as I could. After letting my bag slide to the floor, I kicked it into the small room, and pulled the doors closed.

Looking over at Eileen, I frowned. I pulled the post-it off the door and waved it at her. "Do you know what this is?" I asked.

Eileen glanced up from the reports she was finishing and looked at the note distastefully. "It's a note. From Matron. She wants you to report to her office."

"I got that. Do you know why?"

"Beats me." Eileen rolled her eyes at me. "All I know is that I have a date in an hour and a half, and Matron asked me to stay late until she's finished with you." She sighed and turned back to her report. It looked weird, and I realized far too late it was a magazine hidden inside a manila folder. I resisted the urge to roll my eyes right back at her.

"I'll do my best to be as quick as I possibly can," I said, looking around at our three occupied and peaceful patients, trying not to sound too sarcastic. She didn't look up, so I assumed that I'd succeeded—or she just wasn't listening anymore —and I turned to head downstairs to Matron's office.

I racked my brains, trying to think of something—anything —that I hadn't been fully by-the-book on. The only thing that could come to mind was my altercation with Tam the night before. Subduing Randal was one thing, because he was attacking Polly, but if Matron had gotten wind that I'd engaged with Tam, even if it hadn't escalated beyond words, and she didn't appreciate that, I could be fired. Worst-case scenario, if they'd thought I'd been abusive in my language, or acted dispro- portionately in the situation, I could technically be brought up on assault charges.

I paused on the highest flight of stairs, staring all the way down at the first floor, briefly pinching my eyes closed. Of all the things I didn't want to do right now, moving was definitely in the top three of that particular list. Finding a job as a nurse in Michigan wasn't hard, but with that kind of a mark on my record? Also, uprooting myself once had been hard enough. Twice in three weeks? No thanks.

Once down the stairs, I walked down the long halls toward the approximate area that I remembered Matron's office to be in. I was a little worried for a moment that I would miss it, but as soon as I turned the corner into her hall, I knew I was in the right place. The hall was decked out in fall colors. Not in gaudy decor like some of the other administrative offices closer to the entrance, though. Small trees of every variety and color lined the halls in decorative pots and vines of ivy with red leaves intertwined with the trees, arching over one end of the hall. The fresh smell of the trees seemed to push wakefulness into every corner of my mind, even at this late hour, and I felt an unconscious smile cross my face as I looked at the magical scene.

Crossing the hall, I noticed that the Matron's door was closed, a red light illuminated alongside the placard set in the wall. I was willing to bet Randal's deck of cards that the red light was the "do not disturb" sign, so I settled into one of the dark wood chairs across the hall and waited.

Rather than getting sucked into my own thoughts again, I took in my surroundings. I'd only been in the administration corner of the hospital a handful of times, the last of which had been six days ago on my first day on duty in The Boughs, and none of those times had been particularly conducive to admiring the architecture. The hospital was a beautiful building with little details everywhere if one would just take the time to explore them.

Like the subtle leaf detailing around the archways. I was too far away to tell exactly what the detailing was, but there was something about it that seemed to poke at my brain, telling me to pay attention, probably just as the artist intended. I smiled and wondered how old the building was. It definitely wasn't modern, and yet there were subtle touches that hinted that it wasn't as old as it seemed. It said early 1900's to me, but I wouldn't have sworn by that.

Then my attention turned to the door. It was a beautiful piece of work—red oak, if I wasn't mistaken—and the colored wood gleamed in the fluorescent light of the overhead fixture that was set in the ceiling of the hallway. I found myself wishing that it had different lighting—it needed something different, something softer. Warmer. My eyes narrowed a little, and I focused on the images carved into the wood.

Forest animals—rabbits, deer, foxes—filled the edges, curiously all pointing toward the scene depicted at the center of the door. On first impression, the image was of a celebration, with men and women in flowing medieval-like clothes dancing wildly around a bonfire, movement swirling through every line carved into the wood. At the head of the bonfire, however, there were several solemn figures: a woman, staring at a man on a horse. All of them stood stiller than the wood they were carved into.

I leaned forward in my seat, frowning at the door. The man and the horse seemed to stand in the center of the fire. Unmoving. The man was simply looking back at the woman, letting the flames slowly consume him. This was the focal point of the door —every part of the carving drew attention back to this single point.

I shivered a little bit, recognition sparking in my brain. This had to be the inspiration for Tam's story. He'd arrived on a horse, there were regular bonfires, and Matron was keeping him here for his safety. Of course he would put his situation and the image together. If this was the inspiration, I could see why Tam was troubled. I knew the beauty of art was in the eye of the beholder —and make no mistake, the art on this door was beautifully and masterfully done—but . . . but this was a bit too much. It was disturbing.

I shifted, intent on moving so I wouldn't have to look at it anymore when the door cracked open. Looking up a little guiltily, I saw Matron's face, all smooth skin and sparkling blue eyes, smiling at me.

"Ah, Nurse Margot, I see you got my note," she said pleasantly, opening the door the rest of the way. She noticed my lingering gaze on the door, and the smile widened across her face. Running her hand gently along the shiny red wood gently, she sighed a little. "It's beautiful, isn't it?"

"Yes," I said as I approached. I had no idea what else to say. It was true, no matter how unsettling the subject matter of the door was.

"Its title is '*The Tiend*,'" Matron said reverently, tracing her fingers over the figure of the man in the center of the door. "It's based on a very old legend about a holy ritual of an ancient race. It was also very difficult to get my hands on it. It's a highly-sought-after piece, and the prize of my collection."

"Oh?" I said, looking again at the door.

"Yes. The woodwork is exceptional of course, but the tree that it comes from is also significant. It's made from a single piece—no joints or glue—from one of the Kings of the Wood in

England's oldest forest. There are very few pieces like it in the world."

"That's amazing." The awe in my voice was real.

Matron's smile deepened a little at my words, then she stood back, allowing me access through the door. "Please come in. I called you in for a reason."

Anxiety piled back onto my head, and, nodding a little, I headed into the office. I hadn't actually been in here before. We'd met outside her office before touring the facility, and we had filled out paperwork in one of the general staff rooms. If I'd thought that the door was the oddest thing about her office, I changed my mind the moment I stepped over the threshold.

It wasn't that there was anything on the floor to ceiling shelves as disturbing as the door— there were just many . . . oddities. Paintings, lithographs, and framed illuminations covered all the wall space; terrariums that were bursting with plants; books upon books with fancy covers that looked older than anything that should be allowed outside of a museum, and unrecognizable specimens in jars sat on the shelves. There was one element that every book cover, illumination, and lithograph —and even the art of the stained glass behind her—shared.

"Faeries?" I said, my eyes lingering on the image in the window: a barefoot woman mid-dance, surrounded by drifting autumn leaves. "Interesting hobby."

Matron walked around the desk, smiling a little. "Call it more of a life's pursuit. Please, have a seat. Would you like some tea, or perhaps some shortbread?"

"No, thank you." I sank into the seat on the other side of the desk and looked across at her. "The door. It seems a little . . . on the nose," I said, "considering the members of my ward."

"Oh, they've never been in here," she assured me. "We've done our best to keep everything faerie-related away from Tam and Randal. Polly, too. Though," she looked around the room, "I can see where you might be concerned that an obsession could arise."

Whether said obsession was hers or theirs, I couldn't have told from her tone. Still, no need to beat around the bush. "I'm sorry to be so straightforward, but is there something the matter? I hate to ask, but if I'm not meeting some sort of policy, I would like to—"

"Oh no, Nurse Margot," Matron said. Pearly white teeth were visible behind her lips briefly, then she turned and took a very familiar folder from a stack on one side of her desk.

"Is that Ta—Thomas's file?" I asked.

She glanced up at me briefly, expression unreadable, as she flicked it open. "It is," she said, her voice suddenly more serious than it had previously been. My heart sank. "I was a little concerned about the content of last night's entry, and I wanted to discuss it with you."

"I realize that I had to be firm with Thomas last night, but in order to keep the situation from escalating—"

"That's not what I am talking about," Matron said, her tone patient but not particularly pleased. "I see in here that you have some notes about what Thomas said about one of his ward-mates, Polly."

I frowned before I could stop myself. "About Polly?"

"Yes." Matron's eyes, so blue they were almost violet, studied the folder in the dim light of the office. "It says here that Thomas discussed Polly with you at length, alleging that she was a nurse here by the name of Janet before I . . . 'snapped her wits?'" Her voice lilted up, eyebrows raising as she looked back up at me.

"Yes, it was the story that Thomas told me," I said quietly. "In the file I indicated that I think it's fiction."

"I noticed," Matron leaned back in her chair, chin resting on one of her hands. "However, I also noted that you have not given similar attention to your other patients. In Randal's nightly report two days ago, you did not elaborate on what story he told, and on the night of the twenty-second you didn't include as much detail about Polly's nightmare."

I didn't answer for a moment, until I had the right words.

"Are you insinuating that I am showing some form of favoritism?" I asked, forcing myself to maintain eye contact. *Based on what?* "Or that I am showing signs of the beginning of an improper relationship with Mr. Lynn?" I'd been briefed on those signs before, but I couldn't remember—and doubted—if "reporting too much information" was one of them.

"Only you can answer that," Matron said placidly. "As of yet, no, I do not think so, but I would caution you to not take too much interest in what he says in the future. Tam has very strong delusions, as you have experienced, but he is also very capable of manipulating people into believing his stories. His looks don't hurt in this case, either. To be clear, I do not believe you've been taken in by him and his . . . elaborate fictions, but I wanted to warn you against putting too much stock in what he tells you. Or taking any particular attention he gives you to heart."

"I . . ." I closed my eyes briefly, trying to force down my indignation at her implication. "I can assure you that there is nothing like that going on. Nor will there ever be."

Matron straightened in her chair, an oddly pleased smile on her face. "Well, I trust you will keep it that way. I know I do not have to worry, but some things are simply best said and then never worried about again." She was talking briskly, as though she was trying to get the spiel over with as fast as possible. She stood and held the file out to me. "If you would please take this back up with you, I would very much appreciate it."

I took the file.

Reaching out and touching my arm, she smiled. "Thank you for your time, Nurse Margot, that was all I had to talk with you about."

"Of course," I stood and walked toward the door, my steps somehow slow and clunky. There was a question in my mind, but I wasn't entirely sure what it was yet. But I knew I didn't want to leave until I'd asked it.

"Matron?" I said, turning back.

She looked up from the paper she'd pulled off the top of one of the piles on her desk. "Yes, Nurse Margot?" Her expression was oddly expectant, as if she'd known that I was going to make an additional comment.

I waited for a moment. The question didn't come.

". . . Nothing," I said, oddly disconcerted, and went back upstairs.

If I'd gone by Eileen's reaction, I would have thought that I'd been downstairs for over half the night. As it happened, I'd been downstairs barely thirty minutes, including the time that it took to climb up and down that ridiculous staircase. Just enough time to nearly get lost in the administrative wing, get creeped out by a door, and get warned off of being romantically involved a patient with whom I'd argued the night before.

As Eileen left the ward, slinging her bag over her shoulder and sighing loudly, I didn't watch her. If I had, I wouldn't have been able to control my expression and that would have likely caused a whole other set of problems.

"Anything wrong, Nurse Margot?" Randal asked. He sat at the table, playing solitaire.

Polly sat at the table as well, but rather than playing cards with him, she was doing a puzzle. Looking at their placid faces, I couldn't have decided who had started their personal activity first and left the other out.

Tam, meanwhile, was halfway through another book, this one with a plain red binding. Where did he even get all of them? Did he have a secret stash somewhere?

"No, I'm fine," I said, a little too quietly, as I crossed the room to put the file into the cabinet. When I looked up and around the room again, I caught Tam switching his gaze from me to his book. Pressing my lips together, I moved across the room to the counter. Nothing was on it—I didn't actually know why we had one—but it was somewhere to stand that wasn't in the middle of the room.

"You don't look fi—" Randal started.

I looked up at him and he stopped mid-word.

"Well, there's a look that could crack a bell." His voice was loud and frank, and somehow sharpened the vaguely displeased feelings that were pulling at me into one identifiable emotion.

Anger.

A warning alarm in my brain told me to stop, to think before I spoke. I smothered it. "What does that even mean?" I demanded.

Randal looked up at me patiently. "Do you know how bells are made?" His tone was far less aggressive than mine, but that only made his words grate on my nerves even more.

I struggled to control my expression. I was supposed to be the nurse here. "No," I said flatly, probably harsher than I should have.

"It has to do with that," he said simply, shrugging, as if he recognized my hard tone and didn't want to engage.

I stared down at him, wondering if that was really a door I wanted to open, and then realized the alternative was sitting in the soggy puddle that was the aftermath of my conversation with Matron. As if I wasn't boiling in it already. Sighing, I pushed the frustration aside and I slid into my regular chair.

"Okay, I'll bite, how do you make a bell?"

When he heard the change in my voice, Randal shifted toward me, laying down the excess cards from the deck on the table. "You cast it in a mold, and then you have to let it cool down. If you cool it down too quickly, it cracks." His words were in the simple tone that he usually took with me. I didn't know why he did that; I knew he was smarter than he wanted me to think he was.

I thought for a minute, "So my look was cold?"

"Exactly," Randal said, as though it were obvious, and he picked up his cards again.

I slumped back in the chair and tried not to sigh. I realized that I should probably take the time to read the reports and get caught up for the evening, but I wasn't in the mood. That, and none of my patients seemed to be in danger of exploding at each other, so I took a minute to myself, pinching the bridge of my nose and breathing deeply.

In . . . two . . . three . . . four . . .

Out . . . two . . . three . . . four . . .

I thought about my conversation with Matron. After a moment of reflection, I realized I wasn't upset because she thought I might be showing Tam favoritism, but because she'd insinuated that I was—theoretically—showing favoritism because he was manipulating me into it. If only she knew how very decisively I had previously learned that particular lesson, she would have suspected far, far less of me. It was her lack of knowledge of me that I was galled at, not the accusation itself.

Only, now that I thought about it, was it actually an accusation? It was more of an experienced warning. I could deal with that. It was the responsible thing for a leader to do in their establishment. Right?

After six days?

In . . . two . . . three . . . four . . .

Out . . . two . . . three . . . four . . .

I shouldn't have been surprised when the counting exercise worked, but a moment later, the tension in my shoulders released, and I felt the jumpy, ruffled feeling from the meeting with Matron start to die down. I closed my eyes and savored the moment of calm while it lingered. It was harder and harder to come by these days.

But I was here to do a job.

Taking another deep breath, I opened my eyes and looked around the room. Randal's and Polly's hands were occupied with their individual pursuits, but they were also chattering excitedly with each other about the Hallowe'en preparations they'd helped with earlier that evening. Tam was staring over the top of his book at the door with an absent expression.

I furrowed my brows and tilted my head as I surveyed him. He didn't seem to notice me staring. He gazed off into the distance for a long time, blinking every once in a while, then looking down at his book and turning a page, and then losing focus again. He repeated the cycle over and over.

I checked the reports—nothing earth-shattering had happened that day—then moved on to put together the night-time medications before locking them back in the cabinet.

The chores were done, so I wandered over to Tam, approaching in full line of sight so I wouldn't surprise him. Still, he jumped when he saw me, his book tumbling from his fingertips onto the floor. I picked it up.

"*A Christmas Carol?* In October?" I asked, handing it back to him.

He raised an eyebrow.

"Poor boy has a reading list that he wants to get done by Hallowe'en, don't you?" Randal chimed from across the room.

I sent Randal a small smile, then turned back to Tam. He stared at Randal with an oddly blank expression before looking back up at me and shaking his head.

"Don't tell me you're about to malign the Christmas classics now." The words had just the right amount of sarcasm, and yet they felt hollow.

I sank down on the other end of the couch. "Of course not," I said, a tentative smile on my face. "Dickens is one of my favorite authors."

"Have you actually read any of his books?"

I blinked, now a little uncomfortable. "I've read *A Christmas Carol.* They've also made some half-decent TV adaptations, too. I've seen a lot of them—those are some of my favorites."

"You haven't read Dickens, and yet you know science fiction and fantasy authors off the top of your head?" He was challenging me.

I pulled my chin in defensively. "What, I'm not allowed to prefer one genre over the other?"

"Not when you lie about it," he muttered, bringing the book back in front of his face.

I frowned. "I didn't lie. Dickens came up with one of my favorite stories ever. Since he is still the creator of the work, the medium is irrelevant."

He put the book down. "Name one film adaptation that even comes close to bringing across the author's prose as it was meant to be enjoyed."

"*The Muppet Christmas Carol*," I said promptly. Thank goodness I had actually read the book—short though it was—and could make the comparison.

Tam must have agreed about the film adaptation, because he opened and then closed his mouth, and then turned back to the book. He muttered something else under his breath—I was pretty sure it was swearing—and I fought to keep from smirking.

"So, what's going on?" I asked.

"I'm reading. Or trying to," he said, darting a glare at me.

I pursed my lips, shoving down the annoyance. One of us was going to have to make an effort to cheer up, otherwise yesterday with the almost-altercation was just going to be a benchmark. Okay. Cheerful. I tilted my head to the side, looking across the room pointedly.

Tam's head snapped over to look at me. "What?"

"You've been staring at the door most of the evening," I said. "Either you can see an ephemeral Tiny Tim from here or you've been deep in thought." I squinted at the door. "You know, I can't see him, but—"

Tam sighed and waved his book at me as if shooing me.

"What?"

"Stop it."

I held out my hands. "I didn't know I was doing something?"

He narrowed his eyes. "Please. Just stop." Every sound fell crisp and sharp from his lips. For the barest of moments, I thought about refusing—a taste of his own medicine from last night when he got into my face. Then I remembered how old I was. And where I was. I couldn't let getting rankled by Matron earlier affect how I treated my patients now. It wouldn't be fair in normal life with mentally healthy people, and it was doubly unfair here where patients often had a difficult enough time understanding humanity as a whole. I was a nurse. I was a professional.

I sat back.

"Sorry about that," I said sincerely, settling into the couch cushions and drawing up one leg up against my chest. "But I would still like to know what's wrong."

Tam shook his head, a rueful smile curling up one side of his face, and he glanced over at the table. Randal and Polly had looked over in response to Tam's tone and were still watching.

I shifted a little. My mood settled as cautious concern took over. To be perfectly honest, I wasn't entirely sure what was going on. On one hand, he had apologized last night for his behavior, and I had accepted the apology. On the other hand, if he knew why Matron had called me in . . .

"Tam," I said, once Polly and Randal had gone back to their respective activities. "I know we didn't see eye to eye on things last night, but I am kind of like your doctor. You can tell me anything, and I'll do my best to help."

Tam snorted. "Thank you, but I'd rather not have everything I say make it back to Matron." With that, he pulled his book back up. Conversation . . . closed?

Perhaps if I wasn't in such an argumentative mood—though, with a brief review of the last couple of days, maybe my mood wasn't such an anomaly—I would have left it alone. But I was in an argumentative mood, and so I didn't.

"I'm sorry," I said, contrite but not meek. "I had no idea she read the reports."

Tam looked at me as though I'd told him I was part Martian. "You 'had no idea she read the reports?'" he asked incredulously. He shifted, pulling his book back up to his face more purposefully. Either his vision had gotten exponentially worse in the last three minutes, or he was trying to ignore me on purpose.

"In my experience, if anyone other than people directly involved with patients reads the reports, it's reviewers in the American Nurses Association. Normally, or at least at every other hospital in the US, hospital admin does exactly that—administrate the hospital, not micromanage the patients. I'm sorry I was wrong," I grumbled, pushing myself off the couch and trudging back to the table.

Randal looked up at me as I approached but didn't acknowledge me further than that. Polly pulled my chair over by her and looked at me hopefully.

"Will you help me?" she asked brightly, indicating the puzzle.

I nearly said no. I normally didn't have the patience for puzzles, and with the way today was going, it didn't seem like that was going to be suddenly cured. Then I saw that her eyes held not only an invitation but also a question: *What's actually bothering you?*

Guilt washed over me. The answer, of course, was the meeting with Matron. But I'd just—

Tam's words poured over me, and I knew he was right. I should have realized that other people would have read the report. But I never would have thought Matron would read it. Gwen yes, maybe even Kristen or Eileen. Maybe one of them had reported it? Except Eileen hadn't seemed to know.

It didn't matter. I wrote it more as catharsis for myself, but the detail that I went into was very in depth. Matron was right as well. I had gone overboard on certain details.

Blast it.

"Of course I'll help," I said quietly, sinking into the chair beside Polly.

She reached over and patted my hand. "We all make mistakes," she said soothingly.

Randal, flipping through his hand of cards, hummed in agreement. As usual, a hidden secret danced behind his smile.

"Most of the time they don't prove to be fatal." Polly giggled a little bit, her tone playful. "At least, none of mine have been yet."

She'd said it jokingly, but I had a hard time smiling. It wasn't that I believed Tam—I knew better—but Polly's delicate face, and large grey eyes lent a sort of sad irony to her words. No, she wasn't dead, but she was isolated in a psych ward in a hospital. That didn't exactly scream "living life to the fullest." Again, I wondered why she'd been admitted here.

"That was supposed to cheer you up," Polly said, frowning slightly. "I wouldn't worry about it, Nurse Margot. Matron is up here almost every day. If there was something that you mentioned, it was probably because it was out of the ordinary, and she wanted an explanation."

It hadn't felt like Matron had wanted an explanation. It had felt like a warning based in complete fantasy. Still, if she was up there every day . . . *Wait.*

I turned to Polly suddenly. "Really? Every day?"

Polly blinked at me blankly before shrugging. "Yes. She takes Tam out on walks in the afternoon. Sometimes they go riding."

Randal was looking down at his cards, ignoring us, so I looked over at Tam.

Tam shrugged too, giving me only the most cursory of glances up from his book. "Most days," he amended. "She doesn't usually come on weekends."

With that level of attention paid to him by Matron, it should have been at least mentioned in the report, but it wasn't—in fact, I would have eaten my socks if it was in there. "Why?"

"I don't remember most of it." His voice was calm and matter-of-fact.

My frown deepened.

"Matron sure has taken a shine to dearest Tam," Randal said in a singsong way, finally glancing up at us. Grinning at Tam, he raised his voice to make sure the younger man could hear. "Hasn't she?"

"Do you go out with them?" I asked Polly, before Tam could respond to Randal's obvious bait.

Out of the corner of my eye, I could see Tam's shoulders relax, though he was now sending a smoldering glare over my shoulder at Randal. I sighed a little bit—it just figured that I would have to break up a fight today.

Polly looked up from the puzzle pieces and laughed in surprise. "What, me? Go with them? No, I'm not nearly important enough." Was that relief in her voice? Then she shuddered a little. "Matron . . . takes very good care of those she notices. I'm okay with her not noticing me." With that, she frowned a little and turned back to her puzzle.

"If you don't go out with them, how do you know what they do?" I asked. Polly smiled and pointed out the window over the sink.

"Sneak," Randal said, snapping a card down against the table.

I wished slightly that he'd go back to ignoring everyone. Polly didn't seem too bothered by him though. The poor girl was probably used to it.

"During the day you can see the whole back grounds of the hospital," Polly said. "I've been watching them build the bonfire and set up the decorations over the last couple of days—they're going to have a hayride this time!—but it's always pretty back there, no matter the time of year. Matron always wears a deep blue coat, and you can tell her by her hair. That, and Tam's so big, you'd need a truck or something to hide him."

Tam snorted from the couch. Apparently, he knew about Polly's surveillance, and he didn't seem the least bit bothered by it.

"Says the girl with the hair you can see from space," he said, his voice gently teasing.

Polly's smile grew, and she looked down at the puzzle, placed a piece, and then looked back up at me. "He jokes that that's why they won't let me outside without someone. Aliens will come and take me away." She leaned closer. "Don't worry, I know aliens aren't real."

Polly and Tam hadn't really interacted very much since I had arrived, but whenever they did, Tam—who was normally big and iron and insistent—suddenly became soft and gentle. Guiding instead of pushing. Teasing instead of mocking. Whomever she was to him—Polly or Janet—he treated her with care and deference.

I appreciated that on a professional level, but it was also truly touching to see a person who had a hard time managing his own reality trying to make life easier for someone who had an even harder time.

Polly's train of thought had moved on without me. She was staring at the window again.

"It's fun to watch them build the bonfire. They're stacking the wood in the back so high! It must be twenty feet tall!" Her smile vanished. She looked at me, then at Randal, then at Tam, then back at me, though now she seemed to be looking through me. "That's why it can't snow." Her voice suddenly became soft. "The bonfire won't burn hot enough."

The rest of the night went normally. The patients took their turns in the bathroom and went to bed without much comment. Even Tam forewent his normal bedtime reading to go straight to bed, leaving me all by my lonesome at half past ten. I found myself staring at the reports on the table. Thankfully, there wasn't much to report for the day, just that everyone talked or did their own thing until bedtime.

I'd never had it so obviously suggested to omit detail from my reports, and yet it felt like that was exactly what Matron had asked me to do. Was leaving stuff out even ethical? What if one of my conversations was a critical instance in a long-recurring problem that someone could help with if only they knew about the omitted conversation?

I rubbed my forehead. There was a question in there. Whatever it was, it was the same question that I'd had down in Matron's office, but it just wouldn't come to mind.

There was a question that I did know, however, and a moment later I pulled open Tam's folder. I'd never paid attention to his day schedule before. Whether it was because it didn't pertain to me, or I had just never thought to look, I didn't know, but I looked now.

I ran my finger down the timetable for this week, as I read it out loud. "Breakfast—9 a.m. Group therapy—10 to 11. Gym—11 to 1. Lunch—1 to 2:30. Horseback riding—2:30 to 4:30. Cognitive therapy—4:30-6:30 . . ." The rest of the schedule was normal. Dinner, free time, lights out.

Unlike Randal and Polly, Tam wasn't involved in creating or putting out decorations for Hallowe'en. In fact, except for the group therapy—which had been cancelled today due to a nasty case of the flu going through the rest of the hospital—there wasn't anything except meals that would have him interacting with other patients at all.

Frowning, I flipped through Tam's case file and read through the summaries from each of his activities. I skipped over the few therapy sessions that were in the file. Those were done by the head psychologist in the hospital and wouldn't have involved anyone but the doctor and Tam. I was looking for something— or the lack of something—in particular.

I knew from my research before I came to Our Lady of the Wood Hospital that although Matron was more caught up in running the hospital on a day-to-day basis, she was a fully licensed therapist. If she was the attending therapist during one of Tam's activities, she should have been the one to make the report. Or, if she simply participated and interacted with the patient, she and her work should be at least mentioned in the report.

But she wasn't in here. Kristen and Eileen wrote the reports, having attended each activity as supervisor. There was no mention of Matron. No mention of her accompanying him on walks on the days that there wasn't horseback riding, or riding with him on the days when there was. In fact, there was no mention that he was separated from the group at all.

I wished the records were on a computer; the Find tool would have been ridiculously convenient. I grimaced, manually searching through every record that I could get my hands on. I didn't have a schedule for every week, but Tam himself had said that Matron had been there, day after day.

I had two options: One, Matron was never there, Tam and Polly were lying, and I was looking into this for nothing. But they had no reason to lie, especially not in conjunction with each other. Polly wasn't capable of keeping up a long-term charade, and even though Tam was, neither of them were the type to make trouble on purpose.

Also, although Tam was paranoid, Polly wasn't. Why would she corroborate a story if she hadn't seen it? Judging by what was written in the record, it took her being exposed to something multiple times before it sunk in. Unless, of course, she and Tam had been rehearsing their deception during the day. But that would have definitely have made it into the record, selective editing or not.

Second option: Polly and Tam were telling the truth, and for some reason Matron was being left out of the record, indicating that Matron, Kristen, and Eileen, and possibly Gwen, were in on something. Something to do with Tam. But what? Everything else was in perfect order. Was Tam an ultra-special case?

And if so, I was the nighttime caretaker and a fellow professional nurse. Why not read me in?

Why try to warn me off?

OCTOBER 27

I've never been one to walk out when I spot an oncoming disaster, but I was incredibly tempted when I entered the ward the next night. At first glance, everything seemed normal. Randal was sitting next to Polly and telling her a story, which was common enough. But Tam wasn't sitting on the couch reading his book. He sat in my usual spot at the table, glaring furiously at Randal, rattling off the tail end of something disparaging to the older man.

Now, on closer inspection, Randal appeared puffed up and blustery—which meant he was probably close to exploding—and Polly looked close to tears. Eileen had sunk into the couch where Tam usually sat, hiding behind her "file," pretending everyone was getting along. Random objects lay around the room—blankets, more books than I'd ever seen in here, and even the remnants of a half-eaten sandwich that looked like it had been thrown against the wall.

All in all, a snapshot of a dramatic day, which I was about to inherit.

Yay.

"What's going on?" I asked loudly to the room.

Everyone went silent at once, and all heads rose to look at

me. Eileen snapped her file closed, scooped up her purse that was lying near the couch, and stood to head toward the door. "Oh good, you're here. I'll—"

"You didn't answer my question," I said to her, holding my hand out to stop her, but not touching her. My voice was stern but pleasant.

She stopped in her tracks. "What?" Then she scoffed. "If you want to know what's going on, you're going to have to ask them." She shoved her thumb over her shoulder at the three patients and tried to move past me.

"Oh really?" I fixed her with a look. "You're the attending nurse. Shouldn't you know what the situation is in your own ward? Or is"—I flicked the "file" she was clutching, which was open just enough that I could see the hidden magazine title— "*Glitterati* more important to you than your job?"

Eileen opened her mouth. "You—you wouldn't dare report me to Matron!"

I glowered at her. "Every single time I've come in here, you've either been reading your magazines, ignoring your patients, or both. Not once have I gotten a verbal report. Not once have I seen you do anything remotely resembling your job. You're the nurse here, you should know what's going on and be able to tell me about it."

"Everything's in the report," she said defensively. "There's no need for me to tell you anything."

"Oh really," I said again, gesturing at the patients. "Then the report should tell me about this? What story are they telling, so I can know to watch out for it in the future? Whatever's going on between Ta— between Thomas and Randal, and who started it? Why is Polly crying? I should be able to find all of that in the *real* file?"

She seemed to puff up and scanned the room as if for help. Glancing at the clock, she shook her head. "It's eight thirty-five. It's your shift."

I smiled tightly. "There's fifteen minutes of overlap, something that you have been ignoring regularly. Your shift lasts until eight forty-five." My voice wasn't particularly loud, but I had the attention of every person in the room.

Eileen looked at me, positively fuming. I didn't feel a stitch of guilt. Whatever problem she was trying to escape, she had been there when it started. And so help me, even if I doubted whether Eileen was going to be particularly helpful at solving it, if there were problems here she was going to stay and help me fix things. Or at least try to smooth things out.

"Thomas has had a rough day," Eileen finally said quietly, not looking me in the eye. She seemed penitent, but I couldn't tell if she actually was or if she just wanted to get out of there alive. Maybe both.

"I see." I picked up one of the books from the floor—a collection of short stories by George Eliot—and walked up to the table. Handing the book to Tam, I pointed to the sofa that Eileen had just vacated. "Couch."

"But—"

"Now."

"I'm not a child!" he snapped, standing up, looming over me, nose almost touching mine.

I met his glare calmly. "If you want me to treat you like an adult, you'll have to act like one." I narrowed my eyes and lowered my voice. "You can't intimidate me."

A muscle in his jaw clenched. Then he swiped the book from my hands and stalked toward the couch, expression stormy. I turned back to Eileen, who—props to her—hadn't snuck away. She looked shocked as she watched me and Tam.

"Always had a weakness for the women, Tam, haven't you?" Randal jeered. "Only too happy to follow orders, even when it gets you into more trouble."

I turned, fixing my gaze on him. He wasn't agitated, blast it all. He was preening.

"He's not the only one who can get in trouble, Randal," I said, my voice dripping with honey.

He sucked air through his teeth. "I don't follow orders. I make deals," he said sulkily.

I looked down at him, unimpressed. "How's this: you don't mess with me, and I won't send you to bed immediately."

He raised an eyebrow, expression smoothing out. "That leaves an awful lot of leeway."

I took a deep breath, reminding myself that I'd rather not get in trouble for laying hands on a patient. "Randal, would you please behave? Don't needle Tam. Not right now."

He sighed, as if I'd asked him to give up a beloved toy. Maybe I had. I didn't care.

"Very well," he said. "I will follow your instructions to the letter."

"Great." Then I turned back to Eileen. "If you help me pick up the room, I'll let you go as soon as we're done," I said steadily.

She blinked, glanced between me and Randal, and then nodded, moving toward a blanket that lay on the floor.

"Do you know what's brought all this on?" I asked quietly a moment later, heaving a stack of books onto the counter.

Eileen looked uncomfortable, pushing a comparably large pile beside mine. "We got official word . . . Thomas is being transferred."

I froze. "When?"

"This morning. Oh, I mean, he gets transferred on November first. We found out this morning. Not sure when they'll come for him during the day, but it's official now."

"And Thomas didn't take the news well?" I asked.

Eileen looked down, placing a blanket in the cupboard. It wasn't where it went, but I didn't care at the moment. She nodded uncomfortably. "Randal's been rubbing it in every chance he gets."

"I see." Of course he was.

I looked up at Tam. He clearly could tell what we were talking about—his glare was heated even from across the room where he couldn't clearly hear our whispers. Eileen wouldn't look over at him, as if she were ashamed to look, but when I caught his gaze, he looked away.

"Where do all these books go?" I asked.

Eileen looked at the two enormous stacks by me, then glanced at Tam. "His room," she said, gesturing with her head.

"I'll get him to take care of it."

She looked up at me, as if confused. "You what?"

"They're his books," I said. "If he doesn't put them away, he won't get them back."

She blinked at me several times, as if what I said didn't quite compute. "Okay." She stared at me for a moment longer, as if still trying to figure it out. Suddenly I noticed the bags under her eyes. She really hadn't had an easy day.

"Thanks, Eileen," I said, breaking the awkward silence. "You can head out now if you want."

Noting that it was eight forty-five on the dot, she nodded slowly, and headed toward the exit as if in a daze. I stared after her as she passed through the ward door, the electronic lock beeping and humming loudly in the conspicuously silent room as she closed the door behind her. I was a little mystified at her reaction, but I turned my attention back to the counter.

After heaving one stack of books from the counter to the table, I faced away from the couch to get the other and said, "Tam, could you please take your books back to your room?"

When there was no shift of movement, I glanced over my shoulder at him. He was glaring at me. I raised an eyebrow and was about to voice the threat that I had told Eileen I'd make, when he stood and crossed the room. Refusing to look me in the eyes, he scooped some of the books off the table and made his way into his room to put them away. The light flicked on, and I could see him squatting by a small bookshelf in the corner, slotting in each book carefully, smoothing out the wrinkled pages gently. I didn't approach, just watched and let him go about his business as he entered the main room to get the second stack.

When he was almost done, I pulled out the reports and started to go over them, half-listening to the story Randal had just started telling.

It was a different one today, about a girl in the seventies who had found a man who looked young but was old. Even as she grew older, he didn't, until one day she found out he was under a faerie spell and was doomed to die.

What the—I glanced up at Tam a little nervously, who was now sitting on the couch. At first glance he seemed to not be listening, but his white knuckles wrapping around the cover of his book betrayed him. I kept an eye on him as I scanned through the reports, half wishing that I was on the other side of the table. Partly to play human shield but, having read Tam's file and knowing his particular paranoia, I also felt the inexplicable urge to play a sort of sound barrier as well. Or maybe, hopefully, Randal would be done soon.

No luck there.

It wasn't that the story lasted long; rather, Polly seemed uncharacteristically full of questions tonight. Just as Randal finished answering one question, she would fire off a new inquiry, as if she couldn't help it. I looked over at her. Her face seemed a little pink, and despite the smoothness of her questions, she seemed to be highly uncomfortable. Her gaze flitted around the room as if looking for an escape. Her eyes locked on Tam again and again, her expression earnest.

Randal seemed to notice Polly's targeted looks at Tam. Was that a ghost of a grin on his face? There was definitely an odd sparkle in his eyes as he stared intently at her. What was happening? He could hardly be forcing Polly to ask the questions, but why did Polly keep acting so uncomfortable?

Something was wrong, but I couldn't quite—

"What about—" Polly asked, the words lurching out of her mouth.

"*Stop it,*" Tam said from across the room, though he didn't move from his place on the couch.

Randal looked up, and I shifted in my chair. At once, something seemed to snap in the room's atmosphere, and Polly sank back into her chair, pressing her lips together tightly, inhaling sharply though her nose.

"The lady is simply asking questions, Tam," Randal said, his voice and eyes challenging.

Tam narrowed his gaze until flames practically shot out of them. "Faerie stories are not something that should be talked of." He snapped the book shut. "It'll only bring bad luck down upon our heads."

Randal scoffed. "Bad luck! That talk is only for those who rue the choices that they have made."

"Because a choice brought me here," Tam shot back sarcastically.

Randal smirked. "Perhaps one man's misfortune is another's salvation," he said quietly. "Pity that the choices you did make had such . . . unintended consequences." Randal's gaze drifted over in Polly's direction.

Tam stiffened, and I shifted again in my seat.

"Randal . . ." I said warningly.

He looked over at me, one eyebrow raised. I felt immobilized, despite my own desire to physically jump between the two of them.

"Ah, our watchdog awakes," Randal said. Then, as if I'd done nothing, he turned back to Tam. "I hope you know—"

"I couldn't care less what you hope," Tam spat.

"—that for what it's worth, I appreciate your sacrifice." Randal continued without stopping. "Your future absence will undoubtedly leave a hole in my life, but that's a price that I'm willing—"

"Stuff. It." Tam's tone brooked no argument, and Randal fell silent with a displeased, but almost impressed, look on his face.

"Very well," Randall said finally. "If you insist."

"Amazing," Tam said, voice dry as the desert, "your willingness to grasp the obvious."

Randall did sneer at that, but turned back to the table without further argument, much to my eternal gratitude.

Polly sat there, withdrawn, hands folded limply in her lap. Her mouth was relaxed, and her eyes closed and opened slowly—she seemed a little relieved. Hadn't Tam's words silenced her as well? I shook my head a little. Reaching across the table, I touched Polly's arm. Her expression changed to a frightening sort of muted alarm.

Randal began to flip his cards noisily against the table.

"Are you okay, Polly?" I asked.

She looked down at her hands and nodded silently. My concern seemed to help her to perk up a little after that, though, and after another moment's observation, I turned back to the paperwork in front of me.

When I'd finished with the reports, I took them to the file cabinet, listening to Randal playing with his cards, and Polly, who had pulled another puzzle out, asking about the Hallowe'en festivities.

"Do you think they're going to do the costume contest again this year?" Polly asked. "I didn't see it on the schedule. But then, if they're going to do the big bonfire, they might not have time, huh?"

Randal, glancing over at Tam, shrugged. "I didn't see it on the schedule either, and it's a little late to start constructing costumes."

"Last year they started after . . ." Polly's voice started to drift off, slowly becoming hazier. "Do you know, I don't remember when they started making costumes. After I woke up. I mean, got here. Silly words. Anyway . . ."

I slipped my book from my purse and went over to sit by Tam, who seemed to be growing his own personal rain cloud. He looked at me as if I'd committed a personal offense by coming within a twenty-five-foot radius of him. He could have stretched out his whole arm and still not touched me on the other end of the couch, though, so I ignored him, pulling my knees up to my chest and cracking my book open.

Tam didn't speak right away, as if he were caught between trying to ignore me back and being suddenly interested in what I was reading. Or, conversely, maybe he was trying to find some fault that he could exploit to make me leave. I hadn't thought my reading a book would have been so thought-provoking for him, and yet I realized that this was the first time, aside from Randal's story, that I had actually participated in something that was purely fun for me, and me alone. Perhaps it was a new experience for Tam, seeing me enjoying something. Who knew, maybe it humanized me.

"The Hobbit?" Tam asked finally. I didn't know why I expected his voice to be mocking, but I felt just a bit of shock when it wasn't. Instead, it held a wary sort of interest. Like that of a kid, fresh out of an argument with a parent, watching said parent do something interesting.

"Yes," I said. I waggled the book at him. "Another favorite."

"Fantasy," he pointed out.

I shrugged. "Maybe I'm not so full of surprises as you seem to think I should be."

He took a deep breath, and his stormy expression seemed to flicker back into place.

Settling back into the worn couch, I brought the book back up in front of my face, pretending to read. "So what's wrong?" I asked.

Tam looked at me so fast I was a little worried I'd have to treat him for whiplash. After struggling for words for a moment, he shook his head. "I'm not talking about this with you."

Pretending to be surprised, I blinked and looked away from my book. "Talk about what?" I asked innocently.

Tam frowned at me. "You know exactly what. Randal's been needling me all day. No thank you—I'd rather every nurse from here to the moon didn't know my personal business."

Ignoring the jab, I shook my head, still feigning surprise.

"I'm sure if we were having an official conversation, I might have to put something in the report." I stuck my nose back in my book. "But clearly I'm reading a book. And so are you. Everyone knows you can't read and talk at the same time—it's, like, a cardinal rule. So, I'm talking to myself. If you were to make personal observations about yourself that may or may not correspond with the questions that I'm posing to myself, that's your choice."

Tam looked at me like I was crazy. I didn't exactly blame him, but he also didn't look annoyed, which was my main goal.

"Well, I—"

"If you don't put your book in front of your face, it doesn't count," I said, my nose only an inch away from Bilbo Baggins's name. Tam was probably wondering if I should be a patient here as well.

Then, in a moment that sent triumphant shivers down my spine, Tam raised his book to his face.

I tried to stifle the grin that was taking over my face. After far too long, I cleared my throat and said again, "So, what's wrong?"

"Well," Tam said to *Scenes of Clerical Life* by George Eliot, "I'm feeling a little . . . stressed."

"Stressed?" I said to Bilbo. Simultaneously, I wondered how in the world someone had let me practice any sort of medicine and also realized that somehow this absurd exercise was working.

"In case you haven't picked it up from Randal, I'm . . . going to die soon. Usually people in that situation feel some sort of distress. Or have I been away from the normal world for too long?"

Mom's face flashed through my mind. Calm. Serene. "It depends on the person, I guess," I said, grateful that I'd chosen a larger copy of *The Hobbit* versus the mass market paperback. Better coverage. "If you're feeling stressed about it, it's certainly valid. You're right, though. Fear of the unknown is pretty universal."

"Hmm," he said, turning a page.

I frowned. Had he even been listening?

Noticing that I noticed, he nodded at my book. "Either you're the slowest reader in the universe, or you're not actually reading," he pointed out in mock seriousness.

Nodding in realization, I also turned the page, and said a hello to a drawing of Gandalf. "Clearly I'm just a slow reader," I said.

His lips twitched in what probably would have been a smile if his lips hadn't twitched downward again. On purpose?

"So, you believe that I'm going to die?" he asked. His voice was far more casual than I actually believed he felt. He turned another page. I was sure that neither Eliot's nor Tolkien's works had ever been read that fast at any point in their collective exis-tence, but I turned my page as well.

For the briefest of moments, I thought about agreeing with Tam, but it felt too similar to past mistakes. I couldn't pretend. It didn't help anything.

"I think that you believe you are." I tried to find middle ground. "Officially, you're being transferred, and I know that can feel like dying."

Tam took it better than I expected. "What, you felt like you were dying when you got transferred here?" he asked. There was the barest undercurrent of sarcasm in his words, but it was somehow also a genuine question. I looked over at him. He turned his head to look back at me and raised an eyebrow. "Are you listening to my private conversation over here?" he asked.

I smiled despite myself. "I'm sure I don't know what you're talking about. Gandalf is over here proposing a dwarf rave," I said, motioning at my book.

"Are you sure that's how it goes?"

I scrunched my face, peering closer at the book. "Maybe I'm remembering the movie."

"There was a movie?" He frowned.

"Yeah. Before you were admitted to Our Lady. But I'm reading," I said, tapping the book with the back of my index finger.

He nodded and looked back at his own book.

I flipped another page. I felt the weight of my words pressing against my chest until I opened my mouth to speak. "I felt like I was dying before I moved up here."

"Why?"

I turned to him before I could catch myself and nearly strained my neck yanking my gaze back toward my book. I shrugged, swallowing, trying to keep my tone even. "My parents died."

Tam went still.

I regretted my words immediately. I hadn't even wanted to tell Tam that I practiced jiu-jitsu, and now I told him something that even my employer didn't know? And now goodness knows what was going to happen. Pity, probably. Avoidance, likely. I could only hope that he didn't tell Randal.

But Tam's expression didn't change, though something flickered behind his eyes. Not pity. Worry? "When?"

"About three months ago," I said.

"Do you have any family—"

"We aren't in contact. I haven't actually met my grandparents. I don't know if they're even still living," I said lightly. Or at least tried to.

Tam was quiet for a long time, and after staring at his book longer than it would have taken to actually read the page, he reached up and flipped it.

"I'm sorry for your loss," he finally said. "I lost my parents almost ten years ago now. We weren't on the best of terms when they died. Or before that, actually. They never wanted to be close, and once I learned that, I didn't want to be either. I . . . I hope your situation was different."

I fixed my eyes on the interior of my book and started to bite my lip, stopping when my tongue hit the scar there.

"We were close growing up." My voice was soft. I wasn't sure Tam could actually hear me, but I wasn't about to repeat myself. "Those were the best times. Once I moved away from home, though . . . well, my dad wasn't doing great and was in and out of facilities of one kind or another my whole life. My mom got sick about five years ago . . . " My throat closed, and more out of reflex, I took a deep breath and cleared my throat, hoping that Tam was fixated on his book hard enough that he wouldn't see the sheen of tears in my eyes.

"And your dad?"

"He died in another facility shortly after my mom. He . . . took his own life." The book in my hands dropped a little bit, and I saw Tam shift, fully facing me, his expression open and . . . it wasn't pity on his face. Was it . . . admiration? For me?

I didn't know what to do with that any more than I knew what to do with pity. Clearing my throat again, more out of habit than anything else, I pulled *The Hobbit* back into my point of view. Then I snorted. "Thank goodness we're reading. That would have been a little personal to share here in the ward."

"I appreciate it." Tam's voice was soft, but utterly sincere. "It —it means more than you could ever know."

I looked over at him. His green eyes stood out against the dark blue of his scrubs, and for a moment I sat there, fixated by those eyes. He'd lost his parents too. He knew what I was going through. There, sitting on that worn blue couch, it didn't seem to matter for a moment that we were sitting in a psychiatric hospital as patient and nurse. There, in that moment, there was another person who had traveled with me on a very long, dark road, if only just for a little while.

And that felt like crossing a line. I looked away quickly, turning the page in my book.

"I'm not sure I understand." The words tumbled from my lips. Understand, my foot. To be completely honest, for a moment I couldn't even remember what he had *said*.

Tam didn't seem to mind. He gamely pulled up Eliot again,

and I felt myself relax just a bit. "Just the fact that you want to make a connection with us. It helps. We're not always treated as though—well, actually we are treated as though we're human here. Maybe that's part of the problem."

"I don't understand," I said again, reaching chapter two— "Roast Mutton." I was "reading" too fast. I'd have to retrace my steps later.

"You—" Tam paused, and I glanced over. He looked like he was trying to think of the right thing to say. That wasn't quite the same thing as clamming up, so I let it slide. After a second, he continued. "You treat us like we're capable. And like we're adults. Even if . . . on occasion we don't necessarily act like it."

He didn't return my glance, but the edges of his ears were turning red. I flipped another page in my book, a small smile playing on my face.

"Well," I said, "speaking as a person who threw a bit of a fit herself yesterday, no one can be expected to be mature one hundred percent of the time. Especially in your case. Gwen told me a couple of days ago that Matron's been planning your transfer for a while now. Even if you've known about the change, it can still be hard when—"

His shoulders tensed, and I lost him in a flash. "I'm not being transferred, Mar-Nurse Margot." His voice was stiff and stifling, cutting me off decisively. "I'm dying."

I opened my mouth, the closeness of a moment ago gone in an instant. Then I paused. I knew arguing wasn't going to help anything. I closed my mouth and dropped my book a little.

"You're doing it again," Tam said flatly. "That 'I don't agree, but I don't want to argue' thing. You're going to apologize and put me off nicely, denying everything I said."

"Would you rather have me argue?" I asked, looking stubbornly at the book. "That tactic seems kind of messy to me."

Tam looked over, confused.

I raised an eyebrow. "I saw the state of the room when I

came in. I'll warn you, not only do I throw books harder than you can, but I'll also make you clean it up."

Tam snorted, a smile flashing before he could stop it. "I bet you would, too."

"You can count on it," I said, crossing my legs primly, flipping another page, and coming face-to-face with the hungry trolls. How appropriate. "So, what can I do to help?"

"What?" he asked, dropping his book into his lap.

Polly and I only glanced at Tam, but Randal's head popped up, like a shark picking up the scent of blood. I frowned at Randal.

After jerking his book back up to his face, Tam glanced over at me from behind the pages. He mouthed *What?* at me again.

"What can I do to help?" I repeated, flipping another page.

"With dying?" he asked incredulously.

I thought about it for a moment. "Well, maybe not the actual . . . death part. Is there anything that you know of that I can do to stop it? I mean, maybe help you see it differently? Maybe stop the transfer if it's stressing you out too much?"

"No-o-o," Tam sounded incredibly mystified.

"Then what can I do to make it less stressful in the meantime?"

There was a pause, and then Tam slammed down his book onto the arm of the couch. I jumped and scooted back against the couch instinctively, shocked at the loud noise. My own book fell from my hands.

Tam stood, and I rose warily to my feet as well, stepping backwards over the arm of the couch, never taking my eyes off of him. He took a breath and then bellowed at me.

"You think that in my mind I'm replacing the transfer with death! You're thinking that somehow, I'll pass through this whole experience and be one hundred percent fine and dandy when I get to wherever I'm going. I'm not joking. I'm not making it up. And I'm not getting transferred!"

He was waving *Clerical Life* wildly, and for a moment it looked like he was going to hurl the two-inch-thick book at me. It would have made a good-sized dent in any part of me, but then he took a deep breath, lowering the book to his side. Scowling, he shook his head at me, and broke our eye contact.

"I'm going to bed now," he said. "If you want to help, Nurse Margot, look up 'Janet Christofferson' and 'Fay Avery' on the internet when you get home. See what you find, and then tell me if I'm making anything up."

"Fay Avery is Matron's name," I said blankly, partially still ready to duck, but also starting to straighten back up.

"Exactly," Tam said. He looked at Randal's mildly pleased face and Polly's bewildered expression before turning back to me. Dark green eyes, so sympathetic a moment ago, burned into mine, then he huffed. "I'm going to bed. Unless, of course, you need me for something."

"No," I whispered, still simply grateful that I didn't have an anthology-sized dent in my head. Yet. "I'll have your medication ready for you when you come out."

"Thank you," Tam said, a sneer evident in his voice, before heading to the bathroom.

When he came out, I had everyone's medications measured out, but Randal was playing dead fish and was refusing to go to bed, and insisting that he was going to go outside later. I had cajoled. I had pleaded. I was about to start explaining consequences.

"The moon is up, Nurse Margot, and I must ever heed her call," Randal said, placing his hand over his heart. There was an odd otherworldly quality about him tonight that worried me. I'd have to watch to make sure he didn't make a break for it.

"It's your turn in the bathroom, Randal," I said.

He drew his eyebrows together. "Did I not follow your request earlier?"

"Yes, you did," I said.

"You did not specify how long I had to behave." His voice dropping down low.

I closed my eyes briefly. "I also never agreed to let you go wandering outside tonight!"

"But I fulfilled your demand. Do I not get to make my own demand?" he asked.

I took in a deep, calming breath, willing myself to stay calm. It worked for about two seconds. "Behaving yourself when you're supposed to, Randal, does not equate doing whatever you want. It would be violating policy, not to mention good old-fashioned sense, to let you go out. You have only ever behaved yourself when I have asked you to, which does not make me feel indebted to you at all. Besides all of that, you're my patient. The balance of power is not in your favor."

The words popped out of my mouth before I could stop them. Randal leaned back in the chair a little, his eyebrow raising, as though he were impressed.

"So, you do know a little something about the Fair Folk. And here I thought you were ignorant of the most important aspects of the world."

"I know enough," I said, all but slamming his pills down in front of him. "Enough that I know you do not have a firm enough footing to demand recompense, and you are trying to take advantage of me."

Randal stared at me for the briefest of moments. Then, quietly, he sighed.

Tam, who'd been listening carefully, approached from the bathroom like a vengeful shadow in the dimmed lighting. Darting behind him, Polly made a break for the bathroom door from her bedroom, belongings squeezed tight to her chest.

"Randal?" Tam's deep voice rumbled through the room. "Are you causing trouble?"

Randal's eyebrows drew together. "Did I not fulfill her requirements earlier?" He bent his head backward to look at the other man. "I thought you said you were going straight to bed."

"I need my medication. Are you causing trouble?" Tam repeated.

Randal seemed to think about it. "No more than a usual amount."

"Nurse Margot seems . . . harried."

"Yes, well, she's had to deal with you," Randal pointed out.

I was too frustrated to smile, and I shut my eyes tightly again. After breathing in deeply, for a moment, I spoke quietly. "Randal, if you don't go to bed right now, I'll write a report, and then they won't let you go to the Hallowe'en bonfire."

The effect was immediate. Randal hissed and shot up to his feet, his eyes blazing with fury. "You wouldn't dare."

I did my best to keep my expression the same, but I could feel my eyes narrow. I slowly shook my head. "I don't bluff, Randal." Somehow, I kept my voice calm. Frustration beat so strongly through my system that I could feel my pulse in my palms. Only sheer will was keeping my voice from wavering with fury. "I've tried nicely every way that I can think of to get you to go to bed peacefully, but you've been resistant and rude, and I cannot tolerate that. I know you know better."

"I want to go down to the bonfire." It wasn't actually a request. Randal was looking into my eyes, and there was a sparkly sort of deepness there. It almost reminded me of when he told a story to me and Polly. He was *demanding*.

But he must have been truly insane if he thought I was going to let him go out on his own now.

"No."

"But it's only three days before—You couldn't possibly—"

"Randal, *no*," I said.

His mouth snapped closed, and he looked back at Tam, fury building. There was an odd sort of energy in the air, like static electricity building before a strike of lightning. "This is your influence," he said, lifting a shaking finger to Tam's face. "If you—"

"*Randal*," I barked, done with his nonsense.

The energy in the room died, and he jerked back and saw my face. He stiffened, though he kept looking at me with all the aplomb of an offended king—nose in the air, chest puffed out to twice its normal volume.

"I will not forget this," Randal said darkly, then he shoved past Tam to get to the bathroom.

Polly, having just snuck back out of the facilities, was now watching from the safety of her own bedroom. Now she crept out for her medication. She had that odd, blank look on her face again, and I felt a stab of concern for her. Was she going into another of her episodes?

"You all right, Polly?" I asked.

"I'm . . . I'm fine," she said. She didn't look like it. She looked pale, weak, and shaky.

I felt that if I mentioned it she might get worse, so instead of commenting on her physical state, I offered her the chair that Randal had just vacated. "Sit down while you wait for Randal to get out of the bathroom."

She blinked a little. "I . . . I can't. That's Randal's chair."

Now I blinked too. It had never been an issue before. Granted, most of the time that Polly was sitting, it was when we were all out here together. There was no need for her to sit anywhere else. Then again, she never sat in my spot. Or in Tam's spot on the couch, for that matter.

"Sit in yours, then," Tam said, pushing Randal's chair under the table and pulling hers into place.

Smiling gratefully at Tam, she sank into the chair. Her hands were still shaking.

"Do you need anything, Polly?" I asked, squatting down in front of her. "If you'd like, I can grab you some orange juice or something like that." I didn't think she had low blood sugar, but if something had stressed her out, it could have sapped her energy.

She stared up at me as if trying to solve a calculus equation. Then, grimacing, she pressed the heel of her hand to her temple. "I—I don't know." Suddenly she seemed a little tearful.

Taking her hand gently, I looked her in the eyes.

"Did something happen?" I asked quietly, at a loss. I didn't see how there could have been an incident. There was nothing in Eileen's reports, and I had been in here the whole time during my shift. I hadn't seen anything suspicious, even while Tam and I had been talking behind books—I had seen Polly out of the corner of my eye. Maybe it was her condition at play? But despite what Gwen had said earlier, she wasn't actually schizophrenic; she didn't have auditory or visual hallucinations, and she wasn't disorganized or have trouble controlling her body, even on her bad days. She didn't even have delusions to the level of Tam or Randal. She had acted normally when I came in at the beginning of the shift, and her behavior had only changed after she had asked Randal all those questions about the story. But then, she had acted normal a moment later.

Again, I felt like I was missing something important that lacked a face and a name. I didn't like the feeling.

"Let me grab something from the office," I said, looking up at Tam. He nodded, resting reassuring hands on Polly's shoulders, and she sat back, closing her eyes in relief.

In the office, I opened the mini fridge that held my lunch and grabbed the can of orange juice that I'd slipped last-minute into my lunch box.

Tam's brow raised in surprise when I handed the juice to Polly. "Outside food?" he asked.

"Yes, of course." Like I had anything else.

"The hospital has a cafeteria. Yet you bring food."

"I guess. I've never really enjoyed food that I don't prepare myself." I struggled to control the involuntarily uncomfortable look on my face, before finally wiping it off my face. "Besides, I'm night shift, and the cafeteria closes at night. Plus, if I left to eat, who would watch you?"

Tam shrugged. "Gwen would leave us sometimes."

Of course she would.

"Thank you for the juice," Polly said, looking up at me and Tam, "I'm feeling much better. May I take the rest to my room?"

Behind Tam, Randal sulked from the bathroom to his bedroom.

"Of course," I said, patting Polly on the shoulder. She smiled and walked back to her room, crossing to the bathroom a moment later.

Tam stood there, leaning on the back of Polly's chair, staring at the floor. I noticed the laughably small robe barely covering his shoulders over his pajamas, lending a sort of ridiculousness to his aura, belying his solemn attitude.

"I . . . need to offer you an apology," he said.

I put up a hand. "Tam—"

"No," he said firmly. "I do." His dark eyes were now boring into mine. "Every time we interact, I . . . no one—no one treats me—us—like you do, Nurse Margot. I've forgotten what it's like to act like a normal human, so I haven't been. The things . . ." He trailed off and shook his head. "Would you look up those names?"

"Tam—" I started to refuse.

"Just—just the two," he said. "Just those. Please."

I sighed. It wouldn't hurt anything. Maybe it would give me a little insight into his relationship with the outside world. "Fine. I will."

He hesitated, and then nodded, as though he'd expected he would have to fight a little harder.

After fighting with him before, and then with Randal, and now worrying about Polly, I just didn't have the energy. Besides, a mere two minutes on Google, and my promise would be fulfilled. If smartphones had been allowed in Our Lady, I probably would have done it right then and there.

We stood there for a moment longer, Tam shifting like he didn't know what to do with himself. When he didn't say or do anything else, I picked up his pills and water and offered them to him. He thanked me, and then went to bed. A few moments later, Polly left the bathroom, entered her bedroom, and flicked the light off.

I sunk into Polly's chair, looking at the three closed bedroom doors. Then I looked at the clock.

Ten forty-five.

I wanted a nap. I wouldn't take one, of course. Not after raking Eileen over the coals like I had done, but there was the temptation.

I remembered my first day . . . a week ago? Had it been that long already? Had it only been a week? Well, here I was, sitting at least a little comfortably in my own ward, with my own three patients, looking forward to a quiet evening.

I shouldn't have thought it. Not for even a second. I didn't believe in jinxes, but if they were going to exist, of course they would exist here.

At about three in the morning, whatever had shaken Polly right before bed came back full force.

"Let me OUT!" she shrieked, her voice blasting through the walls like they were made of paper.

I bolted up from where I had definitely *hadn't* been dozing on the couch with a book in my hands. I shot toward her door and threw it open, then I turned her room's light up halfway, so I could see what was going on.

She thrashed in her bed, sheets tangled around her as she jerked back and forth. Nightmare.

"Where is it?" she yelled, banging on the wall so hard I heard a small pop. Had she just broken her hand?

"Polly!" Throwing caution to the wind, I grabbed her by her shoulders, and hoisted her upright. I saw her eyelids flicker, but her head drooped. I tried to remember the medications she was taking. Unlike Tam, she didn't take a sleeping pill. What was keeping her asleep?

"Where is it?" Her voice was now a murmur. "Where is the oak? I can't find it."

"I don't know where the oak is, Polly!" I said. I shook her gently. "Wake up. You're asleep."

She opened her eyes then, but I knew she wasn't awake. Polly looked at me with unnatural recognition in her face, and cold seeped into my veins.

"Ah, Matron," she whispered, her voice low and grating. "Come to finish the job?"

I steeled myself. "I'm not Matron, Polly," I said. "I'm Margot—Nurse Margot. Wake up. Come on, Polly."

"I don't think there are any oak leaves here, Matron," Polly said quietly. "I think you lied. It's just you and your thrall."

"Polly!"

"You lied." Her voice broke at the end, and she shook her head. Her sleep-tangled blonde hair fell over her thin shoulders, and tears trickled down her ghostly face. "You lied. Poor girl. Poor girl. Poor girl, lost in the ivy."

❦

She never really woke up. After more mumblings where she mentioned The Boughs a couple of times, she lay back down. With my penlight, I examined her hand. No obvious break, if there was one, and no bruises were forming. I'd leave a note for Kristen to have someone look at it in the morning if Polly complained of pain.

And then I stared at the wall for a while, trying to lower my heart rate. I kept on doing my breathing exercises, trying to remind myself that Polly was just dreaming. But I kept hearing her terrified voice in my head, her words repeating over and over, and I couldn't shake the little piece of dread that had burrowed into my soul.

It wasn't real. Polly hadn't been in thrall. Thralls were made by faeries. Faeries weren't real. If they were . . .

I shut that down before the thought finished. *If* they were, then I should have seen some cold, hard proof by now. My parents had been just as obsessed as anyone in this ward, once upon a time, and they had spent their lives warning me about how to avoid them. Mom had backed off once I'd

gotten into college and realized that they were a story, but . .
.

But Bill was different.

No, my dear father Bill, having wandered through most of the psychiatric facilities of southern Michigan, had been convinced they were out to get him, that his time in one of their cults forty-some years ago was a secret they wanted kept, and so they were going to try to snap his wits.

I blinked back the tears in my eyes, hugging myself, feeling the bumpy scar on my arm under my shirt sleeve. Turns out Bill didn't need faeries to go crazy.

Tam's words echoed through my head. *"What, you felt like you were dying when you got transferred here?"*

No, I thought, pressing my fists into my forehead. *I felt like I'd escaped.* How could I have known I was wrong?

Thankfully, in the morning, Kristen was on time. With one look at my face and the pristine common room, she shook her head before I said anything.

"Just go," she said.

"Are you sure—" I said.

She waved me off. "You look like you're going to get in an accident on the way home if you stay a minute longer."

I stared at her for a long time, debating about whether I should argue. I didn't even have the energy to debate with myself. "Thank you," I said, though it was more of a sigh.

She gave me an odd look. "Fine," she said uncomfortably, turning away from me.

I nearly ran out of the building, rubbing furiously at my eyes to keep myself awake as I stumped down the stairs past Matron, who was on her way up.

I didn't have an accident on the way home, but I was moderately grateful that the one traffic light into Carterhall was green and the streets were empty as I daydreamed my way into my driveway. My brain was maxed out, my nerves frazzled.

I thought there was something that I needed to do, but as

soon as I had flopped down on my bed I decided that, no matter what it was, it could wait.

Wasn't it looking up something for Tam?

I groaned out loud. Whatever it was I'd do it in a minute. I'd just close my eyes for a bit . . .

OCTOBER 28

I never thought I would be late to work when my shift started at eight-thirty at night, but after getting up at seven-thirty in the evening—feeling surprisingly refreshed, but ultimately just very shocked—I had to rush to get my lunch prepared, get showered and dressed, answer a couple of urgent emails from Mr. Campion's representative, and then rush out the door.

I didn't remember my promise to Tam until I saw his expectant look as I walked in the door. Remembering his earnestness the night before, I literally groaned, cutting the sound off as quickly as it started. As his expression darkened, I paused in the doorway, rhetorically wondering I could walk right back out.

To his credit, he didn't confront me immediately. Instead, he glared at me over the top of his book-of-the-day while he waited for Eileen to leave the ward. I could feel his eyes on me, and the more he glared, the higher my anxiety climbed. He definitely knew that I hadn't researched the names. But honestly, how in the world could I have taken care of that when I'd barely had enough time to make my lunch? But I'd promised.

The minute the door lock beeped behind Eileen, Tam put his book down.

"Nurse Margot," he said, his voice casual. "Can I talk to you?"

I suddenly knew how the Fly felt in the Spider's parlor. Alarm bells rang at the back of my mind as I shrugged nonchalantly and walked over.

"What's up?" I asked.

Tam looked up at me, his face blank. "You said you were going to do something for me last night," he said. "I was wondering about whether or not you were able to do that."

I looked away.

"No, I—"

"You said you were going to."

"Tam, I fell asleep. I work night shifts; I go home to sleep—"

"And I just have years and years of time before I leave, is that it?" he asked coolly.

I looked down at him, full in the face. His dark eyes were intense, but for the life of me, I couldn't tell if he was hurt or angry. For the barest of seconds I wanted to sit, grab his hand, and apologize like I would have if he were my mom.

And then Bill flashed through my mind, and then Matron. I shifted a little. *Apologize, manage expectations, move forward,* I told myself. *Just like with every patient.*

"Tam, I realize I told you I would do something, and then I didn't," I said quietly. "And I'm sorry about that. Please understand that I do have a life—and needs—outside of working here. Going home is my only chance to rest, and—"

Tam shot to his feet, chest heaving in anger.

"You are wasting time that I don't have!" he shouted into my face, closer than he'd ever been before. The room went silent, and Polly and Randal turned to watch. I barely noticed; Tam's imposing presence was taking up all of my attention. Fear blistered through me.

"Tam, stop it," I said sternly, my hands going to hover above his arms, and he stepped even closer, pushing into me. I stepped carefully off to an angle. I didn't know what he was working up to, but I didn't want to come out on the wrong end of it. I saw the emergency button by the door. Would I have time to make it there? Would I have time for people to get to me?

He's not Bill, something whispered in me. And yet, all I could see was Bill's grey eyes, bare inches from mine as he raised the large iron lamp above his head.

"There's nothing to stop, Margot!" he shouted back, pressing me back across the room. "I am a *dead man*! I'm walking around, with barely two days left to live, and you all are just waltzing around like that means nothing. You are heartless! You will never understand, you—"

He jerked his arms up. Whether it was to just grab or strike me, I had no idea, but my ingrained training took hold, fear and adrenaline fueling my muscles. I pressed into him in a trice, protecting my head from any blows as I buried it into his chest. My old jiu-jitsu instructor's words whispered through my mind, as though he was there, walking me through the technique. *Hug him low, gable grip behind the hips just off center. Pull him toward you as you step deep, push your head forward under his chin. Change his balance.*

Sweep the leg.

I hesitated. I couldn't make him lose balance. It would be worth my job.

But there was no one else here. He'd come at me—He—

Bill grinned at me and swung the lamp down.

Sweep the leg.

Tam went down, arms flailing. I was briefly grateful that we didn't have a coffee table, as he went down harder than I wanted him to, landing with a thud. He didn't know how to fall properly — he landed flat on his back and his breath arrested painfully. He tried to get back up right away. Taking one hand, I twisted it behind him, like I had done to Randal—using the leverage to turn Tam over onto his stomach. He thrashed, and I tightened the armlock, kneeling on his hand and pressing it into his back.

"Stop struggling, Tam!"

"Let me up!"

"I can't until you stop struggling," I said, reaching out and securing his other arm.

"I—I wasn't going to hit you! I wasn't!" he protested, trying to bring his knees under him.

"Stop moving, Tam, you're going to hurt yourself," I said sharply.

He jerked again, nearly separating his own shoulder. I put my other knee on the small of his back. It would hardly be comfortable, not by a long shot, but it would help keep him still until his head caught up with the situation.

"Then let me go!"

"I can't do that, Tam," I said as calmly as I could, my hammering heart making my voice shake. I hoped he couldn't feel it in my hands. "I want to let you up, but I can't until I feel safe, and I don't feel safe right now, Tam."

"I don't either!" he exclaimed. His breath was getting faster and faster, and I could feel his muscles tense through the armlock. I watched him carefully. Anticipation? Or panic?

"You put yourself in this situation," I reminded him, keeping my voice calm. "Look, whichever it is—dying or being transferred, the bottom line is you're scared, and I know that. But lashing out at me doesn't help anyone, and I *know* you know that. I've read your file. I've seen how you help Polly, and even Randal. You don't do violence. So why now?"

"It—This is different."

"Why?"

Tam's breath was coming in shorter and shorter gasps now, teeth gritted as he pushed his head into the carpet. "No one— you're not—you're not listening!"

As if he couldn't hold it back anymore Tam, every muscle taut, breaths so fast he practically wasn't breathing anymore, pressed his face into the carpet and screamed. Holding him down, I couldn't resist the shiver that ran through my entire body as he wailed into the short, rough carpet. His chest heaved, and his voice rasped with the volume and intensity of the wordless sound. Fighting for breath. Fighting for control. I'd never heard anything like that. Not from any patient in the last decade that I'd been practicing.

Not even from Bill.

It seemed to last forever, and yet when the sound stopped, it seemed as though something was missing from the room. Tam lay there, face down, breath ragged with tears. His body had gone limp, and for a moment the only thing that anyone could hear in the room were those deep, shaking breaths.

Briefly, I wondered if he was faking it, and I dashed the thought away as soon as it presented itself. Even Bill couldn't possibly have faked something like this.

That scream . . .

I leaned back onto my toes, lightening the pressure off his back bit by bit, just in case he was even better than Bill. But no, as I released his arms, I placed each of them by his sides, and they stayed there. Still cautious, I settled into a sitting position by him, and rested a hand on his back as he cried. I glanced over at my other two patients. Polly was hugging her stained, white cardigan to herself, looking like she was ready to jump out of her seat to come and help, but then my eyes were drawn to Randal.

He wasn't looking at me. I don't think he even knew that I had turned my head. No, Randal stared down at Tam on the edge of his seat, taking in every inch of Tam's wretched, prone form, eyes sparkling with malevolence.

Randal was smiling.

Tam stirred, and Polly couldn't take it anymore, fluttering over as I helped him turn onto his side. Tam seemed deflated, almost limp as he lay there. I ran a comforting hand over his arm as Polly approached with a mountain of facial tissue, looking down at him in extreme concern. Before Polly was within earshot, he looked up at me, and shook his head.

"If you don't help me, Margot, I don't have a prayer," he whispered. I looked down at him, hand still resting on his arm. My heart hurt for him, but I couldn't quite bring myself to say anything. Instead, I helped him stand up, and helped him walk under his own power to his bedroom. He lay down on his bed, accepting the wad of tissue from Polly, and looked up at me as I was about to walk out.

"Will you stay, Nurse Margot? Just for a moment?" he asked, his voice hoarse and quiet.

I paused in the doorway, looking back at him briefly.

"For a moment," I agreed quietly in return.

There was almost no space in the bedroom for me. Pulling a small stool from beside the desk, I sat down next to his bed, looking at him as he stared up at the ceiling with tears in his eyes once more. He shifted every once in a while, his breath still shaky and just a little too shallow. I knew those symptoms, but for once not from Bill.

Reaching out, I took his hand. It was cold. "Do you know what this is called? What you're feeling right now?" I asked quietly.

He looked over at me, lips pinched closed, and shook his head.

"You're having a panic attack," I said quietly.

"Is that supposed to help make it go away or something?" he gasped.

I squeezed his hand a little bit. "Sometimes giving the feeling a name helps it make seem a little less scary. Have you experienced anything like this before?"

"Not since . . . not since I came here. I never . . . let anyone see." He swallowed. "You don't understand. I'm not a . . . a nervous person. I can handle myself. I'm not—I'm not sick."

I looked down for a second, and then back up at him, shaking my head. "There's nothing wrong with having a mental illness, whether permanent or temporary. Even I—" I broke off a little. "I've had panic attacks. I know that fear that you can't quite shake."

"Do you still . . ." Tam paused, closing his eyes briefly as he caught his breath. "Do you still feel that?"

I thought of seeing Bill's face superimposed over Tam's a few moments before, and looked away.

"Not often," I admitted. "But sometimes, yes. Not as much as before. I had to get help to make it better. Actual help, not just random suggestions from well-meaning friends. For what it's worth, Tam, despite your habit of yelling in my face, I don't think you belong in here."

He looked up at me. "What?"

"Despite your—" I looked at the still figure in front of me "—thing with faeries, I don't think you're dangerous. Frustrated, yes. Scared, yes. Maybe a bit overbearing and dramatic—"

"Thanks." His voice was a little less breathless now, his sarcastic tone deep in the tiny room.

I smiled. "But these . . . the anxiety and panic . . . these are things that can be treated, and I think that's what they're trying to help you with here. It's why you're here, really."

Tam turned to me, his expression falling a little bit. For a minute I thought it was going to send him back into an anxious fit, but instead, he just sighed sadly.

"I'm here because I was raised to do this," he said, looking up at the ceiling. "My parents sold me to the fae when I was a child. They raised me—if you can call it that—but solely for . . . for this. I wasn't allowed friends or material possessions, although my parents could be described as the ultimate of the nouveau riche. I never saw any magic, though. So I didn't believe.

"I didn't understand why I couldn't have friends, why my studies included folklore over science. Magic over maths. Every attempt to find and to learn something new was a point of argument. 'There is no point,' my parents would say. 'You were born for bigger and greater things.'

"When they finally died, I thought I was free. I went to college. I got a degree, even. Engineering, though I had to fight long and hard to even understand the math behind it. And then, after my schooling was done . . .

"I don't know when I got the idea to move to America. I'm

not sure it was . . . entirely my idea. But when I did move, I didn't tell anyone. I didn't have any family left, and I didn't want to say goodbye and make all my friends over there sad. I was just going to move, settle, and then invite everyone over when I'd found my place here. Then, the day before I was supposed to move—October twenty-eighth . . . I got a message from my uncle."

"Your uncle?" I repeated. Hadn't he just said—

"Not my real uncle." Tam sucked in a deep breath through his nose. "How am I supposed to explain this? There was a man . . . an old man who made the deal with my parents. For me. I knew him as my uncle. He contacted me to let me know that he wasn't doing well, and that he wanted me to visit. I . . . I accepted."

"Then no one knew you were going to be here?" I asked.

He shook his head.

"I was never supposed to come to Michigan. I flew to Detroit from New York, but I was planning on settling somewhere in Colorado. Or maybe California. My credit card was locked—I'd forgotten to inform my bank I was going to be over here, so it had been frozen earlier that day. My uncle said he'd send a car for me, and he did. I followed the directions to his home. From there they brought me here." The disgust in his voice implied volumes, and I frowned.

"If you acted on good faith, Tam, it's not your fault you . . . came here."

"Allow me to disagree." He turned his face toward the wall, the shadow swallowing his expression.

"Where did the horse come from?" I asked, changing the subject.

He sighed, shaking my head again, a little helplessly.

"A gift. The real reason why he wanted me to visit, or so he'd said. When he'd visited England, he'd taken me to an estate with horses."

"Safe to assume they're your favorite animal, then?" I asked, smiling a little.

He smiled in return, a small genuine smile. I'd never seen him smile like that before. The moment seemed to pause as I studied his face.

"Yes," he said. Then, slowly, the smile faded.

"Matron's kept me under lock and key in a haze by either magic or medication for the last seven years, almost to the day now. I've tried to, well, escape a couple of times now. But it's never—I never—"

"It's never worked," I said quietly.

He shook his head. "My co-conspirators—the people that were crazy enough to deal in with me—were either driven mad like Polly or were met with . . . accidents."

I swallowed. "You mean—"

"They died," he said simply, his tone physically incapable of becoming more emotionless. "Falls, mostly. But then there was the odd . . . falling into a bonfire. Or choking on nothing. Or suicide."

I shook my head. "I'm so sorry."

Tam looked up at me earnestly. "This is not a good place, Margot. If you can, please save me. If not, please just make sure you get out alive, preferably sooner rather than later."

"Tam—"

"I mean it, Margot. If it looks like there's no escape . . . just go."

I didn't respond to that, letting the words sit heavily between the two of us. He stared up at the ceiling, his expression distant.

"Nurse Margot, I know you don't have any reason to believe me—I've done everything wrong, given you every reason to think I'm an abusive, insane freak—but please look up those two names. Just the two. Janet Christofferson and Fay Avery. Just give me a chance. Just give me one more chance."

He turned slightly to fix his eyes on mine for one lingering, terrified instant before turning to look back up at the ceiling. "I just want a chance to be away from all of this. To live. I just want to live."

I looked down at him as he was laying on his back, staring up almost listlessly at the ceiling. No, not listlessly. Hopelessly. I couldn't answer him. Instead, I sat by him for a few more moments, and before I could think better of it, I squeezed his hand briefly. Slowly, and tenderly, just like my mother had always done. I couldn't become involved, but I knew how it felt—like there was no way out. No way up. I just couldn't let him feel like he'd have to go through that alone. It was why I'd stayed in mental health after what had happened with Bill. So no one—at least no one within my radius of influence—would ever have to feel that way again.

I watched Tam for a moment longer, contemplatively tracing the line where the long scar on my head would have showed if it hadn't been covered up by hair. His eyes had slipped closed, the comforting sound of his long breaths telling me he'd slipped off to sleep. Unable to bring myself to smile, I touched his shoulder gently, and left the room.

I walked out into the common area to find both Randal and Polly ready for bed, each wrapped up in their robes. Upon seeing my look, Polly stood, pinching the edges of her robe together around her neck.

"Is he going to be okay?" she asked. Behind her, Randal looked up at the blonde woman, a serious look on his face.

"Of course he is. He's sound in mind and body." It was a formal, oddly almost-defensive tone, and I looked down at him, wondering if something of the smile that I had seen earlier would still be there on his face given his explanation. I didn't see it, but his face was relaxed and emotionless, nothing like Polly's shaking shoulders and quivering bottom lip.

"Yes, Polly," I said quietly. "He's going to be fine." Then I forced a smile onto my face. "And look at you two, all ready for bed!"

"She made me," Randal said, glaring at Polly, his voice dropping into a definite sulk. "You people are so mean. At this rate, I'll never be able to commune with the stars before the night of nights. If I cannot before the payment is made, I will not be fully prepared when the time comes."

"The payment?" I asked.

He glanced up, and a condescending smile crossed his face. "Don't worry yourself about it, Nurse Margot. It has nothing to do with you. Unless," he broke off, looking at me seriously, "you want it to."

If whatever the payment was made me as creepy as him, I would never want it as long as I breathed.

"No, thank you," I said. Then I walked over to the cabinet and pulled out the medication cups. After handing two of them to Randal and Polly and sending them off to bed, I grabbed Tam's cup and headed back into his room. I could tell by his breathing he was still asleep, one arm over his head, the other hugging his pillow to his chest. Frowning regretfully, I looked from him down to the cup in my hands. I hated to wake him, but unfortunately as a nurse, it was practically part of my job description.

"Tam?" I said quietly.

He jerked awake, looking up at me. I smiled down at him.

"Oh, it's you," he said, taking in a deep breath, letting it out slowly.

"We didn't do your meds before you went to sleep," I explained. "Sorry for waking you up."

"You're fine," he said, pulling himself into a sitting position. "I was just worried it was already morning. Time has been moving too quick already."

I nodded, handing him the plastic cup of pills and some water. Taking them, he looked down at them, his expression full of regret and disgust, like he knew he had to take them, but couldn't quite make himself do it yet.

"What is it?" I asked.

He blinked, as if remembering I was there, and shook his head.

"Nothing." Then he quietly took his pills and went to sleep.

❧

The rest of the night passed peacefully, which oddly felt like more than I deserved. I couldn't quite get Tam's hollow sobbing out of my head, nor the image of him pressing his face into the carpet as he screamed.

Or the story about his parents. It chilled me. It had to be a story, right? Just like everything else he'd ever said. No one would deliberately give up their child for fame and fortune, would they? Who would even offer something like that?

Even if it were only partly true, like if his parents were only narcissists or something, compounded with their deaths . . .

Only narcissists? Are you even listening to yourself? I shrunk into myself in the dark room. Not even the book that I'd brought with me could console me, and I ended up half curled up on the couch staring at the door, hoping that someone, anyone would come and save me from myself.

No one did. It was me and Tam's words, repeating themselves over and over in my brain. Those quiet, hopeless words.

I just want to live.

OCTOBER 29

When Nurse Kirsten came in, we spent a couple of minutes making sure that the common room was set up for the day before I dragged my sorry carcass out of the ward. I felt wrung out. I must have looked wrung out as well, because after I managed to not fall down the four flights of stairs, I bumped into Gwen as I made my way through the admin wing.

"Margot?" Her hand on my arm was gentle, but for some reason made me very uncomfortable.

"Morning, Gwen." Did she ever sleep? I couldn't decide whether she had the same shifts as me, or just never slept at all. Same with Matron. I knew she was here as late as 9:30 at night, and yet I saw her wandering around at 6:00 am as well? What was wrong with this place?

"You look really pale, are you doing okay?" she asked.

I sighed and nodded. It felt like a lie, but it wasn't like I was going to admit that I felt overwhelmed by what everyone thought was an easy assignment, and that I really, really needed backup, no matter how much people thought that I didn't.

"I'm fine." I ignored how my voice cracked just a little bit.

"Did something happen last night?" she asked.

I didn't answer right away. I had put in the report that Tam had had a rough night, but not the fact that I'd had to restrain him. If I had, I would have had to put why, and I didn't know what part of last night Matron would take exception to more: the fact that I broke every single type of ethical code by using a takedown on a patient, the fact that I'd sat there and listened to his stories again, or the fact that I was planning on looking up the information he wanted me to.

"No," I said, my voice surprisingly even. "I just think night shift isn't agreeing with me."

Gwen nodded, looking around at the offices. Not many people were in yet, just the night crew, who shuffled as though they were half asleep around the place. "Margot . . ." her voice was soft and almost tentative, "why don't you take the night off tonight?"

I opened and then closed my mouth, shaking my head. "Gwen, you're short-handed."

"I'm assigned as a floater nurse tonight. I'll watch the ward, and you can get some sleep. You're not a machine, Margot. You're human."

"Yeah, but—"

"It's been four days since your last day off, right? You should have been scheduled for one today or tomorrow anyway."

I stared at her. It wasn't that I thought she couldn't do nice things. In fact, in light of the last couple of times we'd interacted, she was acting pretty normal. But taking over a shift for me?

"Do you even have the authority to do that?" I asked.

Gwen smiled. "Sure I do. I'm Matron's right-hand woman around here. Nothing would get done without me, anyway."

Unable, or maybe just unwilling, to fight her arguments any longer, I nodded. "Okay. Thank you. Would you be sure to put it on the schedule? I don't want to be fired on accident."

Gwen smiled, curling her arm around my shoulders as she

walked me to the door. "I'll put it on the schedule. Rest well, Margot."

The seat of my car was the single most comfortable piece of furniture that I'd ever sat on when I managed to heave my body into the vehicle. I didn't dare stop there, though my body almost ached with the thought of laying back my seat and just sleeping in the parking lot. It wasn't like I hadn't done it before, but even with the cool crispness of the morning air, it was like there was something pressing in on every side that pushed me to leave. Go home. Stay there until I was rested.

Waiting for the guardsman was an exercise in self-mastery. I still wasn't sure why it took him so long to process my badge—it didn't have a bar code, QR code, or secret code on it, and by now he must know my face. Maybe it was the only place where he could assert control in his job. As far as I'd been able to see, there weren't any dedicated security personnel in the building, just the male nurses. He could just be—

"Here's your badge." The guard threaded it through the crack in my window. Jumping, I took it and rolled my window down a little more, grabbing the plastic card.

"Thank you," I said. Then, inexplicably, and a little unnervingly, I sat there.

"The gates are open," the guard said. "You can leave."

I looked at the gates. They were three or four inches deep—whatever metal they were, they must have weighed a literal ton. "What are you looking for?" I asked.

The guard—a good-looking man, probably in his forties or fifties with a sweep of grey to match—raised an eyebrow. "Nothing you need to worry about." His voice was suddenly slightly good humored, and ever so slightly condescending, like an adult to a child who had asked a precocious question.

Shaking my head a little, I smiled a little bit abashedly. It wasn't like they were going to tell me if they had some sort of security measures in place. That would be silly—and potentially dangerous—if that information got out. Still, what did he think, that I had a patient in my trunk?

I had a couple of patients that probably would have been amenable to that. Still . . .

"Sorry," I said, and put my car into gear. Rolling out of the gate, I watched the heavy doors close in my rearview mirror. In the red glow of my tail lights, I could see some sort of vine hung over each door, slithering through the intricate metalwork. It must have been my imagination—I was definitely tired enough —but in the dim light of the morning, combined with the low light of the gate house it was almost like the vines crawled over the crack in the gate and sealed it closed as I drove away.

I knew I should have gotten on the computer the moment I got home, but bed was inviting, and given the shadow-driven night I just had, even though I was only going to research two names, I wanted to do it with the proper mentality.

I slept like a rock. Even if I'd had work that evening, I would have been tempted to skip, simply because of how comfortable and relaxed I felt when I woke up in near darkness. I lay there for a while, almost able to slip right back into slumber, until my eyes rested on the clock at the foot of my bed.

Seven o'clock.

I bolted upright. I'd slept for *twelve hours?* Was I sick? I felt my forehead. It was warm from sleep, but no warmer than usual. My brain felt normal and clear. Actually, considering how long I slept, I felt better than normal. Energized. Rested.

It was weird.

Swinging my legs out of bed, I stood, stretching a little bit. I was stiff from sleeping for so long, but that didn't stop me from padding across my bedroom, pulling sweatpants and a long-sleeved T-shirt from my dresser. One shower later, I looked out of my kitchen window at Sharon-the-grocer returning home. She glanced over at my house, seemingly surprised at the illuminated room, and waved a little when she saw me.

I waved back, and once she entered her house, I shut the curtains as hurriedly as I could without seeming rude. I pulled out a frozen container of Stone Soup and stuck it into the microwave to thaw. In order for it to achieve my desired temperature—roughly fifty degrees cooler than the sun—I pressed the 5-minute express button, and headed to start up my computer.

Two names. Two easy internet searches, and then I could reassure Tam that nothing was wrong. His mood had been contagious last night, and I wanted to kick myself for getting sucked into that. I left the kitchen, padding up the hall into the office. Flicking on the light in the room, I frowned at the dimness before weaving my way around the stacks of boxes that I hadn't even looked at yet.

And here I thought I'd purged some of my belongings before I came. Well, I had. And then over the last couple of days, everything I wasn't actively using got stuffed in here. Come to think of it, my winter coat was probably somewhere in here.

Finally making it to my computer hutch, I leaned over the chair and pressed the on switch. My computer was an older model, so it'd probably take a minute for it to warm up. If nothing else, there would be enough time for me to grab my soup and bring it back to the computer. This would only take a minute, and heaven knew I'd earned a cat video or two.

A box and a letter caught my attention, and I looked at my mother's ring box and my father's letter. I should probably read that today as well. No sense putting it off forever. Sighing, I headed back to the kitchen, grabbed a potholder and teased the flaming-hot container out of the microwave without causing myself third-degree burns.

Two minutes later, feeling far too smug about how gracefully I'd navigated my cardboard jungle, I plopped down in front of my computer, crossed my legs in my oversized computer chair, and dug my spoon into the soup.

After eight days of writing hand-written reports morning and night, typing even something as familiar as my password seemed almost foreign, as did the harsh white glare of the computer screen as it started to load my desktop.

Maybe Beth was right—I did need blue filter glasses. Sitting back, I pushed the soup onto the desk, and grabbed my mom's ring box. Flipping it open, I ran my fingers over the wood and iron, letting my mind drift off for a moment. Beth Borden. She was the one who had referred me to Our Lady of the Wood Psychiatric Hospital in the first place. It was interesting. Beth almost looked like Gwen. The same straight nose. The shape of their eyes. The same high cheekbones. If I didn't know better, I would say they could have been sisters.

The desktop flicked up onto the screen. Sitting up, I closed the ring box and put it back on the desk on top of Bill's letter and opened an internet browser. Waiting a second for the internet to remember that it worked, I typed in Matron's name, picking at the keyboard with my index fingers: Fay Avery.

I pressed enter. The first result was Fay's—Matron's—professional profile. Interested, I clicked on it. Her face popped up on the screen, as beautiful and youthful as ever. There wasn't much on her page other than a request for funding that seemed to run every couple of months with barely any variation. Realizing that I wasn't going to get much more than that from her general page, I clicked on the "About" section that was under her photograph.

> *Fay Avery*
>
> *Head Administrator for Our Lady of the Wood Psychiatric Hospital*
>
> *48 Years old.*

I blinked and leaned in closer to the screen. Maybe it was a typo...? But no, her birthday was there. December 22, 1977, almost forty-nine years ago. I frowned a little. I wasn't one to begrudge someone who tried to look younger than they were. Heaven knew once I'd hit my thirties I'd dabbled in different moisturizers and thought about coloring my hair. But this . . . it seemed to go beyond age. It was in her bearing. This was not a middle-aged woman trying to look younger. The woman that I knew was in her prime, or frighteningly good at faking it.

Does that mean you believe Tam now? The sardonic voice in the back of my head seemed to grin at me. Frowning at the computer, I shifted a little and opened Matron's photo, looking closely. The youth was there, or at least the imitation of it. But here and there, you could see the smile lines, the little wrinkles, and above all her eyes that were much older than she was.

No, I could believe it. She was practically a magician, but I could believe it.

Done ogling your boss? The smarmy voice was back again and I sighed. This was ridiculous. Tam was . . . troubled. I knew that. He was in Our Lady for a reason. Why was I doing this?

Because I said I would. I sat back, glaring at Matron's smiling face. There was a twinkle in those eyes, and for a moment, it felt like she was watching me. I could just see her in the office tomorrow, leaning over her desk, grinning maniacally, saying something like *"Didn't I tell you that Tam would manipulate you? He's so* handsome" as she fired me.

I exited the browser, frowning. It wasn't because of Tam's looks, it was because of his . . . his vulnerability. If what Tam said was true and he'd been taught to be resilient and self-sufficient, whether by abuse, neglect, or just sheer necessity, there was no way he would have melted down like he did. Not in front of me. Not in front of Randal.

I sighed, and reached out, swiping Bill's letter and Mom's ring off the table. I wasn't going to solve that mystery tonight. I might as well solve another one.

Holding the letter didn't make me want to open it any more than I had when I first received it. I didn't know all the details of my father's death—whether by accident or by Mr. Campion's design to protect me, I wasn't sure—but it had been highly implied that he had taken his own life.

What if this was his . . . note?

I wouldn't be able to handle that. I tried so hard to be strong. I was strong, but he was my father. But if I didn't read it today, when would I? In five years? In ten? When I was on my own deathbed?

I cracked the seal on the envelope. That drew a smirk out. Ever the dramatic one, Bill. The wax seal had the sun emblazoned on it. At first, I wondered who in their right mind would let a permanent patient have a wax stamp in the mental hospital, then I shook it off as visions of bookshelves and heavy lamps from The Boughs floated through my head.

And then I drew out the letter. I recognized Bill's handwriting, and it squeezed my heart.

He'd written almost every week that he was away—at first to my mother, but when she'd lost her ability to write, he'd started addressing them to me. I did the best I could for the longest time, but there were only so many times I could write "she's a little worse" without coming out and saying it before I lost the taste for it. This one was addressed to me again, the bold cursive flowing and practiced. The date—the day after Mom died. Three days before he died.

July 23, 2026

    My dearest Margot,

    If you are reading this, then I am dead.

I crumpled up the letter, throwing it across the room. I was going to kill Mr. Campion. How dare he send me this? What did he think he was going to accomplish by sending me the last—

I closed my eyes, taking a deep breath. Mr. Campion wouldn't have known. The seal wasn't broken. Besides, hadn't there been a note with the body? Something like three pages of it? *Calm down, Margot,* I said to myself. *Bill wouldn't do that to me. He wouldn't.* And neither would Mr. Campion.

Still, I stared at the crumpled bit of paper for a good long while before I could stand up and pick it up off the floor. There were four pages, actually, with writing front and back. Bill had had a lot to say. He always did. I smoothed out the pages.

If you are reading this, then I am dead. I'm afraid news of your mother has brought me very low, and my heart is broken into so many pieces that I am afraid I might not be able to piece myself back together again. My consolation, the consolation of my entire life, is that you are safe, and that is all that matters to me from now on.

There is a certain sort of realization that a man has when confronted with his own mortality. In the light of that setting sun, I've come to realize that as much as we tried to teach you—your mother and I—there were things that we've lived, mistakes that we made that we've hidden because of our shame. Things that, if you are not aware of them, could put you in grave danger.

We have taught you your whole life that there are creatures in this world that look human but are not. They are the Fae: Fairies, The Fair Folk. They are the shining beauties lurking in the shadows. The speakers of glorious words wrapped around the most cunning and disgusting of lies.

I stared down at the page, disappointed, but not particularly surprised. Words of warning. Of course he would want to warn me. It was almost verbatim to what he'd told me growing up. Next he would tell me that he and Mom were taken in by their lies, but go into no further detail, and tell me to never eat food from strangers, never make an idle bargain, and never give them your name. Then he would leave it at that.

You know from your mother and I that we were taken in by their lies, brought into their court at a young age. But we've never told you the whole story. This is largely your mother's influence—she never thought you were ready for it as a child, and by the time you were an adult, you had decided your own path and were protected by the veil of disbelief. I hope you are always so protected.

The story begins back in 1985. Your mother and I had just met at university, where I was in my fourth year, studying mythology, and she had just started as a general studies student. She was the prettiest woman that I had ever seen, even at eighteen years old, and it was barely a year before I asked her to marry me. Shortly after, we were married, and were approached by a mutual friend of an acquaintance and were asked if we knew anything about faeries.

Neither of us did, and so we were invited up north to a festival on the Upper Peninsula, deep in the Marquette National Forest. I can't begin to describe the party that we had, even if I remembered most of it. Spiced wine, dancing, an enormous fire in the cool autumn air, it felt as close to magical as anything I've ever felt. While we were there, the mutual friend—a beautiful young woman with long auburn hair— approached your mother and told her that her father wanted to speak with her.

We went, and her father, a distinguished, older-looking gentleman offered us a place in the community. I'd just finished my studies that summer, and your mother wanted to start a family, so we accepted, and we moved to Carterhall, Michigan.

I sat back, staring at my father's cursive, wondering if I'd read it wrong. They couldn't have possibly lived here. Wouldn't they have told me?

Why would they have told you? My inner voice challenged. *You only decided to live here after they both died. And since when did you ever ask about their life before you?*

Shame burned in my cheeks. I'd never meant for my separate —specifically, non-faerie—lifestyle to become a hedge between us, and yet it had, with me unconsciously sifting out or not asking about anything that could possibly circle back to faeries. How much of their lives had I missed out on?

Life was normal, for a time. We lived in the town for about three years, communing with the people who had also moved there to be part of the Avery community. It was during that time that we were slowly introduced to the world of the Faeries. There was never one Great Revelation, but the reality of magic in our lives soon became a constant instead of a farfetched children's story. No one was ever sick. The people were happy and healthy, and no one could even fathom the thought of leaving.

In the fall of 1990, your mother learned that she was pregnant with you. There was much rejoicing in the community, and after almost four years of trying to have children, we were thrilled. You were a healthy child, even then, and we were able to rejoice until the next June.

Then the unthinkable happened.

I sat back, worrying for the child until I realized that it was me—I'd lived. Not only that, but I had been healthy and strong.

One month before you were born, we were approached by Mr. Avery, the leader of the community, who summoned us to meet with him. Up until that point, we'd been told that we were welcome to live in the community, but there would be a price to be paid, one that only we would be able to pay. We assumed it would be to pay some sort of sum, or host one of their parties.

We were asked—

I lowered the letter, looking up blankly at the office around me, swallowing hard. I felt as though I knew what was coming, but I couldn't bear to look at the letter in front of me. If they asked of them what I suspected that they asked of them . . .

I pinched my eyes closed, kneading my forehead with my fist. I couldn't read more, and yet my eyes cracked open.

We were asked to give you up. No, that's not quite right. We were asked to sell you. We were told that in the future—the very distant future, we were assured—you would be a priceless human sacrifice, a Tiend, to keep the magic that we experienced every day going. We would be treated like royalty, with everything that we ever desired, and you would want for nothing.

We owe everything to your mother. Before I had a chance to do anything, say anything, think anything, she told him under no uncertain terms that she would never give up her child. Not for all the gold, riches, and power in the world. Avery was angry. He warned her that if she did not pay her debt, that we would pay a different cost, one that would cost us more than would ever compare to giving you up.

I think he meant to frighten her. But my sweet Alexandra laughed in his face, telling him he knew nothing of a mother's capability to protect her child. As long as she lived, she declared, this child would be safe from the likes of him, and she would take any danger head on to keep it that way. Avery, unprepared for her counterattack, blustered, and swore that he would have you, whether by right or design, and she straightened up. Margot, you can imagine queens, angels, and even gods. Nothing compares to your mother in that moment, looking the King in his eyes, and proclaiming to him, "You will have to come through me first."

We left that night under the cover of darkness. We didn't take our car, simply gathering our legal documents and sneaking out on the first bus out of town, taking us anywhere away from Carterhall. We went south first, and then east. When we kept noticing faces we recognized, we changed our names. You were born in New York, as Margot Knight.

We never told you, but you were named after your only living grandparent, my mother, Margaret Henley. As of the writing of this letter, she is still living in Arizona. Do not visit her until you are safe.

And now, a warning. Magic is real. Faeries are real, and they hate us. Do not be flattered or enticed by the sweet smiles and charming words. Humans are chattel, mere puffs in the wind of their unnaturally long lives, tools to get what they want. I know you don't believe, and for that purpose, I have provided you proof.

I sat there, frozen in the chair, staring at the word.
Proof.

He had proof.

I've asked Mr. Campion to send you your mother's wedding ring along with this letter. We had it made after we fled Carterhall. The iron is to repel fae, and the fir wood is to provide discernment. Sight.

In this envelope, I have included two pictures with this letter, both of our time in Carterhall. The first is your mother and I on the steps of our house. It's a happier time, and how I want you to remember us.

I looked at the photo and brought my hand up to my mouth. It was an old photograph, one that I'd never seen. A small white house, with Mom and Bill sitting out on the doorstep. Bill had his arm around Mom's shoulders, pressing a kiss to the side of her head as she was caught mid-laugh.

The second is us with the woman that recruited us. I hope you never meet her. She is the one that Avery sent after us. His daughter. Her cruelty and viciousness continue to leave me in awe. She only ever caught up to me once, to pronounce a curse on us—that our lives would be cut short, driven mad by the very thing that had once been our strengths. Do not be fooled by her appearance—the ring will reveal everything. If you ever see her, run. Just run.

I pulled the second picture slowly from the envelope, and my heart clenched as I recognized the red hair, the piercing blue eyes, and the wide smile.

Matron.

Fay Avery looked exactly the same, a stark contrast to my youthful parents. She stood between them, head tilted to the side, one hand resting protectively on my mother's pregnant belly as she grinned for the camera. I ran my thumb over the picture, a sudden panic gripping my chest. There had to be some mistake. Photoshop or something, something to explain the unexplainable . . .

But it was an ordinary photograph. Bill didn't know that I'd met her—he'd died before even I knew I was going to move up here.

But was it the same person? It couldn't be. It couldn't possibly. Bill hadn't mentioned her by name. I flipped the photo over.

Alexandra and David Christopherson with Fae Avery, June 1991.

But—

The ring, I thought, plucking it off the desk. Coincidence. Nothing more. Nothing more. I slipped the ring out of its nest, and slipped it onto my finger, and then I looked at the picture again.

It had changed. There, in front of my eyes, the woman in the middle of the photograph, Matron, had transformed from a young woman to an old lady. Her hair was still straight, but long and white, framing a face that was lined and slightly worn, as she smiled. That smile. Twisted and almost profane. Looking at the woman, I had no doubt that she could raise a child to be slaughtered. I traced my finger down her arm, to where the hand— almost a claw—hooked over my mother's stomach.

My mouth was dry. It had to be a trick. It *had* to be a trick. But how could I possibly check— the internet.

I slammed the photos down onto the desk, opening the browser and typing before the buffer could catch up with me. I clicked on the link, hissing under my breath as it took longer to load than it ever had before.

And then her face popped up, and I collapsed back in my seat. The same witch stared back at me, dark blue eyes glittering back with a twisted smirk, as if she knew she was hiding in plain sight.

I took off the ring, wondering if it was some trick from beyond the grave. But no, as the ring lifted from my finger, the auburn hair and soft smile returned. Young and professional. Beautiful and innocent.

I couldn't stop then.

I struggled to enter in Janet's name into the search engine. Or rather, I got the Janet part down right, but for the life of me I couldn't spell Christofferson—Kristoffersen? Son? Sen? Sin? Christophersen? I tried every iteration that I could think of, but none of them seemed quite right. I'd seen the actual nurse's name, of course. Since Tam's file went back that far, she had been responsible for writing up the reports—just a few lines at a time. She'd printed it at the bottom of every single entry—why couldn't I think of it?

Nerves already frazzled and threatening to pick me apart at the seams, I picked up Mom's ring and slipped it onto my finger, and suddenly I could see the spelling to Janet's last name. Thinking about it properly, I thought I'd already searched for that particular spelling, but upon hitting enter, a page of search results that I definitely hadn't seen before popped up. Shifting my weight and running my thumb along Mom's ring, I leaned closer to the computer.

I clicked on the first link and the world seemed to tilt on its side.

It was from the Carterhall Oracle. It wasn't so much an article as an ad. A banner, from last Christmas.

Missing: Janet Christofferson

    Birthdate: July 15, 1991

    Age: 35

    Hair: Blonde

    Eyes: Grey

    Height: 5'5"

    Weight: 120 lbs

    Last seen: 16 October, 2025 at Our Lady of the Wood Psychiatric Hospital. Please forward any information to Detective Michael Ansel at Carterhall Police Department. Victim is possibly confused and disoriented. Be gentle on approach.

Then, below the text, a single picture of a woman I knew very well indeed.

Polly.

It was undoubtedly her. From the wide eyes to the tousled blonde hair and gentle, winning smile, if it was not Polly, it was the best doppelgänger in the history of the world. But according to this page, updated at the beginning of this October, she still hadn't been found. She was less than an hour away, how could she not have been found?

I knew the answer even as I thought the question.

Because no one would be looking for Janet at the hospital she had supposedly left. The Boughs was a closed ward. No visitors. No technology. No possibility for an accidental picture to be taken of her. No possibility for someone to hear her voice on the phone if someone called out. No possibility of her being found.

My world spun a little and I bit my lip.

But this would mean Tam—

I stopped the thought before it finished. I wasn't done. If I was going to do this, I was going to do it right. Pulling myself forward in the seat, I clicked into the search bar, and typed in my new parameters.

"Disappearances—Our Lady of the Wood Psychiatric Hospital."

I don't know how many websites I pulled up. News outlet after news outlet, missing person after missing person, accidental death after accidental death. Only one thing connected them— Our Lady of the Wood Hospital. Matron. She'd made a statement to the Carterhall Oracle on the occasion of each incident. *"It is with deepest sorrow . . ."*

There was a sort of whiteness in my brain. A lightness, as though I wasn't quite sitting at my computer in my office. Balling my hands into fists, I looked down at them, feeling almost as though they weren't mine. They were shaking.

Taking a deep breath, I pressed both hands against the dark wood of the desk. I ran my fingers over the grain of the wood, focusing on the realness. My thumb accidentally stroked Mom's ring as well, and I looked down at the polished wood. Protection, Mom and Bill had said, and discernment.

I couldn't stop now. I looked through what I'd found again, switching between the windows that I had open. There were four men—Thomas Rider and two others, each almost carbon copies of each other—and Tam. The resemblance was undeniable. The other deaths were almost exclusively staff. Accidental drownings in the nearby river, suicides, accidents at home. Nothing capable of being explicitly tied back to Matron. It was important, but not exactly what I was looking for.

And then I found it. A small clipping from a Detroit newspaper after searching Tam's name. A request from a Mr. Danny Vering from London for any available information about a Mr. Thomas Lynn, who was last seen boarding a flight to Detroit on the twenty-fifth of October, 2019.

Any information to the whereabouts of Thomas Lynn or his uncle would be greatly appreciated.

"What was the uncle's name?" I whispered to myself as I read. My question was answered in the next line. My heart stopped.

Name of uncle unknown. Possibly Ramsey or Randolph.

I dropped my hands into my lap, and stared helplessly at the screen of the computer. Everything that Tam had told me had seemed characteristic of someone with paranoia—someone out to get him. But could it have been that he had been chosen?

Like I had been.

We were asked to sell you.

Tam's own words came to mind. *"My parents sold me to the fae when I was a child. They raised me—if you can call it that—but solely for . . . for this."*

It couldn't . . . it couldn't be. But here were the pictures. The evidence. The ring . . .

"But why did you stay, Tam?" I whispered at his internet photo. "Why not sneak out?"

"I had promised to stay until someone claimed me," Tam had said.

I thought back to the night that Randal had told his story. *"If you make a deal with the Fae, you may expect it be honored to the very letter. And the greatest calamities be heaped upon you should you not live up to your own end of the agreement."*

I had been flippant. *"And . . . that's it? Honor or calamity?"*

"Yes."

Tam was special to Matron. I knew that. People had been telling me that and showing me that since I'd arrived in The Boughs. The question that had somehow eluded me for the last week seemed to linger in front of me, obvious and simple, freezing me in place.

Why?

Why was Tam so special?

It was obvious now. Randal—*"It's special. It's the All Hallows Eve Bonfire."*

Matron with the door. *"Its title is 'The Tiend,"*

Polly. *"It's the year that Matron kills someone."*

And then, crushingly, Bill. *"You would be a priceless human sacrifice, a Tiend, to keep the magic that we experienced every day going."*

I held my hand to my mouth, the air hissing through my fingers roughly, as the reality of the situation bore down on me, crashing into me again as inconsistency after inconsistency became clear, as though I'd put a pair of glasses on a near-sighted past. The odd feel of the hospital, and Matron's policies: the handwritten records, me in a ward by myself, the small, isolated hovel that was The Boughs.

Why would they have a nurse constantly watch over the patients night and day? Why not an aide like in every other hospital? Why was I alone in The Boughs? Where was my back up? Why did Matron turn a blind eye to most everything that happened in there? Why didn't Matron put someone in there with me after the first incident? Where was the attending doctor? Who was this Dr. Ingen? There were no doctor's notes in my patient's files, no handwriting other than the nurses'. No supervisory notes other than Matron's.

I had been a nurse for over ten years. How could I have possibly not noticed all of this?

There was a moment of stillness, of absolute silence as even my breathing stopped, the only sensation the cool metal of my mother's ring against my lips. The next instant I knew. My hand dropped from my mouth, drifting up to my hair, where the evidence of forty-one stitches left an indent in my scalp. I bit my lip and traced the pucker there with my tongue. My fingers moved to the outside of my shoulder, pressing into the line of the scar.

I could hear Bill screaming at me, pounding the iron lamp into my flesh over and over.

"You should have listened to me, Margot! They're everywhere! They've gotten to you, and you didn't even know! *You! Didn't! Even! Know!*"

Nurse Borden . . . She looked like she could have been Gwen's sister . . .

Struggling to take in a deep breath, I pressed the back of my head into my chair, swallowing hard. Faeries. Magic. The Tiend —the act of sacrificing a human to keep faerie magic alive. I looked at the screen of my computer. The evidence. The missing people. The deaths. I squeezed my eyes shut tight, jaw clenched and hands balled into fists. I couldn't deny it any longer.

Tam wasn't delusional. He wasn't paranoid. He wasn't even crazy. And neither was Bill, or at least not at first.

They were exactly right.

And we were in incredible danger.

OCTOBER 30

I didn't know how to conduct myself when I went in for work the next night. It was as though I had too many limbs, or maybe I had just forgotten how to use them all cohesively. Either way, someone was certainly going to know something was up simply by the way I was acting. The Headless Horseman was probably more subtle than I was being, and he paraded around without a head and murdered people.

My only hope was to avoid any other staff. I wasn't really worried about Randal or Polly—Janet. Randal would notice I was out of sorts but would hopefully pass it off as something else. Polly might not notice. I wasn't sure what I was going to do with her. I couldn't rescue her at the same time as Tam. As much as I wanted to, it would be risky enough getting Tam out without someone sounding the alarm. If two-thirds of my ward went missing, there was no hiding that I had done it. If I was right, and Randal was the one who tricked Tam into coming here, having Randal figure it out would be . . . well, I just hoped that he wouldn't find out. Regardless, it wouldn't be long before Polly or Randal realized that we were gone, but hopefully I could get a police presence here before the alarm was sounded.

Hopefully.

Passing through the administrative wing to punch my time-card, I ran into Gwen. My heart nearly gave out at the bad luck. She smiled at me, apparently on her way to her assigned ward. I offered a weak smile in response, looking down at the ground, hoping that she'd just carry on with her day—or night, as the case was. She was almost past me when she did a double take.

"Margot, are you alright?" she asked, grabbing my arm and pulling me around to face her.

"Me?" I squeaked, blinking a little blankly at her. I could only hope that my blank stare looked the same as innocent, as my expression seemed to be frozen as it was, with no possible hope of change.

"Yes," Gwen said, concern creating the slightest wrinkle between her brows as she peered at me closely. "You're still looking a little pale. And here I thought the day off would have done you a world of good. Are you sure you're okay?"

Oh. I closed my eyes briefly, suddenly remarkably grateful for the endless tossing and turning that I had experienced as I'd tried to sleep today. There were upsides to looking half-dead, it seemed.

"Yes," I said. "I didn't get a lot of sleep last nig—well, today, I guess. I'm a little worried that I might be getting sick. Either that or night shift is just not doing good things to me"

"Oh," Gwen said, the line between her eyebrows running deeper. "Are you sure you don't need to take the day off?" Her question was perfectly normal, even considerate, but the anxious little monster situated in my chest squeezed painfully, an emphatic 'no'. I agreed. Of all the things that would help me feel better, going home would be a definitive step in the wrong direction.

"Yes," I said, managing to smile a bit. "I'm just tired at this point. If that changes, though, I'll be sure to tell you."

Gwen ran her hand down my arm, a comforting touch that made my arm feel as though it was on fire. I dropped my arm out of reach and clenched my fist.

"Okay, then," she said, "but if that changes, let me know. Matron's asked me to ask you if you could come a little earlier than normal to help with the Hallowe'en festivities—nothing crazy, just getting here at maybe six-thirty, instead of eight-thirty? The day nurses will be staying late as well. We just want to make sure there are no . . . accidents."

Like the forty-plus fatalities over the last thirty-five years since Our Lady was founded? I forced a smile onto my face.

"I'll tell you if I need help," I promised. "And I'll come early tomorrow."

"Good to hear. You're such a hard worker, Margot. I'm glad you've come," Gwen said. Smiling, I smoothed my hands over my hair, and Gwen caught sight of my ring. Her lips parted, and a curious expression came over her face. Not curious as in irrepressibly interested, but curious as in I couldn't quite figure out what she was thinking.

"That's a beautiful ring," she said finally. "Where did you get it?"

"It was my mother's," I said holding it out to look at it. "She passed recently. It's one of her keepsakes."

She shifted a little bit. "You do realize that jewelry isn't encouraged as part of the dress code here? I can't stop you from wearing it, you understand, but it's far too easy for someone to steal it or injure your hands."

"I understand," I said, trying to think of an excuse to keep wearing it that didn't involve the fact that it was definitely a ward against whatever faerie spells that might be thrown at me. That would have put me in The Boughs for sure—as a permanent resident. "I've been having a rough couple of days. Moving has put her death into perspective, and I've just been missing her. I thought maybe the ring might help me feel closer to her."

It was a better explanation than I'd expected, probably because it was closer to the truth than I really wanted to admit. I had to be careful to not look too self-congratulatory. It must have worked, though, because Gwen didn't seem to question it at all and even went so far as to pat me on the shoulder.

"I'm sorry you've been having a rough time," she said sincerely. "Let me know if you need anything from Matron or me?"

Aside from a signed confession?

"I will," I said, smiling at her.

She nodded and walked out of the staff room. Breathing out a sigh of relief, I finished punching my timecard and ran up to the ward just as the clock hit eight-thirty. Eileen looked up at me as I entered and stood to start cleaning things up for my shift.

I stood there for a moment, shocked into complete silence, before moving almost robotically to follow suit. I knew better than to look at Tam. I could tell by his posture that he was watching me, but I also knew that if I looked up at him I would flush red. Considering that Eileen was either a victim of or privy to whatever Matron had up her sleeve, discretion was key, and I was going to have to be careful.

As grateful as I was for Eileen's help, and actually feeling quite pleased that what I had said to her had stuck with her so fervently, the fifteen extra minutes that she stayed lasted several hundred years. It was almost painful to move through the routine movements, putting away the day's activities, and making sure that everything was settled for the evening, all the while listening to Eileen tell me about the mundane highlights of the day. A perfectly normal day. Nothing to worry about.

Until me.

Did bank robbers feel like this? Could my plan to rescue Tam even equate to the same thing? Probably. Except with the bank robbers, they'd just go to prison if they got caught. I had more than forty people who could attest to the fact that there was significantly more at stake for me.

At last, the clock hit eight forty-five, and Eileen looked up at me expectantly.

"Thank you for your help, Eileen," I said, smiling slightly.

Nodding in response, she waved at the patients and left the ward. The electronic beep of the lock sounded like music to my ears. I turned toward my patients, and found Randal staring up at me from where he was seated at the table.

"You're acting weird," he said.

I looked down at him. If I was right, he was involved in—possibly even directly responsible for—Tam's disappearance. That being said, I also knew by Eileen's treatment of him, and the lack of Matron's involvement, that either he was under deep cover or he was actually insane and Matron was just using him to get what she wanted—Tam. Either way, it was probably safest to keep my plans away from both him and Polly. Janet.

Polly. I knew her as Polly. More importantly, they knew her as Polly.

"I'm very tired," I finally answered, fighting a completely genuine yawn. "I didn't sleep well last night. Or, well, today."

"No?" Randal asked, as if the concept had never occurred to him. "And what disturbed your sleep?"

The fact that you are likely an accessory to attempted murder? At the least?

"Personal issues," I said simply. "Nothing that you need to worry about. I'll be fine."

"Heavy problems lead to heavy issues."

I raised an eyebrow. "What?"

"Usually, it's heavy problems that disrupt one's rest. Heavy problems always lead to problems with other things. Peace. Health. Sanity." He said it meaningfully, and I knew why. Following his gaze, first to Polly and then to Tam, I nodded.

"It's true that I have heavy problems," I admitted. "But isn't health more in how you deal with the problem, rather than the problem itself?"

Randal smirked and leaned forward onto his elbows. "I should think that it entirely depends on the problem." He looked up at me expectantly, as if he was expecting an answer from me.

It probably would have helped if I knew the question he was asking. I looked at him and decided to answer as honestly as I could.

"I think you're absolutely right," I said, before walking away to look over Polly's shoulder at her puzzle. Glancing back at Randal, he looked confused and almost disappointed, as if I had missed the boat on something painfully obvious. It rankled me a little because I suddenly wondered what I'd missed. I shrugged it off. Knowing Randal, it was probably something mean-spirited, slightly sadistic, or had nothing to do with anything.

As much as I hated to admit it, I had been listening all those years that Bill had ranted and raved about faeries. I knew about their twisty, tricky ways, and I knew for a fact that I was not smart enough to go head-to-head with one and come out on top. If I wanted to get Tam out I'd have to play the 'avoid' and 'pretend ignorance' cards, and for now, I was playing them against Randal.

I wondered what his deal was. What he'd bargained for—presumably with Matron—in exchange for Tam. What was Tam's soul worth to Randal?

Speaking of Tam, I needed to talk to him. If he didn't already have a plan, or at least a small part of one on how to escape, I'd eat his way-too-small robe.

Not that I got the chance anytime soon. Randal seemed determined to be as needy as possible—everything from needing a blanket to losing one of his face cards that we eventually found in the pocket of his robe. Then he moved to picking on Polly, for which I banished him to read in his room for fifteen minutes. Polly realized I was standing behind her a couple of moments after that. She craned her head up to look at me and smiled.

"Isn't it pretty, Nurse Margot?" she said, gesturing to her puzzle. It was a fall scene from somewhere along the coast of the peninsula. "Will you help me finish it?"

I opened and then closed my mouth, nodding. "Although," I said, "I do need to do the reports really quick."

"Okay," Polly said cheerfully. "Nothing really happened today, though. Really, Nurse Margot, you do look quite peaked." She touched my arm, looking up to my face. I briefly wondered if she could tell what I was thinking. She'd been in my place. Done what I had done.

And failed.

"I'm fine," I assured her, walking to the file cabinet. I pulling out the three files, and headed back, smiling at her as I sat down.

She uneasily smiled back. "You promise?" she asked.

I looked up, a little taken aback. Could I honestly answer that question? I was nervous, yes. Scared that someone might catch me? Absolutely. But . . . I couldn't just let Tam die. Not when I could try to do something about it. I wished I had proof. I could have called the police and let them take care of it. But no. I had no proof right now. Hopefully, I could change that tonight.

I felt the weight of my phone in my pocket. I was breaking about eighty rules—or at least One Very Big One—by even having it on my person, but if I could prove that Tam and Polly were here, it would be almost shockingly easy to get the police out. If that didn't work for some reason . . .

I shoved the thought away. My plan had to work. And I had made the choice to put it in motion. Was there an alternative that I was okay with? No.

And so . . . the answer to Polly's question was yes. I was fine.

"Yes," I said quietly. "I promise I'm fine."

She looked at me a moment longer, and then down at her puzzle, nodding. "Good."

I waited for a little longer for Polly to say something else, but she didn't. Nodding to myself, I applied myself to the reports. And then to Polly's puzzle. And then a card game. By the time bedtime drew near, I was reminded just why it was that I preferred public hospitals over private ones. Here I was, aging several hundred years during a round of gin rummy. At a normal hospital I would at least have had rounds to do.

Tam kept looking over at me, too. I could see him off to my left on the couch, by all appearances deep in his book. But every once in a while, my own glances over in his direction somehow managed to correspond with his glances at me. But they were just slightly out of sync, so although I'd see him begin to look at me, or just barely look away, our eyes never met.

I was grateful for it. I needed to hold myself together.

Finally, sometime around my three hundredth birthday, it was time for bed. Polly went to the bathroom first, emerging so quickly that I actually checked to make sure she'd done everything. Surprisingly, she had. Either that, or she had gargled with toothpaste, but if she'd gone to that much trouble to get around brushing her teeth, I was going to let her win that battle. Patting her on the shoulder, I watched her swallow the pills from the little cup and sent her off to her room.

Randal was a different story. He whined and hemmed and hawed, jabbering on and on about seeing the stars. I had not been in the mood for his mania about the stars before, but now that I knew he was essentially whining about not being able to prepare properly for Tam's death, I was two steps short of shaking him until his eyeballs rattled, much like he'd done with Polly. I opened my mouth to say something that was probably going to be regrettable, when I saw the shadow of someone step up behind me.

"Randal," Tam said quietly from over my shoulder. "There will be plenty of time to revel tomorrow. Go to bed now. Rest. Rejuvenate." I turned to look at him, and he looked down at me patiently, as if knowing that I had been fast approaching the end of my rope.

"It will not be the same," Randal said sulkily, folding his arms.

"I expect not, Randal," Tam said quietly. "But things will be different starting tomorrow anyway."

For a moment I thought Tam had given the whole game away, and yet when I looked between them, a small sinister smile slipped over Randal's face.

"You're right," Randal said quietly. He stood then, and there was a smooth grace that I wasn't expecting, as though he shed a couple of decades as he rose. Looking between Tam and I, Randal nodded regally, his rumpled clothes and wild grey hair almost making the movement funny, and then he seemed to float toward his room.

"He's one—"

"Shh." Tam cut my shocked whisper off and grabbed my wrist to reinforce his word. I looked down at it. He did the same, and let go of it quickly, redness creeping up his neck and ears. He looked away quickly. "Not yet." Then he went and sat on the couch again.

Randal was also uncharacteristically quick in the bathroom before gliding over and taking his medication from me. Tam was out of the bathroom and ready for bed before Randal had finished swallowing the last of his pills. Glancing at Tam strangely, Randal seemed to descend from the lordliness that had seemed to inhabit him.

"That was fast," he remarked.

Tam looked up at him, as if he wasn't sure what he was talking about. "I need to rest for tomorrow," Tam said quietly. "It will be an . . . eventful day."

Randal seemed appeased by this answer. "You're right," he murmured again, regality restored, and he slipped into his room.

Tam exhaled slowly.

"And I'm the one who nearly let the cat out of the—" I started to grumble,

"Please Nurse Margot." Tam cut me off. Looking down at me, he just shook his head. "Please." We waited for a moment, staring at each other in silence until the light in Randal's room flicked off.

"I believe you," I whispered, getting straight to the point. "You're right. There's way too much going on here to be coincidental, and too many things that I should have noticed and didn't to lead me to any other conclusion. It's not—" I broke off, considering my words carefully. "This is not . . . what I thought would be real. And it scares me." It was a vast, vast understatement of how I actually felt about it, and the admission tasted like sawdust in my mouth. I looked away from Tam.

"Hey."

When I looked up at Tam, his face was compassionate.

"What?" I asked.

He smiled, his regular half-smile. "I don't think this is what anyone wanted for themselves, Margot."

The use of my name without the prefix touched me a little. It was highly inappropriate, of course, for here at Our Lady, but in the moment, I didn't care much. He and I were alike. Unattached. Alone, even.

If Tam had been brought here because he was unclaimed, was it possible that I was, too?

"What are you thinking about?" Tam asked.

I looked up, his words surprising me out of my reverie. I shook my head. "Just . . . things."

"Well, let's have a seat and talk for a minute, shall we?" he said. Moving behind me, he pulled out my chair, and gestured for me to sit.

"Thank you," I said a little blankly, sitting down as he pushed the chair in to accommodate me.

"You are very welcome," he said, the words sounding a little awkward coming from him, before walking around me and sitting to my right. Then he waited.

I had never been afraid of silence, but this one seemed to sit on my chest, waiting for me to speak, as if anything and everything about the quiet screamed that I was insane, and that I was breaking all sorts of rules by even thinking about this plan. This reality.

Maybe I was.

Too late for that now.

Taking in a deep breath, I looked him in the eyes. "I believe you," I said again. "And I know I need to get you and Polly—

Janet—out. It . . . I don't think I can get the both of you out at once." It was a painful admission, and I saw a flicker of disappointment cross his face. I shook my head. "Maybe if I was more experienced, or there was going to be less going on . . . I just can't see a way that I can get you both out safely. Not with the condition that she's in."

"I understand."

I thought carefully about what I was going to say before I continued, "I think . . . since your situation is a little more dire that I would get you out first, then come back for her. She doesn't know anything, she—"

"It . . . might not matter," Tam's voice cracked a little, and I looked up. Tam shook his head. "Margot, if we leave and Matron and her cronies find out, if they find out that we left, they might kill anyone who is a liability. Janet is a missing person. What would they do, give her back her wits? If she's here and she's alive and we expose them, they're liable for unlawful imprisonment and kidnapping."

I thought about it for a second. Bringing her along may very well kill us all, but bringing both her and Tam would guarantee a police presence. That, and . . . well, could I actually leave her here with that hanging over my head?

"Okay," I said, nodding, trying to ignore the feeling of overwhelming anxiety that accompanied the commitment.

Tam nodded in return. "Now, I have a plan."

"Wait a second," I said, I reached into my pocket. Tam looked mystified as I pulled my smartphone out of my pocket. He looked at it.

"What is that?"

"My phone?" I swiped it on, opening the camera function. For a second I was worried that it wouldn't turn on—that the reason that we weren't allowed technology was because the magic in the building made the technology go haywire. Then the screen lit, showing the table through the front view camera. I held it up.

"Say cheese."

"What?"

"Good enough," I said, snapping the photo, then clicking the result. Tam looked concerned in the photo, but it was his face. Thank goodness. I could go to the police, and show them the picture—

"Well, that's a problem," Tam said.

I tore my eyes away from the photo and looked up at him, confused.

"What is?"

"The photo."

"Why? You look like that. That's your face." I looked closer at the photo. The edge of Tam's jawline, the lines across his forehead, they were his.

Tam took the phone away from me. "This . . . this isn't me. Did you . . ." He looked up from the screen, his eyes scanning over me, as if looking for something. When his eyes rested on my hand, his eyes focused on the ring. "Is that iron?"

I looked down at the ring. "Yes, iron and fir. Why?"

"May I see it?"

I met his eyes, a sudden stab of fear lancing through me. I hadn't taken it off since I'd put it on last night. Frankly, I had no plan on removing it ever again. If I did—

No one is trying to enchant you, I thought, taking a deep breath. *Not right now. It's safe.* I nodded, sliding the ring off my finger and placing it in the palm of his hand.

He nodded at the phone. "Now look at the photo."

I did, and my mouth dropped open. It wasn't him anymore. It looked similar, but was definitely someone who would never pass a closer inspection. Certainly not by anyone who was looking for Tam.

"But—"

Tam shook his head before I finished the syllable. "It was a good thought, but there's a glamour on the whole place. On us. Just in case."

"Maybe if I took the ring . . ." I trailed off as Tam shook his head.

He slipped the ring on his pinkie, and looked down at the photo. "Was this made for someone in particular?"

"My mom."

He took the ring off and placed it back into my hand, closing my fingers over it. "Then it's probably attuned to your bloodline. These sorts of things usually are."

I sat back in my chair, sliding the ring back onto my finger. If I couldn't come back tomorrow with a police force at my back, how in the world was I supposed to get Polly and Tam out? I couldn't leave them behind. I couldn't just walk away either.

Tam read my expression. "Like I said, I've got a plan. Last time, we—Janet and I—tried to get out too soon. The last couple of years have been chaotic around the time of the start of the actual bonfire. If we leave when it's dark, when they're setting everything up, then we should be in the clear. We can get to the stables where my horse Acorn is, and there should be mounts for you and Janet as well."

I cleared my throat, fighting down a sudden smile that clashed with the rest of my feelings. "Or we could just take my car."

Tam blinked at me, as if the words didn't compute. "What?"

"You do know that it's the twenty-first century out there, right? I own a vehicle. I drive it here every day."

"Oh."

I smiled. "It's fifty minutes to Carterhall. How did you think I get here?"

He looked a little sheepish. "I guess I didn't really think about it? I know some of the nurses live here."

I grimaced. "No thanks. I might be an undiagnosed worka-holic, but I do have some boundaries."

"Oh good." He thought for a few moments. "Do you have a place to hide that cell phone?"

"I was going to take it back down to my car once you were

asleep. I'd make everyone and their dog suspicious if I had it, even if I said it was an accident."

Tam frowned and nodded, pain flashing his face before he could stop himself.

I looked and bit my lip, tracing the scar inside. "Another . . . incident?"

"Yes." The word was short and painful.

I stared at him, realizing that I did not know the smallest portion of what this man had endured here. I thought of his tender care of Polly. His courteous, pointed, but peaceful pieces of rebellion. The upside-down book. The long, pointed stare until the magic took hold. He was large and fit. He could have done a lot more damage—to others or himself—if he had chosen, but here he was. Kind. Gentle. Peaceful, even.

I looked down at the table, forcing my thoughts to focus on the task at hand. There was a very important question that needed to be asked. "I know you probably don't want to answer this, but I feel as though I need to ask: What are the conditions of your contract with the Fae here?"

Tam looked up, one eyebrow raising. "You do your homework very thoroughly, don't you?"

"It wasn't homework that needed to be done," I said back evenly. "For better or for worse, I was raised on this. If you've made a deal with the faeries that you'll stay here until certain conditions are met, we need to find a way to get you free without impinging on their sense of honor. If we don't, they will hunt us down and kill all of us and feel completely justified in doing so."

I felt like I was preaching to the choir, and the feeling only intensified as Tam ducked his head, nodding abashedly. I searched his face for a moment.

"You've forgotten about it before, haven't you?" I asked.

Tam nodded. "Janet," he said quietly, tracing the grain of the fake wood table. Swallowing, he continued with a grating form of devastating self-deprecation. "My deal was that I would stay here until I was claimed."

"Like how? By whom?" I asked.

He shook his head. "Specifically, someone who will keep me close to their heart forever. Tradition usually dictates someone romantically involved—"

"Um, I'm sorry to interrupt, but there are several laws against that. I mean . . . with us," I pointed out, feeling more than a little uncomfortable.

Tam shrugged. "I know. I'm hoping that the link between savior and the person they're saving will be enough. I know that I will always remember you and appreciate anything you do to help me get out of here. Even if—"

"We won't fail." I cut him off, hoping he'd correct me, saying that he wasn't about to say something like that.

He didn't. Rather, he sighed. "How do you know?"

"Because I don't fail," I said seriously. "And I don't give up. I haven't before, even when things were rough, and I'm not about to start now."

"It—Margot, there are so many things that could go wrong."

"I thought you wanted to get out of here?" I said quietly. He looked at me, long and desperately earnest.

"I do."

"Well then," I said with finality. "We've got the escape route covered. I'll fill my car up with gas on the way to work tomorrow, so we won't have to worry about running out of gas on the way back. The biggest distraction is going to be the bonfire, and I agree, the best time to get you out will be while everyone is busy with the last-minute stuff. The hardest thing to get around is that you're Matron's sacrifice. She's going to keep a close eye on you. How do we make sure that you're not going to be stuck somewhere we can't get you out of?"

Tam looked thoughtful for a moment before shaking his head. "What are the best options?"

I took a turn to think for a minute. "Probably feigning illness? When is your . . . part?" My stomach turned at the thought of Tam being sacrificed. If Matron's door was anything to go by, he was going to burned alive, and that would happen when the fire was at its hottest. Not right away, but not too long after it was set ablaze. I wish I knew when that was.

"I'm not sure," he admitted, his own voice a little rough. "Matron won't give me many details, even when I do ask for them, and there's something that happens during our meetings that makes it very difficult to remember anything she does tell me." At my helpless expression he reached out to take my hand, and then withdrew it quickly, his skin just brushing mine. "It's not right away. There will be a chance for me to slip away, I know it."

I let out the breath I didn't know I was holding and squared my shoulders.

"Then we'll have to find something that will keep you in here until the last possible second," I said, turning to look at the medicine cabinet. Tam followed my look and as I turned back to him, there was a full, genuine smile on his face.

"Now, now, Nurse Margot, are you planning on using your powers for evil?"

"It's possible that I might lose my job over this," I agreed. "But I'm going to lose it anyway, so I might as well go out with a bang. Besides, in this case I don't think it can actually be counted as evil."

"Don't mind if I agree with you," he said, that full smile still on his face. Then, after a moment, the smile dropped off his face.

"What is it?" I asked.

He shook his head. "Don't worry about it."

"Tam?" I said, a warning in my voice.

He shook his head, expression smoothing out. "Nothing, it won't impact our plans. It was just Randal. But if we keep him in the dark, we should be fine."

"What about Randal?"

Tam opened his mouth to speak, and then sighed, shaking his head. "Do you know who he is?"

"A patient? I'm assuming he's a faerie."

"Yes to both. But he's . . . someone special."

"Like what?" I asked, glancing toward Randal's door, hoping beyond hope that he wasn't sitting there behind it, listening to everything we had to say.

"He's . . . he's Matron's father."

"What?"

"Shh!" Tam rocketed to his feet at the loud word, pressing a finger against my lips. I fell silent immediately, holding my breath as we listened for any whisper of movement.

Nothing. We both exhaled.

"Randal is her *father*?" I whispered. "What does that make him, King of the Faeries? Why is he in here?"

"Because he's senile," Tam said, looking toward Randal's door again. "And very, very dangerous. He was the one who told Matron about our plan last time. I don't even know how he found out, but he has some sort of a deal with Matron. If he provides her with a sacrifice, he can get his powers back."

Memories of the power outage as he screamed at Polly the first day flashed through my head. "That's a terrible deal!"

"She'll never follow through, though."

"But she has to!" I said. "If—"

"This is Matron. Besides, I'm not a sacrifice yet. If we're careful, we'll be fine. We'll make it work."

The nervous, paranoid part of my brain wanted to pick him apart, make him tell me more so I could judge for myself, but I forced the feeling down.

We talked about our plans for a while longer, but eventually there wasn't anything left to discuss. We sat there looking at each other for another moment before he tilted his head to the side.

"Why did you come here, Nurse Margot?" Tam asked.

I looked up at him, tracing the edge of the deck of cards that Randal had left out on the table. I smiled a little. "I wonder if I actually know," I said contemplatively. "I thought I'd come here for personal reasons, but I think I might have been tricked into coming here."

Tam raised an eyebrow. "Oh?" he asked.

I looked across the room contemplatively. "Yeah. There's a nurse that worked at my old hospital. She looks a lot like Gwen. She'd worked there for ages, but it was like the minute I told her I needed out, she had a 'Help Wanted' flyer for me for this place. It's like she'd been waiting for it."

"Really?" Tam's voice was light, but there was an undercurrent of concern that made me squirm, just a bit.

I nodded. "I don't have any family left," I admitted. "My parents are dead. I only found out I have a living grandmother last night, but I've never met her." The last part came out with a sigh, but Tam nodded as though he understood.

"I don't have any living family either. I don't even know if my friends from England are around anymore. I loved them, but I was more interested on coming to America and trying my hand at raising horses. Get out of England and away from life there."

"You were raised around horses, then?" I asked.

Tam snorted. "No." An embarrassed smile crossing his face. "But I wanted to learn—something else, like engineering, that would set me apart from my parents. So I sold my parents' company after they died, and headed off into the unknown."

"And ran into faeries first thing?" I asked.

He shook his head. "I never wanted to believe that they were real," he said staring off behind me. "But I always knew. I was raised with no frills. With the barest necessities to keep me mentally sound and healthy, but there was no evidence. By the time I realized what was really happening, I was already here, and . . . well." Tam focused his eyes on me. "What about you?"

"Oh, I was raised on faeries," I said quietly. "I think it's always been a part of my upbringing. 'Look both ways before you cross the street, and don't give your name to the Fair Folk' sort of thing. Everything about them was always presented as fact. I don't think I was really allowed to believe otherwise."

Tam's face twisted in confusion, and—for a moment—I saw anger flash behind his eyes. "If you believed in fae, then why in the world didn't you—"

"But I didn't believe in them," I corrected him. Tam's anger faded, but the confusion stayed. "My parents . . . I saw how it affected their lives. The fear, the paranoia. Take Bill—my dad—for instance. He never let me call him that—Dad, I mean—just in case some faerie was listening who could take advantage of our relationship. His whole adult life, he never went by his given name, David, either. My family called him Bill, his coworkers Evan. He had more fake IDs than most spies. Always hiding. Always vigilant."

"Always distant," Tam finished.

I nodded. "The death of my mother made me want to move," I said, "but Bill's death sealed it. There was just too much . . . Well, Mom was his last connection to reality and reason. He died, and I moved. And, of course, I ran straight into a hotbed of faeries."

Tam nodded, letting a mirthless smile cross his face. Then, seriously, he reached forward and took my hand gently. "Thank you for coming, Margot. Thank you for saving us."

I looked up into his dark eyes and saw the sincerity there. The thought of Bill flashed through my mind, but I pushed it down. Tam, for all his intensity, wasn't Bill. He wasn't even close. Still, there was a wide divide between having a plan and carrying it out.

Smiling uneasily, I gently withdrew my hand. "Don't thank me yet."

OCTOBER 31

When Gwen had told me to report early to the hospital, I thought that I would have actually been put to work on the festivities, but when I asked the attending coordinator, she smiled a little oddly at me.

"Well, go up to your ward, of course. We'll come and get the wards one by one when we're ready to receive them at the bonfire. No need to worry—we won't forget you." The woman—who wore no name tag, and whose name I had yet to learn—tilted her head to the side. She probably thought the gesture was disarming.

"All right," I said. "Is there an estimated time that you're supposed to come and get us?"

The coordinator looked down at her clipboard. "Hmm. Looks like just about nine. An hour or so after the bonfire starts. Your ward has a good view, though. I imagine that you'll be able to watch from the window until someone comes up and gets you."

I nodded slowly, trying not let the worry show on my face. I was sure the smile I gave her turned out sarcastic, but in my defense, I hadn't been able to sleep for the second night in a row. I wasn't sure whether I was tired or slowly going insane, but the fear was starting to wear off. The dawning realization that these people thought I was either completely brainless or blind to the magic flying around the place filled me with incredulity, and the part of me that wasn't incredulous was just a touch insulted.

Maybe that's what went wrong.

I made it up to the ward just fine. I'd expected there to be some sort of hubbub there. There wasn't going to be much in the way of costumes, just the paper-plate masks that everyone had been working on for the last couple of days during craft time. However, instead of a hubbub, it was silent. There was the quiet beep of the electronic lock behind me, and I stared around the quiet, clean ward in absolute horror.

"Hello?" I called. I didn't speak any louder than a regular tone, but it felt as though I'd screamed—a prolonged, desperate plea.

Nothing. My heart hammered so hard I could feel the pulse in my face. Walking up to Polly's room, I pulled the door open.

Empty.

So was Randal's room.

When I came to Tam's door, I noticed my hands were shaking as I pulled it open.

Nothing.

I squeezed my eyes shut. They'd found out. Somehow, they had found out. Did that mean I was in danger? What were they going to do? Should I try to run?

I nearly jumped out of my skin when the door beeped behind me. I whipped around, expecting the Matron and a cohort of male security guards to haul me away to who knows where. Instead, though, in came Eileen, Tam, Randal, Polly, and—to my surprise—Gwen. Gwen looked me up and down, and then looked at the clock.

"You're earlier than I expected," she said mildly.

I looked up at the clock as well. It was just coming on six-thirty now. I shrugged.

"I usually come a little early to make sure I'm on time," I

said, looking at my patients as they filed toward their usual spots in the room. Polly looked like she was having one of her bad days —was she being manipulated somehow?—and Tam looked somewhere between feverish and seasick. Randal looked younger and neater than I had ever seen him, his greyish-white hair practically glowing. "Is everything all right?" I asked.

Gwen followed my eyes, and then looked back at me, calm radiating from her stance. What a pity her glamour couldn't reach me.

"Tam and Polly were very agitated earlier, and sedated. They've been coming out of it just fine, though. I don't imagine they'll need any more. The lingering effects should keep them calm throughout the evening. We would hate for them to miss the festivities tonight entirely."

It took everything I had in me to not answer 'I'll bet' scathingly as Gwen turned smartly and walked out of the ward, but I did it. Patting myself on the back mentally, I shifted my attention to the rest of the room.

Randal sat calm and composed at the table, taking up his deck of cards, but Polly and Tam were a bit of a mess. Walking over to the couch, I noticed that Tam was turning that special sort of bilious pale that always brings up bad things later. Either he wasn't reacting well to whatever they gave him, or whatever mind tricks they'd used on him had a similar effect.

"Tam?" I said, trying to look him in the eye as his head drooped. "Did they give you something?"

"It's in the file," Eileen said casually, glancing over at me.

"Then can you bring me the file?" I asked shortly. She blinked at me owlishly for a moment before turning to head to the cabinet. I squinted after her as she went over to it, hearing the pterodactyl screech as the drawer protested open.

It was brighter in the ward than I was used to. Maybe it was because I could still see the barest remnants of the sun on the horizon as I glanced out the window. It was weird to see any sort of light outside while I was in here, instead of the darkness that was held at bay by the perpetual twilight that inhabited the main room most of my waking hours.

"Here," Eileen said, hitting me in the shoulder with the files and standing back quickly from Tam, as though she recognized his pallor. Flipping through the medical side of things, I ran my finger down the care sheet. He'd been given an anti-psychotic, signed off on by a Dr. Ingen.

But . . . Tam wasn't psychotic. He wasn't even close. He wasn't schizophrenic and didn't have any sort of behavioral disorder. What's more, the thought of him acting out to the point where they would need to dose him with something this strong was almost laughable. Tam got frustrated, but it was like powder in a flash pan. Bright for a moment, and then gone in a puff of smoke.

Plus, would they have actually dosed him with something this strong if they needed him—what had Randal said?—'sound in mind and body'? Wasn't this something that would negate that? This would have needed approval before administration. Who was Dr. Ingen? No doctor in his right mind would have given this drug to Tam. Was the signature faked? Was this doctor even real?

I forced down that last thought, discomfort curdling in my stomach. This was a hospital where faeries were literally murdering people for magical purposes. I doubted getting proper medical authorization rated very highly on their list of priorities.

"Tam," I said quietly, squatting in front of him, looking up into his face. "Did they give you something?"

His eyes seemed to focus on me, but only for a second. Then barely, but enough that I couldn't misunderstand, he microscopically shook his head 'no'. Then, with agonizing slowness, reached up and fingered a bandaid on his arm. Moving a bit closer, I peaked under the bandaid. No blood on the cotton pad. No tell-tale pinprick mark.

They didn't give him anything? Was this a thrall, then?

"I'm going to take Polly into her room," Eileen said. "You going to be all right out here?"

"Yes," I said. "I'm just going to make sure that Tam doesn't throw up all over the couch."

"Thank you," Eileen said fervently, ushering the silent, equally dazed Polly into her room. "We'll let them sleep it off. They should both be ready by the time the bonfire starts."

I stared at her, fury tickling my insides. That settled it. The drug that Tam supposedly had taken, at the time he supposedly took it, would have put him out of commission until the early hours of tomorrow, if not later. He was already way too alert for any amount of that tranquilizer, or any that would work fast enough to calm him down quickly in a fight. Pushing Tam back to lean against the couch, I went and checked Polly's record. Frowning, I checked her weight chart at the front of the file. If Polly had taken the dosage that they said she had, her heart would have stopped.

Suspicion ignited in my breast, and I looked over to Polly's door, just as Eileen emerged.

"Something wrong?" she asked, her voice light. I shrugged and rearranged my face to keep the suspicious expression at bay.

"Not really, I was just wondering who administered these medications to Polly and Tam?" I asked.

Eileen looked down at the file. "Well, I did, of course," she said, as if nothing was wrong with either of the fictional administrations.

Carefully keeping my face blank, I nodded.

"I see," I said. "Well, let's keep a careful watch on them. You know how the side effects can be—I'd hate to see the incontinence side come out at the wrong time—especially tonight. Also be sure to watch them for red bumps on their arms at the injection site. You checked them, of course, for shellfish allergies?"

Lies. Lies, lies, lies.

"Of course I did," Eileen said, confirming my theory. She hadn't administered any drug of any kind. Or, at the very least, if a drug had been administered, she had no idea what she'd given either patient. What worried me more than both of those blood-chilling possibilities, however, was that her voice was completely genuine and believable. She was a very accomplished liar, or else someone who thought I was actually telling the truth, and who would dutifully follow orders whether or not she knew that there were never going to be any such side-effects. But I very much doubted it was the latter.

I fought down my anger. I already knew that she was involved—no need to get hung up over the details now. Now, how to get her out of the ward?

"Good," I said. "I'll go check on Polly before I do the reports. Since I'm taking over, and everything." *And also to make sure that Polly wasn't dosed with the drug listed in her file.* A dose like that would have been an easy mistake to cover their tracks. An 'accident.'

I had to clench my fists to keep them from shaking.

Eileen nodded, unconcerned, standing in my way to Polly's door. "I'm sure she'll wake up soon. That dose shouldn't keep her out for long."

Sure it won't, you medical impostor.

"Of course not," I responded.

Lying, murderous harpy.

I stepped around Eileen, still holding the files, and made my way to Polly's room. Even though I was almost certain that she was just under some sort of thrall, I couldn't help but hold my breath, hoping to hear the sound of her breathing. The air conditioner was too loud, but as soon as I saw her, I could see the steady rise and fall of her chest. When I reached down to take her pulse, a slow, strong, steady heartbeat pumped through her body, and there was no track mark under the bandaid.

And then I could breathe.

She wasn't particularly responsive though—at the very least, no more than Tam was. I picked up her arm and dropped it. It slowed as if she was trying to hold it up, but it still flopped down onto her mattress.

I frowned. How was I supposed to get the two of them out to my car when they were like this? The escape plan was to leave at eight-thirty as it started to get really dark. I was going to use my sleepless night as an excuse to go home early, hiding the two of them in my trunk. They wouldn't check the trunk of a staff member, right? At least, they never had before.

Suddenly I thought of the guardsman, stopping me every time I left. A new thought popped into my head. Had he been using magic to check the vehicles? Was there a way that I could negate that? But why would they check the cars now? On Hallowe'en? Wouldn't the security staff be just as excited to partake in the festivities, especially with their Tiend supposedly hidden up in the hospital, safe under Matron's watch? Surely they had to be in on it. After all, wouldn't they notice if people came in—healthy, normal people—and then just never left?

But if they were in on it, would they see through me?

I clenched my fists tight, feeling the pressure of Mom's ring on my finger.

Whether they did or didn't, I couldn't control that. All I could control—all I could ever control—was how I acted. What I did. How I helped. I'd said my whole life that I was willing to give my life for the good of my patients. I thought I'd done that with Bill, but here was my real test. The reality of knowing that everything could go wrong and knowing that I needed to try anyway.

I took a deep breath, turned, and left the room.

"Eileen," I said, my voice quiet. Eileen looked up at the sound of my voice, but so did Randal. There was something anticipatory in his face as he put down his cards.

"Yes, Margot, what is it?" she asked.

I looked down at the charts. I had to be careful here. I couldn't outright accuse her. Not without drawing far too much attention to myself. The words were just as important as the message. I stared at the reports for what was probably far too long, and then looked back up at her.

"Would you please help me take Tam to bed?" I asked.

Eileen looked from me to the much larger Tam. How far did her deception go? Was she even a real nurse? Had she ever helped move a semi-conscious patient? Regardless, after a moment, she nodded. Begrudgingly, I admired her tenacity. Even if she wasn't a real one, she sure was committed to the charade.

"Of course," she said, walking over gamely to the couch where Tam was sitting.

He looked up at her suspiciously which, if I hadn't already been convinced of her involvement, removed all doubt about who she was. Together, we struggled to bring Tam to his feet, who looked like he was trying to help, but ended up flopping just a little more than actually helping.

Was he faking it?

Either way, it took far too long to get him into his room, but we finally got there, and laid him down gently on his bed. Eileen hightailed it out of the room as quickly as she could, but before I could follow suit, a hand shot out and grabbed my wrist. I glanced back to see Tam, suddenly very conscious, staring up at me.

"I'm all right," he whispered at me. "Just go ahead with the plan."

"But Polly—"

"I'll carry her," he said quietly. "Gym, remember?"

I looked at his broad shoulders and muscled arms and finally nodded. "Keep playing sick until it's time to leave," I said quietly. "I'm going to try to tell them that you can't go to the bonfire."

Worry flickered across Tam's face. I frowned in response.

"They lied in your records, Tam. I've never seen them do that before. They put that you'd taken an anti-psychotic. A strong one. One that they'd never use on you. I think I can claim you by virtue of dishonesty. Saving your life might create that bond. It seems unlikely that I'd forget you after all of this."

"But we're lying, too, by pretending that Polly and I are ill," Tam whispered fiercely. "It would negate our high ground."

"Well, then, let's hope that plan A works," I hissed back, pushing him down onto the bed and walking out the room. I must have still been scowling when I left, because Eileen looked up at me with a worried expression.

"Is everything all right?" She nodded toward Tam's room. "Is he doing all right?"

I glanced back into the room, feeling a little caught off guard. I hadn't planned on starting the plan quite this early, but I could hardly tell her I was frustrated with Tam for pointing out the potential flaw in my plan. So, I shook my head.

Here went nothing.

"He's not doing as well as I would like," I said. It sounded shockingly sincere, and I almost jerked at my tone. I'd never thought of myself as a bad liar, but the cool assurance in my voice was so close to the real thing that I felt guilty almost immediately. Shoving down the feeling I nodded back toward Polly's door. "Polly either. I'm not sure they should go tonight."

I expected Eileen to react, but instead Randal, whom I had somehow forgotten about as he sat peacefully at the table with his deck of his cards made an incredulous noise that was half gasp, half choke. I looked over at him, and Randal gaped up at me in shock.

"Are you okay, Randal?" I asked, stepping toward him.

He spluttered a little bit, and I saw Eileen looking at me, similarly aghast.

"Not—not go?" he stammered. He looked up at Eileen. "Not *go?*"

"Of course they can go," Eileen said to Randal, a little flustered. "I'm sure that the medication will have completely worn off—"

"Eileen, if you gave—" I paused, fury bursting from me just for a moment. I shut that door quickly, taking a deep, calming breath, and holding up the reports for her to see. "Eileen," I started again, "I'm sure they were in quite a state when you administered their doses. But the doses that you gave them were high. The average half-life of the drug you gave to Polly is at least fifteen hours. And with the dose that you gave her, well, the side-effects could last as many as thirty. I can't recommend either of them going somewhere as hazardous as a bonfire in case one or both of them were to lose control of their faculties."

"But—" Eileen said, glancing at the reports in my hand, and then up at the clock. It was nearing seven-thirty. She sighed. "Can we at least wait until it's closer to the time we're supposed to leave before we decide? Maybe they'll wake up more by then."

I looked at her evenly. "Are you going to the bonfire, Eileen?" I asked.

She shrugged, as if she were admitting something she shouldn't. "Just as a guest. I asked Matron if I could," she said.

I raised an eyebrow.

She shuffled her feet again. "I was on night shift last year. Not in The Boughs, but I had fun. I wanted to be here again. That's why I want Polly and Tam to come. They'll be so sad if they miss it."

If by sad she meant dead, then yeah, they'll be sad. At least in Tam's case.

I couldn't put my foot down too hard yet. Sighing a little, I shook my head.

"We'll have to see. If it's still too bad, will you both honor my decision?" I asked, looking at both of them.

Randal still looked horrified, but Eileen's face relaxed, and she nodded. Randal looked at her like she had kicked a puppy. Or disemboweled it.

"It'll be fine, Randal," Eileen said. She walked behind him and patted him on the shoulder. It was the first contact that I'd seen her make with any of the patients.

I tried not to frown.

❧

The next hour passed slowly, and by the end, I was ready to scream. I grimly hoped breaking Tam and Polly out of the hospital would be an acceptable alternative to that. Both of them stayed in their rooms, and every time I looked in on either of them, Tam pretended to still be weak and disoriented. Polly seemed to be waking up, though.

What if I couldn't stop her from going outside? What if she gave the game away? I shook my head. I couldn't think of that. I'd just need to guide her out before she made too much of a fuss. If she was in one of her hazes, then maybe she could just be led.

But no, I needed to tell her, just so she didn't give us away. She was smart, and she needed to get out. Worst case scenario I'd lie to her now and explain when we got to the car.

It was time to check on her again. Then I would ask Eileen to take Randal down to the bonfire, since I would have to stay up here to watch Tam and Polly. And then we would leave.

We were so close.

I opened the door to Polly's room and raised the lights just a little bit. She was awake. She turned toward me as I sat down on the little stool beside her.

"How are you feeling?" I asked.

She shrugged, and the motion looked childish. "Okay, I guess," she said. "A bit tired still."

"That's okay. Polly—" I paused, trying to think of the right words. "I was thinking you could come home with me today. Would that be all right?"

Polly's eyes opened wide at that, and she started to sit up. For a moment, I worried that she was going to protest, so I pressed on her shoulder until she lay down again. However, a delighted smile crossed her face as she lay back against the pillow.

"Really?" she whispered, both hands coming up to cover her mouth.

"Really," I whispered back. "You, me, and Tam. But you can't tell anyone, okay? It's a secret."

A troubled look crossed Polly's face. "Matron doesn't like secrets."

Funny, considering how many secrets she had of her own.

"It's okay," I said. "Someone will tell Matron after we leave."

"Are you sure?" she asked.

I nodded. They'd be in uniform, and hopefully they would be reading her Miranda rights to her as they did so.

"Yep," I said. "All I need you to do is to pretend to sleep until Eileen takes Randal down to the bonfire."

Polly's eyes widened. "You mean we're not going?" she whispered, hands by her mouth again.

I nodded. "Is that okay?" I asked, suddenly unsure.

She exhaled, a relieved smile on her face. "Yes. I'm so frightened of fire, Nurse Margot." She blinked. "But what if they catch us? What then? What if they tell you to find the oak?"

"What?"

Polly raised herself up on her elbow, glanced toward the door, then leaned close to whisper, "Just remember, it's out by the oak leaf—never the bough."

"Polly, what?" I asked, but she had lain back onto the bed again. Smiling her small, gentle smile, she pulled her blanket over her shoulder.

"Call me when you're ready," she whispered, and rolled over.

I stared at her, the confusion overriding my nervousness for a moment, and then I stood, and made my way back out of Polly's room.

Eileen emerged from Tam's room and shook her head at me. "I don't know what's going on," she said helplessly

I shook my head, holding my hands out placatingly. "It'll be all right," I said. "You can take Randal down a little early. He'll want to enjoy the activities longer than Polly and Tam would, anyway. I'll stay up here with them tonight. If they come out of it more, I'll take them down later when our time comes to go down, no problem."

Eileen didn't look like she was convinced. She definitely didn't look happy about it. I sighed, stepping closer and dropped my voice to a whisper. "Eileen, if you don't take him down, and Tam and Polly don't get better, he might not make it down tonight. And we both know how he'll react to that."

That did the trick. Throwing a reluctant look over at the old man, she nodded.

"Fine," Eileen said. "You owe me."

I studied her face. "We can discuss the terms later."

She nodded, unsuspecting. "Deal."

Then she turned to Randal, who was looking expectantly between the two of us. "Well, do you want to go down to the bonfire a little early?" she asked.

Randal looked as though Christmas had come early. "What? Yes! Of course! What a privilege! What a pleasure!"

"O-kay," Eileen said, throwing a look at me that reiterated how much I was in her debt. If she knew . . . Well, if she knew, then there was a good chance that I would not leave here alive. Not tonight.

I counted to ten after they had left the ward and I could see their backs retreating down the hall through the window in the door. Then, calmly, as though I was simply going about my regular chores around this time, I went to check on Tam.

He was already sitting up, stretching his arms above his head.

"You ready?" I asked.

He nodded, standing with almost with a jump. "Ready." He sounded a lot more confident than I felt, and I felt the warm spread of gratitude fill my chest. I wasn't alone in this. I didn't have to get this done all by myself.

I felt his hand on my shoulder.

"Go grab Polly. I'll be out and ready by the time you get her up and moving."

I nodded and went.

Polly must have heard me go into Tam's room. She, too, was sitting up in her bed, and was pulling her hair into a braid. Upon my entry, she looked up and a smart, clear smile crossed her face.

"You ready to go home, Janet?" I asked.

The grin widened. "Absolutely," she said as she stood.

"Is there anything you want to take with you?" I asked.

Janet looked up at me, dead serious. "Absolutely not." With that, she brushed past me. She stopped short in the doorway.

"What, changed your mind?" I asked, pushing her a little to the side to make my way out of the room, looking back at her oddly.

"And just what would she change her mind about?" a cool female voice asked. I froze myself, turning away from Polly to face the one woman in the world that I didn't want to see right now. Snow-white hair stirred against floor-length robes the color of sapphire in a non-existent wind, her robes matching cold eyes that seemed to stare directly through me.

Matron.

She wasn't alone, either. At least four men—each tall and muscled— plus Gwen and another woman that I didn't recognize stood around Matron. The mystery woman looked old. Older than anyone I'd seen here, patient or staff. Older than Randal, even.

"We were just—" I motioned back at Polly and Tam and snuck a glance toward the clock. Eight fifteen. Why in the world would they be here now? Had Matron already had a chance to talk with Eileen?

Tam is their sacrifice, an annoyingly observant voice said in the back of my mind. *Were they not supposed to notice his absence?*

"The medication has seemed to have worn off some, Matron," I said. "We were going to do a couple of exercises, just to make sure they were going to be safe around the fire. By then it would be about—"

"And that explains Tam holding his rucksack as though his life depended on it?" The dark blue of her eyes pierced straight through me as she spoke. Cursing my bad luck, I wanted to turn and look at him, but I couldn't look away from the regal woman.

After a moment, I found my voice. "I can't speak to where or when his mania will manifest itself," I said with my palms extended. "He's delusional. I don't know—"

"Stop pretending," Matron said, her voice a thunderclap in the otherwise-silent room. "I know that you know my true nature."

"You mean the fact that you're Fae?" I asked, the words snapping out of my mouth before I had the time or even the inclination to think.

A cruel curl of a smile appeared on Matron's face. "And there it is." She straightened then, as if a weight has dropped from her shoulders. She looked at me as though there should have been a revelation.

"Were you supposed to look different?" I asked, shifting my weight from one hip to the other, the acidic words rolling off of my tongue.

Matron's smile didn't disappear, or even dim. "Indeed. And I believe that you know that. Given your lineage, though, I should have guessed that you would see through it. Thankfully, these days we live in an age where humans alter their appearance more than I have ever needed to. No, for you I have lifted the veil of perception. You will be able to see things as they really are tonight. Nothing to dim the weight of the world you now live in, or to keep you from your worst fears."

I couldn't help a wry smile. "There's never been anything stopping that before."

Her smile did dim a little then, and she raised a hand. "Gwen."

Gwen stepped forward. She was dressed like the Matron, except emerald green robes draped over her slender frame instead of sapphire. "My Lady," she responded, her voice a low, deferential murmur.

"Please take Margot to my office. I will talk to her after the festivities," she said, loud enough to reach my ears, but quiet enough that I realized I wasn't necessarily supposed to be paying attention. In fact, if I didn't know better, I would have thought that they didn't know I could hear them.

"Of course, My Lady," Gwen said. Then, stepping toward me, she reached out for my arm.

I punched her in the face.

I mean, I sort of meant to, given that it was my arm and I most assuredly didn't want to go anywhere that she was going to take me. However, I was almost as shocked as she was as I watched her stumble back grabbing her nose, a short, strangled gasp ripping through the air. The brunette bowed forward, and then snapped her head up to look at me, black blood dripping down her face. She pointed at me.

"Get her!"

The four men that had accompanied Gwen and Matron turned toward me in unison, and I swore inwardly. It wasn't like I'd never fought more than one person before, but it had been in a room with mats and the ability to tap when things got dangerous.

At least you're not in a skirt, a little voice chimed in, and despite the pounding of my heart ringing in my ears, I felt a small smile creep onto my face. No, I wasn't. And even though I hadn't found a gym yet, I was far from out of practice.

Slipping out of my jacket, I stepped back a couple of steps and hung it on Polly's doorknob. Then, looking up at the men, I lowered into a solid base. They flew at me all at once, frighteningly fast and determined. I didn't know if "get her" was faerie code for "kill her" but I wasn't going to give them the chance.

The first came at me head on, arms reaching out, his hand clasping over my wrist. Bringing my arm around, I broke the grip and grabbed his head, bringing my knee up to collide with his face. I felt his nose crunch against my knee. The second grabbed me from behind almost immediately, trying to pull me up and out of the way, but only succeeding in causing me to drive my knee into the first man's face again.

I leaned down to touch my toes, causing us both to stagger forward. My hands were there to catch me, though, and I moved my hips just enough to be able to step behind him and grabbed his ankle. I hesitated briefly, and then yanked. We flew backward. I landed my full weight on his stomach, felt the air leave him, and then, using my hip as a fulcrum, I yanked as hard as I could, hearing the ligaments and cartilage in his knee crack loudly.

I was already standing, pressing into his leg harder as I went to make sure the man couldn't follow. A sharp cry accompanied the movement, but I ignored it, fear and adrenaline pounding through my brain. The third man swiped at me. I sidestepped, grabbed the sleeve of his jacket as I grabbed his collar, and as he leaned toward me to recover his balance, I sat down and kicked up, sending him flying laterally. I used his momentum, ending up on top, before popping to my feet, and kicking him as hard as I could across the face as I stepped up to face the last man.

A cold hand touched the base of my neck.

"Enough," Matron's voice said in my ear, and I froze, hands snapping to my sides, gasping for breath, fists and jaw pulled tight with anger. "Gwen?"

"I am all right, My Lady."

"Good." Matron looked around at the carnage, looking at each of the injured men as they groaned on the rough blue carpet, a look of unmitigated fury on her face. "Take her downstairs."

"No!"

"Silence, Thomas!" Matron snapped. "I will have no more of this. You will die on that pyre tonight, and I don't care if I have to kill every human in this hospital to do it!"

My breath caught in my throat, and Matron looked at me, and then at Tam. Stalking toward me, she stopped only an inch or two from my face. "So, you would risk your life for his, would you? Well, there just so happens to be a heavy price for what you seek. If you should succeed, then you may have him. But if you don't, his will not be the only death tonight." With that she turned toward the door, blue cloak swirling.

"A moment, My Lady," Gwen said, hand dropping down from her bloody face. Matron stopped, watching Gwen as she stepped close to me. Looking me in the eyes, Gwen fixed me with a look, the crystal in her blue eyes igniting with a fire I recognized from somewhere. "Margot Knight, raise your hand."

The world filled with stars and dreams. It reminded me of something that I couldn't place. My limbs felt light and I could feel one hand drifting up of its own accord. My right hand.

"No!" I heard someone shout from behind me. Was that Tam? My hand kept rising. Something glimmered on one of the fingers. Iron and wood.

"Silence!" Matron snapped. "I have had quite enough of you, Thomas Lynn. You think you can keep on involving outsiders, and expect there can be no repercussions? You are no better than a starving dog—consuming anyone and everyone in your path while you claw your way toward your own needs. You never learned—not even with the constant reminder of your failure in front of you. Their deaths are on your hands and your hands alone. Sit! And be silent. You too, Janet Christofferson. You will be lucky if you do not follow Thomas into the fire tonight."

Silence fell in the room, and my attention drew back to Gwen as she reached out, hand wrapped in the fabric of one emerald sleeve, and harshly twisted something off my finger.

A ring?

"A discernment charm," Gwen said, slipping the ring into a plastic bag and holding it up for Matron to see. "She must have known for days. Thank goodness power of a name still works."

Matron looked at me, beautiful red hair flowing over her shoulders, piercing my soul with her dark blue gaze. Red hair? Something in my head whispered about a glamour, but it was too quiet to hear, even in the stark silence of my thoughts.

"I'm not surprised. Take her down to my office. Give her what she's asked for. If she does not prevail, we kill her at sunrise." Those eyes flicked away from me to another woman across the room, with blonde hair and an innocent face. Janet? "No more mistakes. No more mercy. You are dismissed."

A hand encircled my upper arm.

"Yes, My Lady."

The fog in my mind remained as I was pulled from the room. The hand on my arm was not gentle, but it was probably because I was slow, my limbs jumbling and bumping against each other as I stumbled down the hall alongside Gwen. My head lolled as I tried to keep it aloft.

"I knew Beth made a mistake when she sent you here," Gwen growled. "She said you had a rough history. She said that you wouldn't believe those who knew about our kind. But still you found out. You believe."

The tiny part of my brain that was still aware wanted to murmur something about if Our Lady wanted to keep secrets to not hire intelligent nurses, but the fog was too dense, and as the little thought pushed to the front of my mind it started to evaporate before it could reach my tongue.

Gwen pushed me forward to the top of the steps, pausing as we both looked down the three long flights. Her hand clenched the back of my shirt, and for a moment I thought she was going to push me. But then my legs moved, somehow navigating the stairs safely. She took me to the bottom floor, and practically dragged me into the administrative wing.

"I knew there would be an attempt tonight. I warned My Lady that it would happen, and now look where we are. The Sacrifice was almost claimed, and the Tiend was nearly ruined. What would have happened to us if she had not heeded Randal's warnings? Margot Knight, in here."

I turned sharply to where she pointed, my eyes focusing suddenly on the Matron's door.

It was moving. People danced, animals scurried, and flames

roared where before movement was only implied. I shied back, at once repulsed and entranced by the carving. *How is it doing that? Was it supposed to move? How is it doing that?*

"It's an illusion, Margot. Ignore it," Gwen said gruffly. Her hand moved to the back of my neck again and she shoved me forward. I didn't like it. Something niggled in the back of my brain, and I felt like I should be doing something to stop her. But what?

I couldn't figure it out, so I tripped into the room, nearly falling against some sort of furniture that I couldn't identify in the darkness. Gwen swore viciously behind me and grabbed me by my hair. My hands flew up to my head, grabbing the base of my ponytail instinctively. Something burned within me, telling me to move, Move, MOVE. But there was nothing to tell me how to move. No instructions. No muscle memory. So, I let her pull me up and shove me into a chair with a frightening amount of strength.

The chair rocked dangerously, and for a moment, I thought I was going to tip over backwards without the ability to do more than grab the arms, but a second later the chair righted and settled into place. Gwen leaned in, placing her hands on top of mine, and looked into my eyes. Her crystal eyes were so cold they seemed to crackle with danger.

This was not the woman that I had met my first day.

"Margot Knight," she growled into my face, and any thought other than Gwen's words puffed away, turning into the same mist that shrouded the rest of my brain. The only thing that mattered now were her eyes. They were pulling me in, sinking me deeper.

"Listen to my voice, Margot Knight, and remember my words. You have attempted to lay claim to our Sacrifice, Thomas Lynn. By Faerie Law, you had every right to do so. But such a claim comes at a cost. In order to earn your prize, you must get to him. The methods are yours to determine. If you are able to escape with him, you have earned the right to keep him, and we will trouble you no more. Do you understand me?"

"Yes," I felt the word slip from my lips, slow and slurred. But I did understand, and so I answered.

I could see the cruel grin in Gwen's eyes as she spoke next. "There are three stages. You must first escape your mind. Then the room, then the facility. Any resource here is at your disposal. Thomas will die at midnight, just before the turn to All Saint's Day. You have until then to retrieve your prize." Her hands tightened on my arms for a moment, and then loosened. "Good luck, Margot," she said, her voice deep and hateful. "I'll be back in the morning."

Her hands cinched tight again, and her claw-like nails dug into my arms sharply until I cried out. Then the room pitched sideways. I pinched my eyes shut and screamed as the world spun out of control. Everything inside and outside of me twisted and rolled until I stopped suddenly. The chair rocked, feet clattering against the floor as the world settled into silence.

There were birds singing. I could feel something warm and intense on the back of my head, crackling and coming in waves like a fire. Swallowing hard, I could feel my heart beating painfully in my chest as I opened my eyes, unsure of what I would see. As soon as I saw the yellow wallpaper, printed with climbing ivy reaching toward the ceiling in tentative fingerlings, I knew where I was. Pain, coupled with the deepest grief I could remember feeling, assaulted every sense I had. I could feel it in the trembling of my hands. I could smell it in the salty scent of my own sweat. I pinched my eyes closed again, hoping beyond hope that in a moment I would appear elsewhere—anywhere— other than here.

It was no use. When I opened my eyes, it was the same walls, the same burgundy carpet, the same worn couches with the woven fabric that practically exposed the foam underneath. He would be here. I knew that. Somewhere—

"Margot?"

My heart stopped, and I pressed my lips tightly together before I looked up to see him in the doorway. His long blonde hair fell around his face and framed his grey eyes. His willowy hands, which I knew were deceptively strong by hard experience, were linked in front of him as he peeked around the door into the room.

I struggled to put a smile on my face and pushed myself out of the out-of-place-chair to stand in front of him. "Hi, Bill," I said, my voice weak. That wouldn't do. Clearing my throat, I took a deep breath in and forced myself to relax. "It's been a long time."

"Not really," he said, looking back into the other room. "You were only here last week."

I blinked. Dread that I couldn't quite explain seeped into every corner of my body, filling up every strand of hair, every finger and toe. Somehow, I knew that something horrible was going to happen. Forcing a smile onto my face, I shrugged. "I just wanted to come see you."

Bill looked around and shoved his hands into his pockets. "Really?" he asked. "You've been so busy recently."

"And I'm still busy," I said, mirroring his body language and sticking my hands in my pockets. I looked down. "Bill . . ." I trailed off. I looked away, over at the fireplace. The fire roared in the hearth, staving off the chill that I felt seeping in on every side. I frowned. It was summertime. What an odd choice. I shook it off. I had unpleasant news to deliver. Steeling myself, I sighed. "Bill, you're moving."

He looked up at me, expression sullen. "I know."

I pulled in my chin. "You know?" I repeated. "How could you know? I just decided yesterday. I haven't made any arrangements, but we'll figure out where you're going to togeth—"

"No."

I closed my eyes. "Bill."

"I don't want to leave."

"Bill, it's unethical for me to keep caring for you here. You're my dad."

"Who are you?" The words were harsh and acerbic and I

pulled in my chin, shocked despite my fear. Something niggled at the back of my brain again. Why was I so afraid? This was Bill. My father. He would never do anything to hurt me. I had no reason to be afraid of him. And yet, I couldn't shake the feeling that I knew something about what was going to happen. Then it hit me.

He was going to try to kill me.

"Bill?" I said, my voice breathless. "It's me, Margot."

"You are not Margot," he said, his handsome face twisting as he spat the words. He walked over to a side table, looking darkly at the heavy-looking lamp. "My Margot would never send me away. She's my daughter. She loves me."

I pressed my lips together again, gritting my jaw for good measure. "Bill—"

"She would never—send—me—AWAY!"

Fear blossomed into panic, and I stepped backward. I could feel the warmth coming from the roaring fire, yet none of the heat sank into my skin. It passed right through me as though I wasn't there. What was going on? Outside, the sunshine seemed to dim, and a distant roll of thunder reverberated in the distance, struck up in a chorus with a cacophony of rain. The hair stood up on my arms, and I reached up to rub away the chills. But it was summer. It was June.

It was wrong.

"This isn't how it went," I whispered.

Bill looked up at me, starting, as if he weren't sure what I just said. Fear still pounded through me, but this small kernel of truth stuck in my mind like the tiniest anchor in existence. But it was still an anchor, and I grasped it as firmly as I could.

Bill, recovering from my departure of how the scene was supposed to flow, deepened his frown. "You are not the Margot that I know. Who is controlling you?"

I knew the words. He'd said them to me before, but now they sank in. I looked around. Was I dreaming? Was this a PTSD nightmare?

Suddenly I remembered. This was the day that Bill had found out I'd requested his transfer to another hospital. The day he'd found out that I had had him committed. The next thing he would do was say, 'Some faerie, Margot?'

"Some faerie, Margot? Are you in thrall?" he demanded, hand straying closer and closer to that iron lamp. I stared at him, much like I had during the actual event, struggling to figure out what was going on. Was I in thrall? But faeries weren't real, were they? That's what someone crazy would think. It's what Bill would think.

But it was true, wasn't it? I squeezed my eyes shut, and I saw a pair of crystal blue eyes staring back at me, cold and furious.

Gwen.

"Yes," I whispered involuntarily, opening my eyes. The fear was building again. I had been sent back to the most terrible day of my life, the day where I stared at a man I loved more than anything and had been beaten because of a blight on his own mind. But I hadn't been sent here by Gwen because of my regrets. Nor because of my fear. No, I had been sent here for my mind to be broken, snapped by what already festered in my own soul as I was forced to wallow in an eternal loop of the worst day of my life, trapping me so I would be powerless to save—

Tam.

I felt a new emotion then. One that wasn't part of the memory.

Anger.

I looked up at Bill. His long fingers had wrapped around the base of the lamp. In a moment, he would step close, and I would take my first hit. I had been powerless to stop him then, and every time I'd replayed this memory since. Would I be again? He stepped toward me. I slid my foot back.

No. I couldn't be. I *wouldn't* be. Not now. I needed to be strong.

For Tam.

For Polly.

For me.

"Stop!" I thundered, holding up my hands.

He looked at me, taken aback, the lamp lowering slightly. Then it raised again. "You are not yourself."

"Neither are you," I said, swallowing hard. "You're right. I am sending you away. And I'll send you further away still before you die. But it's all me. I made those choices. Not some faerie pulling the strings. Me. Because you were hurting me, and I was hurting you. Every time I convinced the doctor to try another treatment that I knew wouldn't help. Every time I made excuses for you. Every time I thought I could give you the treatment and the security that you needed, we were hurting each other. Bill," my voice broke, and I shook my head, "faeries are real. But that doesn't matter. You are sick. No faeries are controlling you. None, but you were so far past reality that you were willing to try to kill me. *Me.* Your daughter."

He blinked, and shook his head, the iron lamp tightening in his grasp. "No. No one must ever find out what you are to me. It is my sacrifice to protect you."

"You didn't protect me, Bill. I nearly died. Sixty-six stitches, Bill! A titanium plate in my head. Thank goodness I didn't have any brain damage! I have PTSD, I didn't sleep for two months, I've questioned myself over and over again, trying to think of whether there was an alternative, but there wasn't one! I cared so much, I was so scared for you all the time, but you . . . you couldn't care for me. You were so wrapped up in your own world, even at the end, that even under different circumstances, I know you would make the same choice again and again and again."

Tears streamed down my face. "I wanted to believe that things would be different someday. That we could find a way to protect ourselves, but that day will never come now. Your healing never came from me. And mine can never come from you."

He wouldn't look at me. I couldn't stop myself.

"I miss you. And I miss Mom. I miss you both so much. I wish things were different. I wish I hadn't lost you four days apart. I wish neither of you had gotten sick, and we could have been one of those happy families that you see in the movies. But we never were. We were scared and broken and running. And I can't pretend that we could ever be different now. You're dead. And I'm still here. And I have people to save. People who need me. Who need me more than anyone has ever needed me in my life. They're so scared, Bill. Their minds are not their own, and the only way out is if I come for them. And that means letting you go forever.

"But I can't move on without letting you know that I will love you no matter what you did when you were here, no matter how much it hurt me. I know that doesn't make sense, but you're my dad, and nothing can change that. And that's why I had to send you away. And that's why I'm still not sorry."

Bill was silent for a long moment. The room had changed. Now, instead of the lamp being in his hand, it lay on the floor. A dark wet circle spread between us, and there was blood on his suit. He stared at me with tears in his eyes and blood on his hands, shaking his head slowly.

"I never meant to hurt you."

"I know," I whispered.

"I miss you, too," he whispered.

I could only close my eyes, pulling those words close to me to save for eternity as tears ran down my cheeks.

"What do we do now?"

I opened my eyes and looked around at the room, wiping my eyes and running a shaking hand over my hair. "I . . . I don't know."

"So, you're stuck in a thrall, are you?" Bill looked around at the room with interest. Suddenly, he put his hands on his hips and whipped around, the very image of a galled parent. "What exactly have you been getting up to while I've been away?"

"It wasn't my fault!" I protested. "I moved to Carterhall to avoid faeries! I didn't know that I picked the one hospital in the world that was run by them!"

Bill shook his head and wagged his finger at me. "I told you that your non-believing attitude would get you into trouble one day."

I pinched the bridge of my nose. "This isn't helping me actually get out, Bill."

He shrugged and looked around, apparently unconcerned.

A parental prerogative, I supposed, rolling my eyes. "So . . . what do you see?"

"I dunno."

"Excuse me?"

"This is *your* thrall," he said, gesturing around. "Honestly, that means I'm not actually here. Any realizations have to come from you."

His words weren't that different from normal, to be honest. Back in the day, whenever I would be scared or stuck on a problem, he would always run through the same thing. He would sit me down, stare me deep in the eyes, and ask—

"What do you know?" Bill's voice rumbled around the room.

I opened my mouth to say that I wasn't sure. But then I felt the heat from the fireplace. The heat that went right through me. I was cold, which meant—

"My body is still somewhere else." I thought for a moment. Cold. Dark. "Matron's office."

"Why were you put there?"

"I found out about the faeries," I said. "Tam's going to be sacrificed tonight. It was a place to hold me—while they killed him." A cold shock seeped through me. How long had I been here? What if I was already too late?

"How are you being held here?"

"Magic." I responded. If it was a spell on my mind, then I would have to escape my mind. Gwen's words reverberated through my skull. One of my three tasks. Escape my mind, escape the room, escape the premises. Was there even a way out? I voiced the question.

"Of course there is," Bill responded. "They're faeries. Their sense of fair play means there will be a way out. You just have to earn it. Figure it out, and you can leave."

Unless I was just dealing with a whole host of psychopaths, but I'd worry about that later.

"What is it then?" I said, looking around. The room seemed ordinary. Fireplace, sofa, the window . . . I looked closer. There wasn't a latch. Unless I broke it, no way through there. Maybe if I went the way Bill had come— "Hold on, where's the door?" I said. The room had closed itself in, real ivy boughs winding their way up the walls where a doorway had once been.

Something pricked in the back of my brain, but it left as soon as it came. Bill was pacing now, fingers stroking his smooth chin.

"Do you know anyone else who has been through this?" Bill asked.

I wracked my brain. "Um, Polly-er-Janet, but she never got out. She was driven insane, and Matron kept her around as a lesson for Tam."

Bill turned to me, a smug look on his face. Striding across the room, he leaned down, nose almost to mine. "And what does Polly-er-Janet dream about?"

I opened my mouth, and then closed it. And then opened it and closed it again. The realization, the sheer knowledge that stared me in the face at this very moment . . .

"Oak leaves," I whispered. "And ivy boughs. Bill . . . she dreams of oak and ivy."

He smiled, then. An odd, proud smile. "Out by the oak leaf—"

"—and never a bough."

Janet. Wonderful, sweet, broken Janet would be my salvation. I looked around the room. Ivy, frankly, was everywhere. With holly berries, and winding vines, it was almost overwhelming. There wasn't an oak leaf in sight. I looked high and low for the rounded leaves, under the side tables, around the fireplace, even at the base of the lamp to see if Bill had to complete the memory in order to send me back.

Thankfully, but also disappointingly, it wasn't there. I stood in the middle of the room, hands on hips, looking at all the places in the room. Not in or behind the curtains. Not on the carpet. Not hidden in the wallpaper. The only place that I hadn't checked was the chair.

I started, looking over at the chair that I had arrived in. It wasn't that I hadn't noticed it, but more like I'd . . . slid past it. I'd checked around it. I'd even moved it to look at the design in the carpet. But I hadn't examined the chair itself.

I stepped forward, running my hand over the dark, red-brown wood. The carvings were subtle, highly stylized, but there was no mistaking what they were. The rounded leaves. The large, full trees. Staring at the deep, red color, I stepped back, my hand over my mouth.

"Bill," I gasped, "I found it."

He was at my side in an instant. He looked at the chair, and then at me. "Well? Get in!"

I looked at him uneasily. "Is it that simple?"

"Well, that's how you got here, isn't it?"

I swallowed and looked down at the chair. Then I looked back up at Bill. Time was ticking, but I couldn't leave him quite yet. "You—the real you—he never understood. He died three months ago. I think he only ever forgave me at the end, but he never . . . understood."

Dream Bill nodded sadly. "In a way, he is very similar to your friend Janet—broken from caring for those he loved most, but unable to keep the shadows of fear from merging with the darkness of his reality. He wasn't capable of understanding. He never was."

I nodded, understanding but wishing that I didn't.

Bill nodded in return. "Now, you have a hospital to save."

"I wish I could have saved you."

Bill smiled gently. "I do, too." Turning me around, he centered me above the chair so all I had to do was sit down. I could feel the power growing. "I love you, Margot."

I lowered myself into the chair, trying not to break eye contact.

"I love you, Daddy."

And then I sat, closing my eyes. I felt something snap, and the world tilted again, spitting me out into darkness. I stumbled, falling out of the chair that I had barely sat in. I grabbed onto it, shuddering out a sob, gripping the arms tightly, trying not to dissolve into tears as my heart pounded so hard I was worried it would stop.

"No," I whispered, gritting my teeth. "Not here. Not now."

I had patients to save.

Clearing my throat and wiping the tears from my eyes, I looked around, trying to ascertain exactly where I was. I was in Matron's office, of course, shrouded in shadow, the only light coming from a bobbing line of lights outside the stained glass window.

What time was it?

I didn't remember seeing any clocks in here, but thankfully, I was in the habit of keeping a small plastic watch in the pocket of my scrubs. It was old and battered, but I'd just changed the batteries. If the magic hadn't messed with the electronics, we'd be in business. I pressed the little button to light up the face.

It worked.

The time was . . .

Eleven thirty.

How could that have taken me so long? I could have sworn I was only in the room for a couple of minutes.

Because it was a construct, I thought to myself. I glowered at the watch, resisting the urge to dropkick it through the window. Well, no use wishing for more time. This was what I had. Time to do what I could and leave behind everything I couldn't.

Ignoring the creepiness of the dark room, I rushed to the door. It would probably be locked, but I had to try. It wasn't locked. There was simply no door handle. I bit off a word that I normally would never use, resisting the urge to kick the door, but I still smacked it with the palm of my hand in an attempt to make myself feel better. It didn't work, and I shook my hand as I looked around. Of course it wouldn't be that straightforward. The Fae would know better. They'd want me to prove something. That I could be as smart as them.

Look for the hidden things.

Oak and ivy.

I looked around, trying to find some sort of oak or ivy motif anywhere in the dark room. I thought back to Polly. Janet. She hadn't found it that night. But it would be here. It was in the Boughs—the ivy wrapped around the top of the room. It was also in the fake world I had just escaped. It would be here.

The door was oak, of course, but there was no handle. A red herring? I wouldn't waste any more of my time here. If there was no alternative, I'd come back to it.

It was just so dark. I couldn't see a lamp or a light switch. The only light I had was the little watch light. But that wouldn't be enough to illuminate a paper, let alone the room. No, the only light that I had was coming through the window.

I looked up at it. The woman dancing in the autumn wood. Surrounded by leaves.

Could it be that simple?

With the procession of lights bobbing beyond the stained glass, I could just make out the light of a golden-brown leaf with curved edges laying on the ground of the design, and—invisible in normal lighting—a curved handle sticking out along the bend of the metal frame of the stained glass.

Was it a window?

I rounded the desk, nearly knocking a telephone off of it and bruising my hip in the process, and reached out for the handle. The metal was cool under my hand, and difficult to turn, but when I managed it, it swung inwards, wide and easy.

It was more than big enough to climb through.

I caught my breath in the cool breeze from outside. I had my way out of the room. Now, for the rest of the plan. I looked out the window, just in time to see the end of a long procession of cloaked figures with torches making their way in the direction of where the bonfire was burning. In that moment, I knew what I had to do. I could do this.

I could do this.

⁂

The lawn was slick when I dropped out of the window a few moments later. Matron's office was on the ground floor, but with the added height from the cellar beneath, it was a six-foot drop out of the window. I wasn't a short person, but even six feet seemed like a long way up from the windowsill. I had climbed out backwards, hoping no one would catch me as I was dangling half-way out of the window with my rear end sticking out prominently. I made a mental note: scrubs were not particularly conducive to escaping through windows. That was followed with a more fervent prayer that I would never have to use that information again.

Once I was down, I straightened and started to walk as casually as I could across the lawn. Nothing suspicious about a nurse crossing the lawn. I was just part of the staff. The cold bit at my bare arms, and I wished I'd kept my jacket on before I'd taken on Matron and her cronies, or at least had the wherewithal put it back on before I was dragged from the ward.

Too late for that now.

I headed toward the stables. I hadn't been there before, but I knew where they were. They were on the fire escape plan that I'd been shown during orientation, and I could see the corner of the roof from the Boughs. If Tam was supposed to ride a horse as part of his sacrifice, it would be in the stables.

If Gwen wasn't lying about the time, that is. If she had, I would deal with her later.

I made it to the stables, ducking out of sight behind the open door almost immediately as an enormous roll of drums split the air, and the shuffle of many, many feet began to move. I peeked around the edge of the door and was immediately met with the sight of Tam astride his horse, dressed in golden regalia. He rode side-by-side with Matron, who sat side saddle on a large black horse, bedecked in the same blue robes as before. The blue turned black as night in the dim light, and a crown rested on each of their heads, not of gold or silver, but of wreathes of autumn wood and berries. The King and Queen of the Forest, off to die.

Or at least, Tam was. I noticed their hooded cohort and realized that I was never going to blend in with my blue scrubs. If I was going to stay close enough to be helpful, I'd need to find a disguise.

I'd always sworn to my jiu-jitsu coach that I was going to only use my abilities for good. I felt justified about earlier, and I was saving someone's life, which definitely counted for good, but it didn't completely feel like it as I picked out my target carefully. I grabbed the hooded figure by the shoulders and dragged them back to the stable and out of sight of the procession. I turned the shrouded figure around to face me, and nearly started laughing. Gwen, the devil incarnate, stared back at me.

All feelings of guilt dropped away. Yanking the hood off of her head, I pulled it tight toward me, and reached around the back of her neck with my other hand, pulling the fabric tight against both arteries. The cloak didn't have as much stretch as a hoodie, but it did the job. By the time Gwen thought to cry out, there was no air that could escape her lungs, my wrists tight against her neck, closing her throat.

Her legs gave out as the blood choke took hold, and she looked up at me as I crouched to maintain my grip, a terrified expression crossing her face.

"This just isn't your night, is it? Much as I wouldn't mind, though, this won't kill you," I reassured her sarcastically. "You'll only be unconscious for a few minutes. Next time think long and hard about who you choose to lock up."

The choke did its job. When her eyes rolled up back in her head, I slowly counted to twenty. It would only keep her unconscious for maybe a minute or two, so I would have to act quickly.

I'd chosen my ambush placement well. Lead ropes for the horses hung on the wall, and by the time Gwen had started to stir, bound and gagged, I was throwing her cloak over my shoulders and pulling the hood up over my head. At the last moment, a thought crossed my mind, and I turned back to her as she struggled against the rope.

Mom's ring. I worked swiftly, feeling down her sides until I found the pocket that it was hidden in, and pulled the ring out. Frowning, I shook my head at her, slipping the ring onto my finger.

"Stealing is wrong," I said. Then I paused. "And so is murder." Then I turned, rushing to follow the line of revelers, who had gotten entirely too far ahead. The procession had almost finished curving around the side of the hospital to where the bonfire blazed. I stopped in my tracks as I rounded the building and saw the bonfire for the first time.

It was enormous.

I knew it would be incredibly large. The woodpile had been over twenty feet tall, and now that it burned the flames roared higher still. How was it burning so slowly? Hadn't it been lit at eight?

I shook myself. It was a magic fire. Did it actually matter? I could see Tam's head over the tops of the hoods in front of me. There would be no way to fight through this crowd to reach him, especially once they realized who I was. So how would I get to him?

Then the humming started. I could practically feel my spirit start to lift from my body, despite Mom's ring. Ducking back away from the other revelers, I bent over, stuffing my fingers into my ears, and holding my breath for good measure. I hadn't seen them put something on the fire, but that didn't mean they hadn't.

Creeping along behind the ranks of hooded figures who lined up neatly in almost endless rows around the bonfire, I finally found a place where I could see what they were looking at. Tam stood in his kingly attire and stared solemnly into the fire. Horror twisted in my gut. He would walk in there if Matron told him, I knew it. The weightless feeling faded from the air, as did the barely audible hum, and looking across the crowd, I could see mouths closing. The chant was over.

I pulled my fingers from my ears. It was smokier over here, but if I was having a hard time seeing them, they couldn't see me as easily either. Across the clearing, Matron had dismounted, and was petting the nose of the white horse under Tam. They were both unnaturally calm, despite the sheer heat that was coming off of the fire. Matron was saying something to Tam—I could see her lips moving, but the whoosh and crackle of the fire drowned out her words.

Was she instructing him to walk in? Invoking another spell? How did this work? I ached to move closer, but I knew I couldn't without exposing myself. I'd have to at some point, but it wasn't time yet.

"THOMAS LYNN," Matron suddenly shouted. The whole area stilled. Even the crackling of the flames seemed to quiet a little as the magnificent woman turned toward the crowd in a whoosh of blue velvet.

"Yes, My Lady," Tam's voice returned Matron's call, barely audible over the roar of the flames.

"HAVE YOU FRIENDS?" she cried. The silent anticipation in the crowd was chilling, and I waited with my own bated breath for his answer.

"No," came Tam's soft reply.

"HAVE YOU FAMILY?"

"No," he said again.

"HAVE YOU A LOVER?"

"No." Something twisted inside me. It wasn't regret—I hadn't known Tam long enough for that, and I'd meant everything that

I'd said about not having relationships with patients. But there was something that grated on my soul. Something that whispered of an opportunity almost lost.

But that wasn't why I was here.

"HAVE YOU ANYONE THAT CLAIMS YOU?

"N—"

"Yes!" My voice was shriller than I wanted, a frightened screech in counterpoint to Tam's negative rumble, but it had its intended effect. All heads went up, scanning the crowd of hooded figures, trying to figure out where the sound came from.

I stepped forward from the ranks, and I felt every eye turn to me. I didn't have the inclination to run. It was far too late now, and the end—one way or another—was in sight. I was sure Matron knew exactly who I was even before I drew back my hood, but she waited until the light from the bonfire touched my face before screaming, "YOU!"

"Me," I said evenly, continuing my slow walk toward her and Tam.

He didn't seem to have heard me. Rather, he waited on the horse and stared contemplatively into the flames.

"How did you get out?" Matron hissed, stalking toward me.

"Oak leaves," I said softly, practically inaudible over the noise of the crowd and fire. Matron's expression was as dark as the burning pyre was bright, and only blackened further as she heard my simple explanation. I knew that she knew everything—Polly, the dreams, and the warning.

"Your history is dark," she hissed. "You should have been in your trance for hours."

"It is dark," I agreed softly. "There are things that never should have happened, but my past is behind me."

Her exterior cracked. "How?"

"Hope in the future," I said evenly. "And a frighteningly good therapist."

Her face twisted at that, and she motioned back at Tam. "Then I commend you on your victory over yourself. But you have no claim over Tam. You have denied any romantic attachment to him. You have not known him long enough to be friends. You are not his sister, mother or daughter. You cannot take him."

"That is not the sum of every relationship," I said quietly.

Matron's face twisted mockingly. "What else can there be?"

I smiled faintly. "It's so simple. So after your kind's way—I'm surprised you haven't already thought of it—"

"Tell me!" she growled, her tone dark and dangerous.

"Are you sure you can't figure it out?" I asked, my own dangerous smile crossing my face.

"TELL ME!" she screamed.

I straightened. "I'm his nurse. I came here because he is my patient, someone in need that I have the capabilities to help. So, I claim him. Mine to help. Mine to heal. Mine to free."

"By what authority?" she screeched.

"Yours," I said. "He is mine, because you gave him to me."

"Then I rescind your duties! You're fired! You have no hold over him."

"You can't stop me from caring for someone. You've tried, but that's what brought me back and kept me here, even when you represent everything I fear most in the world." I stepped close to her, narrowing my eyes. "You can't touch me, or my hold over him."

She looked at me, the unbridled fury of fire and brimstone burning behind her eyes, and then it dimmed. A tickle of humor crossed her rosebud lips, and she clapped, nodding her head at me.

"Well done, Margot Knight," she said, and leaned in close to me, that small flame dancing behind her eyes. "But you have not won yet." Turning back to the fire, she stalked away from me. "Even an impure sacrifice is still a sacrifice. Before he entered the trance he agreed to this! I saw as the hope left his eyes and he succumbed. *He* does not claim *you*, and thus I can do what I will with him. Thomas! Proceed!" At the last moment, she turned back to me, sneering, "You must leave the premises to be truly free. If you can stop him, he's free to go."

Tam's horse began to move forward and my stomach dropped in dismay. She was going to kill him anyway.

The fire died a little, as though to let Tam into the midst of his own pyre, and in my desperation, I saw my chance. Rushing forward, I ran toward the flames. Placing my foot on the sturdiest looking beam I could find, and hoping beyond hope I got the angle right, I took another step, gaining height, but feeling the searing pain as the fire scorched my legs. Then I launched myself into the air.

I collided with Tam with enough force that the wind was knocked out of me, but it was nothing compared to hitting the ground. The horse shied, awoken from its own trance by the tackle and it bolted away from the flames. Tam and I hit the ground, just out of reach of the pounding hooves.

Tam landed on top of me, and I felt two of my ribs break on impact, agony stealing my breath before I had the chance to get it back. I forced myself to breathe in, paralyzed with the shock from the pain for the briefest of moments before feeling Tam trying to break away. He wasn't turning toward me to see if I was all right, like I would have expected, he was turning toward the fire, struggling to stand. He was still trying to go into it!

"Tam!" I shrieked, pulling him backwards toward me, hooking my legs into his, wrapping my left arm under his, and my right arm over his shoulder.

He tried to shake me off, turning, twisting, even trying to scoot nearer to the fire. If I'd been too cold before, now I was burning. The bonfire only seemed to grow in intensity as Tam writhed and tried to strike out at me. His arms tried to reach over the top of his head to grab any part of me that he could, digging at the ends of my ponytail and the skin of my face. I tucked my face into his shoulder, just trying to keep control. *Just hold on*, I told myself. That was all I could do.

But could I even do that? My body screamed in protest, my

arms and legs growing weak with pain as I tried to keep a grip, but I held on. There was nothing else I could do to save him.

Just.

Hold.

On.

And then he relaxed. Actually, that wasn't exactly accurate. It was more like he woke up, his body relaxing, and then stiffening, letting the two of us roll to the side, resting on the ground. I couldn't breathe—shallow hiccups were the best that I could manage through clenched teeth.

He turned then, looking over at me. "Margot," he whispered, eyes wide.

I clutched at my side, trying to make some sort of sound. Infuriatingly, nothing would come out, leaving me to grimace at him. Had I won? "I—I saved you," I managed to whisper.

"Not quite," Matron said. I looked past Tam to see her standing in the middle of the sandy clearing, the revelers standing far, far back in silence. She was holding something black and shiny out in front of her.

Was that a gun?

I don't know why I started laughing. The pain combined with the stress, combined with the sheer exhaustion and utter ridiculousness of the situation that I managed to find myself in must have completely broken what was left of my sanity.

Matron certainly thought so, lowering the gun reflexively as she stared at me with a mixture of disgust and contempt. The laughter crackled like lightening through my sides and I started to cry from the pain, so I sat there in the dirt, grubby, burned, and broken, sobbing and shaking from laughter and agony.

"I'm sorry," I gasped mirthlessly, wiping tears from my eyes with trembling fingers. "I mean, all things considered, I am absolutely certain you'll shoot me. But after all this . . . You're just going to pull a gun out? Did-did you run out of magic?"

Matron didn't answer. Instead, she leveled the gun at my head. I bowed my head, grimacing and grasping my side, and turned from her to Tam. Oddly, if I was going to die, I wanted to be looking at the man I had saved.

But I didn't want to die cowering. I grasped Tam's arm. Bile rose in my throat from the strain.

"Help me up," I said, looking into his eyes.

He looked over me, shaking his head almost immediately. "What? No! Margot, look at your legs!"

I categorically refused. I could feel the burning and could smell the smoldering fabric and seared flesh. My scrubs must have caught fire. Everything screamed at me to lie down, to never move again, but I couldn't—I couldn't do that. Not until I had no other option.

"It's fine, Tam," I said, leveling my stare at Matron. "She's going to shoot me anyway."

"That's not going to happen," Tam said firmly.

Matron's scowl was sharp and deadly as she glared between the two of us.

"I think it just might," I said softly, taking his hands. "But it's all right."

"What? Why is it all right?" he demanded, grasping my hands tightly in return.

"Because you're free."

Tam gaped at me, his dark eyes glimmering in the firelight. "What? What are you talking about?"

I turned to Matron. "She said as much. 'Stop him, and he's free to go.' It's after midnight by now. You're no longer capable of being a sacrifice, anyway. And neither am I," I said, my body shaking uncontrollably. Was I in shock? Maybe she wouldn't have to shoot me—maybe I'd just keel over on my own. I swallowed, forcing down the feelings of panic. "And I want you to leave. Now."

"She'll kill you if I leave. Margot, you saved me—"

"She'll kill me if you stay," I said, still not looking away from her. "Midnight or not I'm still under her power until I leave the premises. Get Janet. The extra keys are under the back floor mat of my car."

"How astute of you, Margot," Matron said silkily. "I think I will quite like killing you. Given any other circumstances I might drive you mad and watch you putter around the wards for the rest of your natural life."

"But?" I whispered, bowing my head.

"But I do not take kindly to those who ruin my plans." Matron's expression didn't change, exactly, but there was a different light in her eyes when I met them again. She raised a hand, and I could feel an energy rising. Static electricity? Magic? A manic smile crossed her face. "You. Helpless and broken like the mortal that you are. It's shooting the proverbial fish in a barrel."

Tam stepped in front of me, and Matron laughed harshly.

"Do you not think I'll shoot you, too, Thomas? You've been a thorn in my side for the better part of the past decade. At this point it's a privilege to kill you with my own hands."

"And you've turned me into a cowering dog. I'd rather die like one than see someone like Margot die." He stood straight and proud—taller than I had ever seen him—his expression thunderous.

"Don't try my patience, Thomas!"

"A *dog*, Matron!" His shout was ragged, and not just with the smoke. "How dare you?"

Her eyes narrowed, the white wisps of hair blowing in the backdraft of the fire. "I will do whatever it takes to keep my power. You know that about me. You have *always* known that about me."

"Then I'll do my best to stop you. And to save Margot," he said calmly.

"No, Tam," I whispered. "She'll kill you. You know she will."

Tam was staring at Matron. It could have been from the waves of heat and smoke coming from the fire, but a tear trickled down the side of his face, and yet his face was unlined. Unafraid. "You know that I haven't done much with my life, Margot. I thought that escaping was the only way to fix that. But maybe stopping a bullet for you will make it worth something after all."

I opened my mouth, but nothing would come out.

"At this range I can't miss," Matron sneered. "But the bullet should pass through both of you quite easily. I must admit that the one thing I enjoy about this modern age is the increased technology."

Her eyes narrowed as she aimed carefully at Tam, when suddenly, in the distance, I heard something. Droning, high and low, grew louder and louder until it hurt my ears. I turned toward the source of the sound. Flashing lights from at least a dozen police cars were headed across the field, a red, white, and blue testament to the best-timed rescue in history.

NOVEMBER 1

A loudspeaker ripped through the air. "Fay Avery, drop the gun and put your hands in the air!"

I looked her in the eye, hugging my ribs. "Funny, Matron," I said, swallowing hard. "I'm pretty fond of technology myself."

Her mouth was open, her expression stunned as she looked between me and the approaching squad. "H-how?" she stammered.

"You failed Evil Villain 101. Don't leave a prisoner alone in a room with a telephone. Somewhere in that crowd is a Detective Michael Ansel. He was *very* interested to hear what I had to say about Janet and your hospital."

Matron stared at me, the hand holding her gun dropping to her side. I slumped back onto the sand, sick to my stomach. Tam followed me down and caught me before my head hit the ground, turning back to watch Matron. Spilling out of their cars, police swarmed her, taking the gun and yanking her arms behind her back, one of the officers reading her the Miranda rights.

A sudden thought sparked in my brain, and I reached up to Tam, who was standing over me protectively, and grabbed his hand.

He looked down. "What is it?" he asked.

"Help me up," I said.

"You should not be moving anywhere," he said sternly.

"Yeah, yeah," I said, using his hand as an anchor for one hand, holding my ribcage with the other. Hissing with the pain, I made it to my feet with Tam's help, and staggered over to where Matron was being subdued to by the police officers. She glared at me.

"What do you want?" she hissed.

"Tell me I won," I said.

Matron's face twisted, and for a brief moment I could see the rottenness at her core, usually so carefully masked by her beautiful exterior, rise to the surface like a volcano.

Then it died.

"Of course you won," she grit out. "The magic died at midnight. You saved him. He is safe, and you are free the moment you step foot off the premises."

"No one will come after us?" I looked around the field, which seemed full of people, both cloaked and uniformed, the odd normal patient sprinkled among them. "Any of us?"

"I told you, the magic died—"

"Fay Avery," I whispered, and she looked up at me, her eyes wide. Whatever magic there was left, we both felt it take. "I require your oath."

She stared at me, pale and suddenly shaken. "There will be no repercussions," she whispered. "From any of us to any patients or uninvolved staff, past or present."

I wouldn't thank her, as was the way of her people. I knew what it meant for her, but also that it was my right. The honor given to me as victor. Drawing myself up instead, I nodded to her, accepting her word.

And then I walked away. Tam curled his arm around me, letting me lean on him as we went to find the officer in charge. The world turned sort of hazy then, and halfway across the field my legs buckled under me. The next face that I saw was a paramedic, flashing a bright light into my eyes. I jerked back against the painful brightness, and I heard a murmur of approval. Blinking the brightness away, looking up I could see the bottom of Tam's jaw, and felt the vibrations of him as he spoke another couple of words as I squinted back into awareness.

A crinkly sort of metal blanket was tucked tightly around my body, followed by more actual blankets that were piled on top of me, keeping me warm and pinning my arms close to my body. I tried to struggle against them a little. Pain blistered across my side. Ah, yes. My ribs.

"You're heavy," I whispered to Tam.

He looked down. "Well, hello there," he said softly. "We just got you in the ambulance. We're taking you to the property line."

For a moment, I was unbelievably confused, wondering why in the world they weren't just taking me to the hospital. Then it clicked.

"Fulfilling my bargain." My whisper was almost painful to listen to and I grimaced.

"You would eventually anyway, and Matron did promise to stand down, but I'd rather it was done and dusted," Tam said grimly. "I've been here far too long to trust them otherwise."

He didn't have to tell me twice. The ambulance moved slowly over bumpy ground, but before long we turned onto a smooth road and sped up. I didn't exactly feel anything, but there was a sort of release in my chest, and I could hear Tam exhale as well. I heard a voice I didn't recognize from the front of the ambulance.

"That's outside the gates, Mr. Lynn."

"Perfect. To the hospital?"

"Yes," the other paramedic in the back with us said, "We've got a police officer following to take your statements once Ms. Knight is stable."

We arrived at the hospital thirty minutes later, the first to arrive. My ribs were x-rayed and the surprisingly minor burns on my legs cleaned and pronounced non-life threatening. And then the paperwork started. I was required to issue statements to the sheriffs of two different counties, an FBI agent, and the representatives of at least two nursing organizations. Those interviews were more thorough than either of the Sheriffs' or the FBI and took the better part of two hours. When I was finally finished, I was left to myself, the beeping of the machines, and Tam.

"Why was I talking to the FBI?" I murmured to Tam.

He was wearing an extra set of scrubs now instead of the faerie robe, and had kindly refused to leave my side except to change. "Apparently Matron was funding the hospital through less than legal means," Tam said, shaking his head. At my raised eyebrow, he shrugged and explained. "I talked to the agent during my interview." We sat behind the little curtain partition for a few moments longer in silence.

"She's in a lot of trouble," I remarked. It shouldn't have been a surprise. Not really. And yet, realizing that her law-breaking ways extended past murder and false imprisonment genuinely shocked me. Not that I thought criminals couldn't branch out to more than one type of crime, I just never thought for a second that I would be sucked into the middle of it.

"Yeah," Tam said. "Is this your first police investigation?"

I nearly laughed but caught it in time. "Unfortunately, no."

"No?"

"No." Thanks, Bill.

"You'll have to tell me about it sometime," he said, reaching over and taking my hand—the one without the IV line—in his. It was comforting—an anchor of real in a sea of chaos. More comforting, though, was the fact that he was free. We were free. We'd lived.

"Margot?" Tam's eyes were worried.

What—oh, my history with police investigations. "I will," I promised.

He went quiet, nodding, taking it in. Then he inhaled and turned to me. "You've had an eventful life."

He surprised me with the incredible understatement, and I laughed before I could stop myself, and then practically doubled over with the pain, groaning. Tam half caught me, guiding me to lean back against the bed again.

"You can't do that to me, Tam," I panted, trying not to laugh again. "The pain meds aren't that strong. Besides, I'm—I'm easily surprised."

"Um, I don't think you are, though," he responded.

I breathed out another laugh, and it was at that point, a blonde head poked around the curtain. My mouth dropped open in delight. "Janet!"

The blonde stared at me, her eyes bright and clear.

"Margot, you made it!" she said, rushing toward the bed to embrace me.

Tam stopped her gently. "Not yet, Jan, she's had a rough go of it."

"What?" she asked, looking me up and down. When she caught sight of my bandaged legs, her mouth dropped open. "You—you—" Her forehead creased, as if she were struggling within her mind to make sense of things.

I watched her, compassion blossoming in my chest, and held out my hand. She took the seat on the opposite side of Tam and was holding my hand like it was going to break. We sat there quietly for a moment longer before a nurse entered.

She immediately focused on Janet. "There you are! You left your bed, Janet. I was worried!" The nurse looked at all of us, smiling softly when she saw our linked hands, before turning compassionately to the blonde woman beside Tam and me. She said, "It's getting late. Why don't we come see your friends in the morning?"

Janet perked up a little and smiled. Then the smile dropped off of her face. "I'd rather not take any medications."

The nurse at the edge of the curtain smiled and shook her head reassuringly. "You don't have to." She walked past the partition, and held out her hand to Tam. "I'm Nellie, the psychiatric specialist here. Could I talk to you when you have a minute? I'd love to discuss Janet's care with you. She's given you as her emergency contact until we can get in touch with her family."

"I'd be happy to help in any way I can," Tam confirmed. Then he looked over at Janet. "I'll see you in a bit, hey? Nellie will take great care of you. I'm going to watch over Margot for a bit."

Janet looked a little unsure. "I'll see you tomorrow?"

"Of course you will," Tam said.

Janet looked at me, and I nodded. A peaceful smile crossed her face, and she bobbed her head in return, satisfied.

Watching her go, Tam shook his head regretfully. "It's not going to just go away, is it?"

I shook my head. "It really depends on what Matron did to her." I sighed. "I hope . . . I hope that whatever it is, that it's reversible."

"Me too," Tam whispered, his thumb tracing mine absently, his hand my anchor to reality. As we watched, another large group tramped through the emergency room. This time, going by the outfits, most of them were police officers, with various revelers, who apparently had decided to fight back.

I saw Gwen and was digesting the fact that I really didn't feel sorry at all for what I'd done to her, when I saw a familiar face between two sturdy looking police officers walking down the hall.

"Randal?" I asked. The pain killer drip was definitely working, and my voice was soft, but the old man turned, as if pulled by an invisible rope.

When he saw my face, his face—which was now unnaturally lined and almost horrific in its sudden age—contorted in pure unbridled rage. Pulling the officers to a stop with him, he advanced toward my bed, but was dragged to a halt at the curtain. Death radiated off of him, but whether it was his own dying aura or his desire for me, I didn't know.

"I curse you, Margot Knight," he spat. "I curse you by day

and I curse you by night. I curse you in the fall and in the spring. I curse—"

"Randal," Tam said from beside me, quietly and firmly, "Silence."

Randal cut off, glaring up at him.

Tam fixed him with a look and shook his head firmly. "The magic has run out. There is no more to cast curses."

"I was to have it all!" Randal seethed. "The Queen promised! She promised that I would return to my glory and my position as Lord of the Wood, and this—this—" he inhaled sharply, trying to think of something horrible enough to call me. I lifted my chin, unafraid. His face twisted, a grotesque imitation of himself. "You have ruined everything."

"Your Queen ruined it herself, Randal," I stated. "She made a bargain and lost."

Randal narrowed his eyes, breathing hard, but didn't argue. Keeping his dark look on me for as long as he could, he let the police officers lead him away. I watched him go, a deep frown creasing my face.

"Are you sure the magic is dead?" I finally whispered to Tam after I'd been moved to a private, more secure hospital room.

Tam, sitting in the chair next to my bed, shifted his grip on my hand, interlacing his fingers with mine. "I'm sure. The old magic requires more than evil intent and a spoken word," he said reassuringly.

I turned my head to him. "How do you know?"

"Perhaps there's a reason that they chose me. I mean, apart from my sound mind and incredible physique." He grinned, a flash of humor glinting there.

I made a face. "Really? We're going that route?"

Tam grinned but didn't say anything. He simply held onto my hand, his fingers interlaced with mine.

I gripped back tightly and we sat in silence. "Thank you," I whispered.

"For what?" Tam said.

I looked over at him. "For what you did . . . toward the end, with Matron. Standing in front of me."

He looked down. "I couldn't just leave you there."

"But you could have. You were free, she couldn't have stopped you."

He opened his mouth to speak, and then closed it again, shaking his head.

"What?" I said.

His hand, still wrapped around mine squeezed tighter for a second. "I couldn't let her be right."

"Who? About what?"

"Matron. About me. I don't know if you were . . . conscious, but she pointed out that I had gotten so wrapped up with trying to escape, it was all I could focus on. Margot, I put you—quite literally—in mortal danger. And I didn't care. I mean, I did, but it wasn't as important as getting out."

"I chose to help you, Tam."

"And you will forever have my gratitude. But there are parts of myself that I've found that I'm not proud of. That I never want to run into again. That I will do everything I can to get rid of. I want help but . . ." There was a bashful kind of modesty in his expression, and for the last time, I thought of Bill. But this time I smiled.

"I don't think I'm the right person to ask, Tam. Not right now."

He smiled ruefully. "I thought as much. But . . . will you keep in touch? Everything I know—"

"We'll get you the help that you need, Tam. The real help you need, to fix what's happened here."

His eyes fluttered closed. There was another squeeze on my hand. "Thank you, Margot."

I squeezed back.

There was a small window just past Tam, and we watched the sun break over the eastern horizon. Peace, strong and real, spread through me and I smiled as I stared out the window. "What are you going to do now?" I whispered.

Tam didn't look at me, mirroring my smile as I drank in the glorious light. "I think," he said, his voice soft and eyes wet, "I'm going to live."

THE END

ACKNOWLEDGMENTS

There is a crazy long laundry list of people to thank for this book.

The first, of course, is my Heavenly Father. He gave me my talents, and BOY was this a chance to develop not only my writing chops, but also to iron-clad my self esteem. I had a couple of run-ins with a few people who didn't believe in this book as much as I did, and I'm grateful for the opportunity to learn, grow, and strengthen myself, even if I didn't like it very much at the time.

The second is, of course, Sarah. You were surprisingly not as involved in the planning of this book as much you usually are, but thank you for loving me and guiding me out of the path of weird plot development, it's-too-good-to-be-true-isms, and supporting my choice to not try and force Tam and Margot together by the end of chapter 13. To you, and all, I promise: **There will be a chapter 14 available at some point.** No, I haven't written it yet.

Also, thanks to the rest of my beta crew: Jesse, Cate, Caylie, and Steph. As always, your cheering for me (and your threats of violence) have kept me happy and motivated through this whole process. Also, thanks to Jackie Cope, Mathis Boone, and Hollijo Monroe for your eyes and your questions. Jackie, thank you for making sure that Margot got her mom's ring back. Hollijo, thank you for punching me in the gut *just* enough to make sure Tam wasn't interchangeable with a lamp. I hope you'll find him improved.

I have to include, alongside the other beta readers, a special mention to Jacque Stevens, who lent me her precious time to read over an EXTREMELY rough version of Oak and Ivy, and then several more drafts over the last few months. You asked just the right questions to help it move forward and your expertise and experience in nursing have been invaluable. It's your advice that I remembered the most, and which planted the seeds of most of the revisions. Thank you a thousand times. Times a million.

Kayla and Suzanne: You are the most patient sub-editors ever. THANK YOU. You earned every single penny, even though you probably spent most of your time properly formatting my dialogue. Kayla, thank you for getting as excited over developments as I did, and adding just enough encouragement to keep me going as you asked inconvenient questions.

Also thanks to everyone who read this to get rid of my typos and persistent formatting errors (Aka Bekah's Bane). I'm going to forget some of you (SORRY), but especially Kayla, Sarah, Caylie, Jacque, Erin, and Jesse.

To Kaylyn: You give my books faces. I adore your art, I adore you, and I feel truly blessed that I met you. To many more!

To Coach Pease: Thank you for having the patience to at least try to teach my uncoordinated rear Jiu-Jitsu. Thanks for looking through (most of) the jiu-jitsu scenes in this book and helping me fine-tune the technique and what would be most effective. Also, while I'm here, there's no way to adequately thank you (and your family) for basically being my extended family during my college years. It's hard to believe that (as of this writing) it's been almost 10 years. Time flies by when you're having fun! Takedown. Submit. It's that easy.

I am also very grateful to Celestial Seasonings for their Bengal Spice tea. I'm ETERNALLY grateful to Heather, for giving me the recipe for an herbal tea substitute for chai. My diet will never be the same.

I'm grateful for wonderful autumn nights (with the lights on, for this book).

Thanks for ITV and David Suchet for Poirot, along with my creepy playlist on Pandora, both of which fueled the creepy factor of this book. Hence the writing with the lights on.

Lastly, thanks for the creators of NaNoWriMo, who showed me that people CAN write 50,000 word novels in less than a month. I did it—the first draft of this book was 61,000 words in 23 days. Don't get excited—I am NEVER doing that again. At least, of course, until the inevitable future day that I decide I want to.

To any others that I may have forgotten to mention by name: THANK YOU. Your work, effort, love, and influence has been felt and appreciated. You, and those named, have made all the difference by believing in me.

ABOUT THE AUTHOR

Rebekah Isert (pronounced "eyes-hurt") chose to become a writer rather than an optometrist. She enjoys writing, watching martial arts movies, and reading whatever sounds interesting. She loves to write fantasy, but delights in the right to write whatever story captures her imagination. She currently lives in the West, but given her propensity to travel, could realistically turn up anywhere, anytime. Feel free to reach out to her on Facebook, Instagram, and her email at rebekahisert.author@gmail.com.